Dessert First

Dessert First

Dean Gloster

Published by
Merit Press
an imprint of F+W Media, Inc.
10151 Carver Road, Suite 200
Blue Ash, OH 45242. U.S.A.
www.meritpressbooks.com

ISBN 10: 1-4405-9454-6
ISBN 13: 978-1-4405-9454-0
eISBN 10: 1-4405-9455-4
eISBN 13: 978-1-4405-9455-7

Printed in the United States of America.

10   9   8   7   6   5   4   3   2   1

Library of Congress Cataloging-in-Publication Data
Gloster, Dean, author.
Dessert First / Dean Gloster.
Blue Ash, OH: Merit Press, 2016.
LCCN 2015047822 (print) | LCCN 2016021782 (ebook) | ISBN 9781440594540
(hc) | ISBN 1440594546 (hc) | ISBN 9781440594557 (ebook) | ISBN 1440594554
(ebook)
CYAC: Leukemia--Fiction. | Sick--Fiction. | Brothers and sisters--Fiction. | High
schools--Fiction. | Schools--Fiction. | Dating (Social customs)--Fiction. | Family life--
California--Fiction. | San Francisco (Calif.)--Fiction.
LCC PZ7.1.G589 De 2016 (print) | LCC PZ7.1.G589 (ebook) | DDC [Fic]--dc23
LC record available at *https://lccn.loc.gov/2015047822*

Cover design by Colleen Cunningham and Alexandra Artiano.
Cover photography by Frank Rivera.

This book is available at quantity discounts for bulk purchases.
For information, please call 1-800-289-0963.

*For my wife, Nancy Ricci, and our children, Alexandra Hope Gloster
and Jay Antonio Gloster, who keep teaching me how to live.*

1

I've thought a lot about what happens when we die, and I'm pretty sure it's not reincarnation. No loving and merciful God would put us through high school twice.

The first day of school this year, I'd finally forgiven Evan enough to sit next to him again in morning carpool. We were alone in the back of his mom's Camry, surrounded by the smell of leather upholstery, and his hand brushed mine, a light tickle. *Was that deliberate?* Did it mean something? Hope bubbled up in me. Maybe I could fix things with Evan—and the rest of my friends—despite last year's blowup. Then perspective slapped me with a ringtone.

"They're admitting Beep," Mom said through the scratchy cell phone reception, without even hello. She babbled white count and neutrophil numbers, blood labs awful enough to start my twelve-year-old brother on chemo. Again.

That was a soccer cleat kick in the stomach. After I hung up, my mouth wouldn't work for a second.

It had just been a bruise. On his arm where I'd grabbed him three days ago.

"Beep's cancer's back."

"Oh, jeez," Evan said, squirming. He raised an arm to put it around me. I gave him a look, and he plopped his hand back on his knee.

I looked ahead blankly at the elevated BART train tracks past our high school, and then we pulled up at the drop-off area. Evan scooted out of his side, but just stood, looking earnest and like he wanted to help. I was frozen. Clots of kids streamed by the open car door, talking too loud.

Someone honked. I flinched, and Evan's mom turned around in the driver's seat. We were blocking the loading zone. "Should I take you somewhere else, Kat?"

Yes. To someone else's life. I could have used a complete transplant. But since that wasn't medically possible, I shook my head and stumbled out into sophomore year.

᠔

I just wanted to get home to pack Beep's hospital kit. But after school Evan followed me out of our seventh-period French class, catching up at my locker. "Hey." He touched me above my elbow. "I'll walk you home."

All the hairs on my arm stood at attention. I wasn't sure what to say. My silence stretched over the hallway shuffling gabble and slamming of lockers, and my arm tingled where he'd touched it. Evan's serious brown eyes are so pretty they're almost wasted on a guy. Lost freshmen streamed past us while I weighed the heart-hurt risks. I already ached, so how much worse could it get?

"I won't try to make you talk," Evan added.

So Evan walked me home, like we were best friends again, except I wasn't in the mood to make him laugh, or even talk, and he wasn't leaving a trail of gooey footprints from stomping my little heart like last year. I mostly looked down at the gray sidewalk and tugged on my backpack straps, worried about Beep, while red maple leaves swirled past us in wind gusts. It was one of those perfect Bay Area September afternoons, with clear blue skies and just enough breeze to keep it from being too hot. Which made me mad, because it was the day Beep's cancer was back.

Evan finally broke the silence. "I'm sorry about Beep. And also—" He gave me a worried look. "—about last year."

"Me too." I had a hollow misery pit inside. Walking with Evan helped. But enjoying his company had its own dangers. Like Beep's latest cancer relapse, hanging out with Evan scared me and made me think *I can't go through this again.*

We turned onto my block, and I half expected to see our house crushed into lumber scraps by the weight of Mom's anxiety. But there it was, still perched between trees up the stairs from the sidewalk, in its two-tone brown. We both stood at the bottom of the stairs, for so long it got awkward. Evan stuffed his hands into his front pockets, as if he wasn't sure what to do with them.

"So—" He looked down at my knees. "Could we get together and write songs again?"

"Evan, can you think of any *worse* possible time to ask that?"

"Yeah. Pretty much anytime at the end of last year."

That actually made me laugh. "Yeah." He had me there.

He raised his eyebrows and his mouth twitched into a fragile smile.

"Thanks." I shifted under the weight of my backpack. For walking me. And for joking with me again. Someone had to start that. "It was nice."

He gave me the warm flicker of a broader grin, as if the words were a present he'd keep. "Am I forgiven?"

Except for Calley Rose, my other ex-friends had still shunned me at lunch, even in the new school year. Thanks to Evan and his big mouth. "We'll see."

☾☽

Our dog, Skippy, greeted me at the door, a tiny enthusiastic gray mop of leaping joy, trying to dog-cuddle my knees, while I struggled out of my backpack.

Rachel, my older sister, was at the kitchen table, surrounded by books. When she swiveled her head to look at me, her honey blonde hair swung, with actual bounce and body, like some model from a hair commercial. A soaring wail of syrupy pop blared out of her white iPhone. For once, though, I didn't slam her musical taste. I wanted to get along, and maybe even get her help with pulling things together for Beep's latest hospital stay.

Rachel got up from the kitchen table and gave me a stiff hug. After I got over the surprise—she hadn't done anything like that in more than a year—I hugged her back. When I was little, Rachel was my best friend, and I think I was even hers. But that was a long time ago, before she discovered boys. Now my breathing in the same room annoys her. Maybe Beep's cancer relapse would be a common enemy, and we could get along again for one night. Rachel goes to a different school, Berkeley High, where she's a senior. Our house is technically one block across the border in Albany, California, but she got a transfer to go to Berkeley High, for their "nationally famous Latin program" because, apparently, she likes dead languages better than she likes going to school with her live sister—me—at Albany High.

"I'm making dinner," she said, stepping back. "With no carcasses." Rachel doesn't eat meat, because she doesn't believe in cruelty to animals—except, usually, to me. She also doesn't eat eggs or cheese.

The kitchen was full of baking bread-and-onion smell. I peered into the oven, where a frozen vegan pizza was browning to the proper blandness. "How about I put cheese on my half?"

"Really?" Rachel skewered me with her you-immoral-omnivore glare. "Congealed mammary secretions? Of another species?"

I opened the fridge anyway, but the brick of cheddar was gone. Maybe we weren't going to get along tonight. "Did you throw out the cheese?" She'd done that before.

"*Mom* did. It had a spot of mold."

Right. Ever since the last two times Beep had cancer, when fungal infections had tried to snack on him while his immune system was mostly missing, Mom has been a fungus-phobe. Even though I'd explained we should eat lots of mold, to keep the food chain in the right order.

I held up both hands in surrender, or at least peace. We both sat at the table in a stunned, mostly no-talk zone, while the vegan pizza crisped into cardboard. Rachel blew her nose twice, and used hand sanitizer after each time, already doing the Beep-has-a-compromised-immune-system drill. We took turns petting Skippy, who shuttled between us, his scruffy tail wagging, panting with the effort of trying to cheer us up, his collar jangling with every wiggling round trip.

"Except for Beep's cancer coming back," Rachel finally said, "how was your day?"

I looked up from petting Skippy. Rachel doesn't usually ask about my life, except to find out when I'll be out of her way. "Weird. Evan walked me home." I wasn't sure how I felt about that. A little scared. A little hopeful.

"*Um hmm.*" Rachel raised one of her perfect eyebrows, then went on to what she was probably planning to say anyway. "Mom doesn't want me coming to the hospital tonight, because of my cold. And I don't want to just sit around here worrying. So I might go out with Brian. Unless . . ."

"Really?" Brian was Rachel's latest boyfriend, as of a whole two months, nearly Rachel-record time before a guy bored her into dumping him. Rachel's boyfriend-of-the-month club somehow drove Mom insane (well, more insane than her anxiety-spiking usual) even when Rachel wasn't dating some college frat boy. "*Tonight* you have to go Brian-snuggling? Your hickey collection isn't already complete?" As soon as that was out of my mouth, I knew it was the wrong thing to say, but it was already out there annoying her like a buzzing wasp.

She pressed her lips into a tight white line. "Since you put it that way, yeah." She grabbed her phone, which killed the "music" and then she started texting furiously, jabbing at it with her thumbs. "Less painful than hanging out with you. But don't you dare tell Mom."

The oven buzzer went off. Rachel sneezed and gave herself another hand-sanitizer self-massage, so I pulled out our alleged dinner.

After two pizza slices, Rachel pocketed her phone and shoved her plate in the dishwasher. "Sure you don't want me to stay?"

Her back was still angry stiff, though, and she'd already half turned away, with her purse on her shoulder. It wasn't a serious offer. Besides, we'd had a semi-peaceful dinner. Better to quit before we snarked on each other even more. "Nah, I got this." I'd get Beep's stuff together and take it to the hospital. "Have . . . fun."

She frowned, as if that was a dig, spun on a heel, and muttered on her way out. The door slam echoed in the empty house. I walked to the front window. Down at the bottom of the steps, Rachel slid into Brian's blue Nissan. Before dinner, being in the same room was bearable—our shared misery had squashed the fight out of us for half an hour. Maybe someday we could work out a longer truce.

⚭

After Rachel disappeared with Brian, I jammed my plate into the dishwasher, rattling the glassware when I slammed it shut. Rachel had left me alone to deal with Beep's cancer. But if I had a boyfriend or even multiple friends, I'd probably hang out with them too.

Mom had stayed at UCSF hospital all day with Beep, while the docs put in the Broviac line. Dad was supposed to go there from his work, which was also in San Francisco. After a quick call with Mom, which I had to cut off before the list expanded forever, I emptied my backpack and filled it with Beep's essentials:

1. A toothbrush.
2. His pajama bottoms with pictures of NFL football helmets on them, and some underwear.
3. His Xbox game console, controllers, cables, and a game headset, together with dozens of shooter videogames, their discs in plastic sleeves. Also *FIFA World Cup Soccer*, which unlike the rest isn't bad. The only shooting is shots on goal.

4. His old stuffed animal Ted E. Bear, tan, worn, and with a drooping eye, who I fetched from the top shelf in Beep's closet where he was hidden behind Beep's baseball glove. T.E. Bear came to every hospital stay. By now, he'd seen better days. "Me too," I told him, setting him on top of the videogames.

I bustled down to Mom's room, passing my open door and glimpsing my Fender Stratocaster, sitting mournfully in its stand. Since I'd stopped writing songs with Evan, I hadn't played much guitar. Not the time to think about that now. I grabbed Mom's pajamas out of her dresser and the family iPad off the top of it, and fetched the Xanax and Valium for her out of the medicine cabinet in her and Dad's bathroom.

Then, after I walked Skippy, I pedaled my bike to the El Cerrito Plaza BART station. My backpack bulged with enough pajamas and gaming equipment to impersonate a boy headed to a slumber party. But instead I was taking the train in to San Francisco, to catch the N-Judah streetcar to UCSF hospital again, through falling darkness.

When I transferred to the N-Judah, I got the last seat, flopping down next to an old guy with curly white eyebrows so tangled they looked like shoots migrating to re-seed his scalp. To make space for me to sit, he had to move a plastic bag of take-out cartons reeking of garlic. Beep was back in that awful hospital bed. And here I was again, in a streetcar full of strangers, a box of moving light headed through a dark tunnel toward the hospital, in Muni garlic stink-o-vision.

My phone dinged. I unlocked it to see Evan's post, a picture of a piece of paper reading "Good Thoughts." *Sending these to my friend Kat and her brother Beep,* he'd posted. *Get well soon, Beep.* A sweet thing to send, but I gave it a long exhale.

What was I going to do about Evan? Since the blowup late last school year, I hadn't exchanged texts or even online messages with him, except in my alternate Cipher identity, which no one knew was me. There was no way I could go back to writing songs with Evan. He's an amazing musician, and I mostly do the lyrics. Eventually, if we wrote more songs, we'd do one about crushes or heartbreak, and Evan had been both of those to me, even if he didn't completely know it. With Beep's cancer back, there was already enough to deal with, without prying open an artery in front of Evan.

Responding to Evan—even online—scared me. Still, I hit "like." I appreciated the borrowed good thoughts. Then I texted Calley Rose about being on my way to the hospital to see Beep and asked her to text back. I checked my email—nothing—then checked the email for my alternate online identity, ciphergirl2@gmail.com.

Waiting in Cipher's inbox was an email from Drowningirl. I hadn't heard from her in weeks. Drowningirl is another cancer sib—sibling of a cancer kid—like me. I'd met her on the blood cancer Facebook page when I was logged in as Cipher. We'd started an online friendship, because she's the only person with a life twice as miserable as mine.

She only emailed me (well, Cipher) when things got overwhelming. I'd hoped that when her brother went into remission months ago, she'd gone on to become happy. But here was an email. She sent a poem, in haiku form. She emailed them sometimes, little torn pieces of her heart.

Night fog, life is gray.
Slick pavement gleams wet, so dark:
Even stone now cries.

She ended her email, *Sorry to be a bummer. Be well.*
The Muni streetcar was getting close to UCSF, so I didn't have time to send her a long message. And I wasn't about to bum her out more with my news about my brother.

14

Drowningirl—
Hope you're finding some light, too. Are you okay? Friendhugs,
Cipher.

She always finished her emails to me with "Be well." I finished mine to her the way I always do, with the prevention hotline numbers. *1-800-SUICIDE (784-2433) 1-800-273-TALK (8255).*

2

UCSF is a fifteen-story hospital in San Francisco. Beep was just on their regular kids' floor, not yet in their intensive care unit, called the PICU. ("Pee, I see you," which Beep says makes sense, what with the bedpans.) He didn't have to share his room with anyone, though. With his immune system on blood cancer vacation, they weren't sticking another kid in there to cough on him.

I stood at the door. Beep was watching TV, so he didn't notice me. Beep looked even smaller than usual, propped up in the big hospital bed. He had short hair, and his ears and eyes were slightly too big, like he was still growing into them. He was pale underneath his spray of freckles, and the white bendy tube of a Broviac line stuck out of the gauze dressing on his chest, like he'd been harpooned with a giant drinking straw. A drip was going in through the Broviac, but it wasn't chemo. The bag was dark red, blood products—because Beep's cancer-mutated cells otherwise weren't so good with the basics, like carrying oxygen and clotting. Weirdly, the visitor's chair was empty—no Mom or Dad. Was Dad still at *work*?

"Hey, Beepster."

"Oh, hey." He flicked off the TV.

"Brought your stuff from home. Where are the parent units?"

"Dinner." Beep frowned. "Dad just got here. I said I wanted to be alone."

That was probably code for having a sore neck from watching Mom bounce off walls. It didn't apply to me. Anyway, I had Beep's videogames. "Is Mom freaked?"

"Naaah," he stretched it out, deadpan, earning a smile from me. "But she tried to get them to move me because a kid was coughing—two doors down. And she made them refill the hand sanitizer, because it was more than half empty."

The hand sanitizer on the wall was full now. He probably wasn't making that up. "No holes in the ceiling, though," I said, glancing at it. "So Mom didn't actually hit the roof." I put my backpack in the visitor's chair and hugged Beep, careful not to mash the tube in his chest, collecting a nice Beep hug back while he sat up in bed. He still had his regular-person Beep smell, the warm yeasty smell of person, not the faint chemo-sweat stink of hot metal. "I'm so sorry."

"Me too." We hugged for ten seconds, then he let go. I kept my part of the hug going, rubbing his small back for another couple of seconds.

I turned away and dabbed at my eyes where he couldn't see. I cleared my throat. "Brought your Xbox." Beep has gone so many times from the pediatric floor to the PICU to the step-down unit at UCSF, then to George Mark Children's House, to home, to the emergency room, and back, bouncing between hospitals like a little bald Ping-Pong ball. So I'm the only girl in the universe who can set up an Xbox and have the controllers and headset working in sixty seconds.

"How are you?" I got one question in before I pulled out the packet of game disks and he could disappear into videogame gunfire.

"Okay. I was getting tired of having hair anyway." He didn't even pick up the Xbox controller. "Can you find out what's wrong? Mom got weird. Something with the blood tests. It's—" He frowned. "Bad. Cancer again but mutated or something—they didn't explain well."

A hot pang of fear shot through me. "Sure." I sat down on his oversized bed. What was to explain? He'd relapsed, which meant his ALL—acute lymphocytic leukemia—was back, and he'd spit and hurl his way through another treatment plan to get rid of it. Ninety-five percent of the time, the docs get kids with ALL into remission.

"And Mom." He shook his head. Mom's freak-out meter is useless in signaling between Bad, Really Bad, and OMG.

"Kat." Mom's voice came from the doorway behind me, and I jumped. "Have you eaten?"

"Just some cardboard with Rachel."

"The cafeteria here is still safe," Beep said. "They're not recycling my barf. Yet."

Gross.

"Can I talk to you, honey?" Mom used her forced cheerful voice. "Maybe get a bite?"

I nodded. Beep raised his eyebrows. *You'll find out for me?* I winked and picked up my backpack, which was lighter without Beep's stuff.

"Hi, Kat," Dad said, then "Hey—Xbox," actually recognizing the controller appendage next to Beep. Dad set a bowl of quivering gelatin cubes for Beep on the bedside tray. "I'll play you, Beepster." That was great, because Beep would mop the screen with Dad, which would be good for Beep's morale.

I wandered off with Mom to complete my spy mission.

On our way down, Mom sputtered about Rachel. "I've called her ten times in the last hour." Impressive. "She's not picking up. Something's wrong."

Right. Only if neck hickeys are really wrong. I wouldn't know. "I'm sure she's fine."

"*Something* happened."

Like, she happened to be ignoring Mom. "Rachel turns her ringer off when she can't deal. Can you think of any new reason she's having trouble with that tonight?" I waved my arm around at the hospital cafeteria and vaguely up toward Beep's room. "Send her a text." I grabbed an orange tray and peered down the counter to find the least gross cafeteria choice. Hospitals serve cruddy food, like school lunch, but for dinner. If they make the food bad enough, they figure patients will get well to escape it. The little sign claimed mine was "beef bourguignon," but it was just brown sludge with gray meat and mushy carrots. It almost made Rachel's vegan pizza seem appealing. Almost.

At the table, Mom texted Rachel some version of the Inquisition, then finally looked up. "Your Dad can give you a ride back to BART."

"Not all the way home?" It was already almost eight and dark. Mom was, no doubt, staying at the hospital overnight.

"He's going back to work." She pressed her lips into a tight frown. "He has a filing tomorrow." A filing means turning some long legal pleading paper in to the judge. Like lawyer homework, but I guess you can't get an extension because of a little thing like your kid has a cancer relapse.

"Great." I stabbed a carrot with my fork, to underline how not great. "What's with Beep?"

Mom crinkled her mouth into a worried frown. "It's terrible. He's also got AML."

My stomach tensed. AML—acute myeloid leukemia—is bad, period, which I knew from the blood cancer Facebook page and from my online flirt-buddy Hunter Lange, who had it. It's a different kind of blood cancer you can sometimes get as a side effect of the chemo and radiation. Survival odds were worse.

"If they can't get Beep into remission," Mom said, "we might need you to donate bone marrow."

"Of course." Rachel and I had both been tested after Beep's prior relapse. Neither of us was a perfect match, but I was closer.

Mom blew out a long breath. "They're still figuring out how bad it is. So don't tell Beep about the AML. I don't want to worry him."

I gritted my teeth. Beep would worry way more if no one told him what was wrong.

"Can I have the iPad?" Mom asked. "We should check for clinical trials."

Clinical trials test new things that are more effective than the standard treatment. Beep was in one in his first two go-arounds with the ALL to get him into remission, so we got all his expensive cancer drugs for free—a good thing, because Mom had joked that otherwise we would have had to sell our house to pay for them. I'm not sure it was a joke. I frowned at Mom. "If UCSF has clinical trials, they'll tell you about it."

"What if it's at a different hospital? Or they forgot?"

She had me there. I passed her the iPad. Maybe I could get three bites of "beef bourguignon" in peace. But all I could manage was pushing around the gray lumps, while Mom pecked at the screen. "There's nothing," she said finally. "Except numbers about mortality rates."

I tugged it away from her and clicked back on the browser to Google. Her search terms included "mortality," "morbidity," and "risk of death." *Please don't let insanity be hereditary.* "No one uses words like 'fatality' to name a clinical trial. They don't *scare* people away. Tonight, back home, I'll look online." I shoved my bowl away. Another bite of beef bourguignon would have killed my appetite anyway.

Mom's heels clicked on the corridor tiles while we marched back toward Beep's room, under the too-bright fluorescent light, passing through the pine-disinfectant hospital hallway smell. Back in Beep's room, Dad was still playing the videogame, running around onscreen in a spacesuit while Beep, smiling his little kid grin, blasted him with a laser rifle.

After Beep finished Dad off with the sizzling boom of an onscreen explosion, Dad scurried into the hallway with Mom for a mysterious parent conference before he bolted back to work. I used the break from hovering Mom zone to tell Beep about the AML.

"How bad is that?" he asked.

"Not great. Harder to get rid of, but probably easier in kids than in grownups. Mom didn't want to tell you yet."

"How come?"

"She's insane."

He snorted. "You're supposed to tell me the stuff I *don't* know."

"Well, they're figuring it out exactly with tests. She didn't want you to worry."

"Right. I'm back in the hospital, with a relapse. But not, you know, *worried.* So. What'll they do?"

I sat on Beep's bed next to him. "Well, they'll start chemo, but maybe with different drugs." I took his hand. "Tonight we'll check for an even better, newer treatment program. And if the chemo doesn't get you into remission, you might get a bone marrow transplant, to get rid of the cancer, forever."

"From who?"

"Me."

"Cool," Beep said. "About time someone else in the family got jabbed with a needle."

3

On the BART ride back to the East Bay, I checked my phone. *Sorry—at a movie*, was the only text back from Calley Rose. Going to movies must be nice. But her family has a no-text rule after 10 P.M., and she actually follows rules, so there was no catching up with her.

On Facebook, my online flirt-buddy Hunter had updated his Facebook status. *Thinking of a great summer job—collecting on my life insurance. Profit$$$! And I don't even have to show up!*

I usually enjoy Hunter's sense of humor, which is seriously sick and totally irreverent. But tonight I wasn't in the mood. Mostly, I entertained him. Tonight maybe he could help me. I sent him a Facebook private message. *Hey, handsome shiny-headed guy with a sick sense of humor (even sicker than your blood)—know anything about AML clinical trials? Beep just got diagnosed with AML too. Rough day.*

Of course, it was already after 1 A.M. on the East Coast, where he was. So no quick reply.

Evan had also texted me. *Future indie-band-mate: How is Beep? Email or text me. Or call.*

It's scary, I sent. *Now he also has AML—a worse blood cancer. I promised Mom I'd look online for clinical trials.*

Whoa. So sorry. Can I help?

It would help to have two people looking, because you phrase your searches differently and find different things. *Sure. I'll call you when I get home. Unless it's too late.*

Call anytime. I dream of hanging out with you, even by phone.

Was that an over-the-top flirt? Or was he being sarcastic? Evan was probably just trying to make me feel okay about imposing in the middle of the night. *You have weird dreams, indie-boy,* I finally sent. *But I'll call anyway.*

I sat there fantasizing about saving Beep, as darkness and lights flicked by and I passed Berkeley rooftops: If my bone marrow could fix Beep, somehow that might start fixing everything—my whole life. Instead of hating on each other, maybe Rachel and I could go back to getting along, like we did before Beep got sick. If Beep could survive cancer, maybe Mom could let go of worrying about every other little possibility. Or at least we could remind her that Beepster survived cancer, for perspective. Maybe Dad could stop stressing about money or how it felt to have a son with cancer or keeping our health insurance or whatever sent him running to work all the time.

Maybe I could give up being angry long enough to stop jabbing at everyone with sarcasm. And have multiple friends again. And even get my schoolwork done.

Or not. But, worst case, if not, I might still barely be okay: I could always say, "Sure, I had to repeat a high school grade—but I saved my brother's *life.*"

๑๑

For anyone who's not a serious cancer sibling geek like me, it might be easy to miss what a horrible person those last thoughts make me.

Because "It would be really cool to save Beep with my bone marrow" really translates to "Wouldn't it be neat if Beep's horrible chemo and radiation *failed,* so he needed my bone marrow?" Transplant is a last resort. It comes with a lifetime of immune system–whacking drugs to keep your body from fighting off sis's bone marrow. Which shouldn't be a big issue because it's not like *I* often get rejected.

I just hadn't thought it through. What I did instead was check my Cipher email to see if Drowningirl had answered. Nope. Maybe Drowningirl had an actual life, full of friends and even a boyfriend.

Although if she had lots of friends, it's hard to see how she'd be that miserable. And if she was that miserable, maybe she had as much trouble as I do making new friends.

☯

By the time I bicycled home through darkness from the El Cerrito BART station to our empty house, it was 11:45. Skippy greeted me with four hours of pent-up enthusiasm. I petted his little belly and scratched his ears, which he loved, for so long that I realized I was doing it partly to put off the call to Evan. So after I gave Skippy his time in the back yard, I carried him upstairs to my room for moral support. I turned on my computer and sat at my desk. *Don't cross the line into flirting.* I took a deep breath and called Evan. Maybe it was so late he'd gone to bed.

He picked up on the first ring. "Hi Kat. Thanks for calling." His voice was quiet, like he was trying not to wake his parents up.

"Thanks, uh, for helping." My pauses between words were so long it sounded like I was translating French.

"I've missed talking to you so much," he said.

Which was like a stab in my chest. I almost gasped at the quick razor-cut-through-my-heart sharpness of it, because of how I've missed Evan. "I was really mad at you," I said. "You wouldn't have enjoyed talking to me."

"I'm enjoying it now," Evan said. "So maybe that means you're not as mad anymore?"

Long pause, on my end. "If you help me find a clinical trial for Beep, we might be able to work things out."

"Enough to write songs together again?"

"Don't press it," I said, and I had to clamp my teeth together to keep from calling him Skinnyboy, which is what I call him when I'm in my secret online identity of Cipher, who no one knew was me. It had been a long day, and I was almost dizzy. Talking to Evan felt like walking on a high wire. "Maybe if we find a complete cure for Beep's cancer."

"Well, then," he said, "let's *find* this cancer cure."

I laughed, a nervous bark of scared, and we were off. I explained we were looking for phase III clinical trials for pediatric AML and then Evan pounded away on Google, while I searched the different blood cancer sites. We shot links back and forth by email about leads we were turning up.

The official Monroe house rule, instituted because of Rachel, is no calls after 11 P.M. But Mom was at the hospital, Dad was back at work, Rachel was off fogging car windows, and we were fighting cancer. Forget the rules.

Evan found it first: www.clinicaltrials.gov, the searchable trial database of the National Institutes of Health.

Then it was a slog. The descriptions were in medical jargon about as readable as medieval French. In the middle of our search, Rachel came home and at one point banged on the wall, because I was talking so excitedly with Evan. I ignored her. After we turned up a bunch of random phase I trials, I finally stumbled on "Bortezomib and Sorafenib Tosylate in Treating Patients with Newly Diagnosed Acute Myeloid Leukemia," a promising phase III trial accepting patients at 140 different hospitals, including UCSF Benioff Children's, where Beep was.

The chemicals were supposed to generally stomp little misshapen leukocyte butt, seven different ways. The trial was limited to patients with "High Allelic Ratio FLT3/ITD." I had no idea what that meant, even as a serious cancer sibling geek, but for once I hoped it described my brother. Unless it was bad.

"Wow," I said when we were done. It had taken almost two hours, and by then we were giddy, having won the online scavenger hunt, making unpronounceable cancer drug name jokes. It was after 2 A.M., and I was sitting in the dark in my room, lit only by the computer screen. The door thudded closed downstairs, from Dad finally getting home from work, after Skippy's quick who-woke-me-up bark. "Evan, you're my hero, and officially great."

"Whew. You finally noticed."

I don't know what he meant by that, but I had to hang up. "Dad just got in. I'm not supposed to be on the phone after eleven."

"It'll be our secret. Good-night. Sweet dreams."

"Uh, you too. See you tomorrow."

"You mean today."

I laughed. "Right. 'Bye. See you today."

I sat back in my chair in the darkness and smiled at the glowing blue computer screen. I'd done exactly zero homework, which put me one day behind, but it was still early, not like the deep, undone homework crater at the end of last year. Plenty of time to dig out. *Yes.* We would help Beep stomp cancer. I emailed Mom, put in the links about the trial, and told her Evan and I had found it. I sent Evan a bcc, to make sure he knew I was giving him full credit. I even copied Dad's work email, which I figured Dad would check again before bed because it was only 2 A.M. I hit send. It felt great.

ॐ

It was a shame to waste that nice feeling on being asleep, because the next morning Rachel exploded at me by 7:03. We share one bathroom, so we have a schedule. I shower first, then Rachel takes twice as long, since she has actual gorgeousness to assemble.

Tired from being up late, I played tag with the snooze alarm. That put me behind, so Rachel pounded on the bathroom door. Mom had spent the night at the hospital, and Dad had already left for work.

"Why don't you take less time?" I opened the door, wrapped in a towel, letting steam escape. "And settle for almost completely stunning."

"Why don't you stop being a selfish jerk?"

Okay, game on. "Oh—you need extra blow dryer time? To inflate your air head?"

"What I need is sleep. You kept me up all night yelling through the wall on the phone."

Exaggeration. Evan and I had been talking excitedly, not yelling, and Rachel hadn't gotten home until after midnight, long after school-night curfew.

"For your information, I was finding Beep a clinical trial."

"Because you're so damned perfect."

I don't know where that came from, especially from perfect Rachel. I was still annoyed that she'd left everything to me. "At least I was doing something. Not abandoning everyone."

"You're awful." She barged past me. "No wonder you have no friends." Okay, ouch.

She slammed the bathroom door in my face, so I yelled through it. "Except you were doing something. With Brian. Moaning the theme song of the Berkeley back seat petting zoo."

While she was trying to assemble a response, I added, "Which you've moaned to so many boyfriends, guys at your school probably hum it when you walk by."

"Bitch" was the nicest word I could make out, muffled through the door.

ᘐ

I was still in a bad mood when I was picked up by carpool. Mad at Rachel and mad at myself for getting in a fight with her, again.

Evan was smiling, but when he saw my grumpy expression, it faded. "Thought you'd be in a better mood."

"I was, but Rachel started hating on me." And reminding me I'm a total loser. I slid into the back seat next to him. "Sorry. Just the usual." I've complained about Rachel before.

"Well," he said a minute later, when we pulled up to Tyler's house to pick him up, "at least you know Beep's relapse isn't disrupting things at home."

I rewarded that effort with a weak smile, which was the best I could manage. Actually, until Beep got cancer the first time, Rachel and I got along.

෧෬

"Hey, Crazy Kat." Tracie Walsh, my soccer teammate and least favorite person, blocked my path in the hall that morning between second and third period.

I was not in the mood to deal with Tracie, but her hanger-on friend Ashley had me blocked too, so I stopped.

"This year, don't be a flunktard." Tracie looked down at me from under her blonde hair and over her California surfer-girl freckles. She's the head of a little in-crowd of self-congratulating girls everyone had called "the Tracies" since grade school.

"What?" I said. Some guy bumped me hard in the back then went around us.

"I hear you're ineligible for volleyball this fall." Her expression was vague disgust.

I was, because of my grades, at least until the first quarter ended on November 1. It was annoying, though, to have Tracie remind me. With the prior go-around of Beep's cancer, losing all my friends, and my "major depressive episode," the end of last year had turned into a handed-in-homework-free zone. "What's it to you?"

"You're not a dumbshit." She shook her head. "Pull your grades up before soccer season."

I frowned at her. Her interest almost made sense. I was one of the best players on the soccer team, and because of years of playing club-league soccer with Tracie, I could practically read her mind, so when she stripped the ball and inevitably dribbled up field instead of passing, I'd cover her position.

"Saw you with Evan yesterday," Tracie said. She crinkled her lips as if she had a sour taste in her mouth.

Ah. The real reason for our motivational chat.

"Maybe this year you should concentrate on your schoolwork," she said. "Instead of musicians. So we can have a decent soccer season."

If that advice had come from anyone else, I might have paid more attention. "Maybe you should learn how to pass the ball. That might help, too." But I wasn't done being annoyed or done talking. "You threw Evan away. *Three times.*" And had made sure everyone in the Berkeley-Albany-Oakland area knew that it was her choice.

She smirked down at me. That was part of her ultimate in-girl mystique: She always broke up with the guy first, even the hot, talented guy. "So?"

"So you don't get to decide who he talks to anymore." Even I knew that much about how the boyfriend thing works.

She frowned at me. "He only hangs out with you out of pity."

Ouch. Had Evan told her that, along with everything else, back when she was his girlfriend? My insides felt scooped out, but I didn't let that show. "He doesn't hang out with you at all. Maybe he's over you."

Tracie's eyes narrowed, her expression fierce. "Ha. If I wanted Evan, I could get him back like *that.*" She snapped her fingers, annoyingly close to my face, a quick flash of pink nail polish. She stepped forward, crowding me.

I didn't back up, and I don't do intimidated. I put my left shoulder forward, like we were on a soccer field, and drove between her and Ashley, bumping them both, hard.

Ashley dropped her binder. "Watch it!"

"Get your grades up," Tracie's voice followed me, loud over the hallway noise. "Or there'll be *consequences.*"

Ooh. Consequences. What was she going to do now? She'd already wrecked everything last year. And whatever she had in mind, it wasn't as bad as cancer.

ೄ

To the shock of everyone, by the middle of freshman year, I had somehow wormed my way into best-friend status with Evan. Along with writing songs and playing music together after school every day, we were spending lunches together, in plain view of humanity and even Tracie Walsh. But Evan is an awesome musician and super-hot, so then Tracie swooped in and scooped him up as her boyfriend. So much for my lunches with Evan. He was dragged around instead by Tracie, like a cute new purse with legs. How could he be with her? Tracie was the ruler of her toxic in-group, commanding its endless convulsions of expelling someone through threats that if the other girls didn't exclude her social victim-of-the-week, they'd be next.

I'd nearly hurled the first time I'd seen Evan making out with Tracie behind the gym, his hand tangled in her long blonde hair. Glurg. A picture of that sweaty clinch would have made an awesome diet aid, taped to the fridge at home, but about then Beep was going through his earlier round of chemo, so there was already plenty of mealtime nausea for the Monroes.

Then, when Tracie broke up with Evan, it was all he wanted to talk about—how sad he was. A topic, weirdly, I wasn't super interested in. I tried to be sympathetic, but then they got back together. Then she drop-kicked him away again. And then the blonde spit-burp from hell got together with him *again*, and he didn't believe me, that she was horrible, because somehow her lip lock was more persuasive than my mere words.

Tracie hated me even more than I hated her. Maybe my friendship with Evan was a threat. Unfortunately, as the leader of the popular clique, Tracie was in a position to do something about that hate. And when the Tracies crank up your misery, they're thorough. While

Tracie was using Evan as her yo-yo boy toy, she and the rest of her in-crowd also got to all my girl friends—Calley Rose, Amber, and even Elizabeth. Breathless promises of admission to the Tracie-Wannabe set were dangled, or threats of total social death, or both. Also, Tracie passed on to those girls some semi-horrible funny jokes I'd made about them. Jokes Evan had helpfully shared with Tracie.

With Beep's cancer and the start of fighting with Rachel last year, I was cranky. And during my hundreds of hours with Evan, I'd vented some of that anger, joking just between the two of us. I might have been a teensy sarcastic when I talked about things like Amber's shopping obsession and Elizabeth's endlessly-repeated dramatic hair flip. Evan apparently thought my lines were so funny, he repeated them to his new girlfriend, Tracie. Who scuttled over to Elizabeth and Calley Rose and Amber, pointing out how amusingly Kat had slammed them. Thanks, Evan.

I wasn't invited to Elizabeth's or Amber's birthday sleepovers. Those girls cut me off. Completely. So basically, I'd lost everyone. Lost my other friends because of my big mouth. Lost Evan because every other week he was lip-locked to Tracie's big mouth. It broke my heart.

After that, to avoid the lemon-juice-on-paper-cut sting of sitting next to Evan on carpool days, I scooted myself into the front seat for the rest of freshman year. I'm not sure Tyler, in morning stupor mode next to Evan, noticed. But Evan did. Every day, he asked me how I was.

"Fine," I said in an empty voice that meant not fine, and didn't ask how he was.

Sometimes, Evan's mother tried gently, "How's your brother doing?"

Vomiting everything, thanks, but no one wants to hear that right after breakfast. "He has *cancer*," I said, to shut her up, which worked. "I don't want to talk about it." I put in my ear buds to listen to music and pulled the hood of my sweatshirt over my sullen face.

Everyone tries to fit in somewhere in high school, but there's no My Brother Has Cancer Club. I guess at the end of last year I could have done other school activities. Maybe even combined them with a service project: if not a blood drive, maybe I could have introduced the boys in chess club to the mysterious toothbrush. But somehow, Beep's struggle with cancer seemed more important.

4

After school that day, Mom called to say Beep "looked punky," but that was just Mom's report so I didn't worry much. Anyone back for a third round with cancer would look a little down. So, unaware of the growing problem, while I was at the computer and supposed to be doing my homework, I went on Facebook. I was way overdue in posting an update for Beep.

Beep doesn't really Facebook, but for the last two times he had cancer, I set up an account to share how he was doing, so we didn't have to answer a zillion calls from distant relatives, family friends, and classmates' parents. It helps to let everyone know what's going on, to take the edge off worry. Which is a public service, because cancer practically pulls worried people out of passing cars.

But the only way to prevent three time zones of mass freakout and a babbled avalanche of untested home cancer cures is to post in the language of Mom Calmese. In Mom Calmese, problems are past tense, obstacles are overcome, and there's always a plan to deal with the current situation, which is never dire. We're cheerful, positive, thankful, and optimistic. We never freak out.

My mom, with an actual anxiety disorder since I was little—which Beep's cancer hasn't exactly made better—is useless at Mom Calmese. So I write Beep's updates. I pretend I'm the exact opposite of my actual mom. Even in Calmese, though, I had a hard time posting about Beep's relapse. But no one else was going to—heaven forbid we let Mom near the Internet. I sat clattering at the keyboard, messing with wording.

A little setback this week. Beep's blood test came back with some
concerns, so he's at UCSF for another chemo round to get back into

33

remission. Beep is back in his temporary home away from home, surrounded by a great team.

Mom Calmese is the perfect language for lying by telling the truth. Every word was true, but what I left out—how scared I was for Beep and how much I wished he could skip the misery of chemo again—made the whole post a hollow lie.

I logged out of Beep's account and logged in on my own. I still Facebook, not just because I post Beep's updates for everyone. Lots of kids in the cancer community, like Hunter, still use Facebook, because it's better than CaringBridge, which is similar but only for sick people, so it's medical-information-filled, with posts about "bowel movement frequency." Eww. I'm not exaggerating. A large part of the sick child mortality rate is probably kids dying of embarrassment when they find out what their parents posted on CaringBridge.

Hunter, my online flirt-buddy who also has leukemia, had replied to my Facebook message about clinical trials. *Yeah. I'm on one. Borte-something-Tonsylate. Not fun.*

Of course not. It was freaking chemo. *Thanks for the info. How are other things? Besides possibly dying?* I added that, because Hunter almost always responded "possibly dying, but otherwise fine." Although currently cancer bald, Hunter was a hot senior—even when he wasn't extra warm from radiation treatments. He was some kind of basketball star back at his high school in Maryland. He played point guard, which is sort of the basketball equivalent of center midfielder in soccer, the position I play. He had even gotten some scholarship to play basketball in college, which was looking less and less likely, since—as Hunter put it—he couldn't even pass the physical for a Mighty Mites team, whatever that was.

There was also a status update from Evan, a selfie picture with his eyes closed. *Tired*, he posted. *Up half last night talking medical research with a cute girl.*

Evan thought I was cute? My heart flipped a little somersault. Evan is another reason I Facebook. Because he's a musician, he uses it to get the word out about upcoming gigs and to "connect with his audience." I wasn't sure how to respond to the cute girl post, though. I'd sworn off flirting with Evan, except in my online secret alter ego Cipher. So I went and got the iPad, so I could also log in separately as Cipher.

Ooh, Skinnyboy, I commented as Cipher, picking up on the "medical topic": *Concerned about a rash?*

Evan: *Nah. Was researching cancer clinical trials.*

Evan knew Cipher as my online "good friend" from the cancer community. Cipher posted lots of comments on my cancer blog and had friended Evan on Facebook, where they flirted with appalling frequency. *Whew!* I responded as Cipher. *I should definitely get to know you better. Maybe even wrap my tentacles around you.* Somehow, back last year when I invented my Cipher identity to keep talking to Evan online, even though I was officially furious, I'd said, as Cipher, that I had tentacles and a poisonous stinger, and it had become a thing.

But if Evan was being specific that he was looking up cancer treatments with a girl, people would know it was with Kat Monroe, especially after his post the day before about giving Beep and me good thoughts—and they'd probably hassle him for bad eyesight, for calling me cute. I went back to the computer keyboard, where I was logged in as me. *Evan is my hero,* I commented as Kat. *(*Sends Evan 10,000 great friend points*)*

Tracie: *Now Kat's trying to bribe boys to be her friend.*

Evan: *(*Sigh*)*

Was he sighing at my comment, or Tracie's dig or Cipher wanting to get to know him better? But it was a problem that Tracie had posted a comment. Once Tracie posts something, the rest of her crowd piles on.

Ashley: *Bribe—ha. Kat's parents don't have enough money to buy her a friend.*

I went to the iPad to post as Cipher.

Cipher: *Kat's brother just had a cancer relapse. You must be a real caring person to make fun of their spending their money on cancer drugs.*

Ashley: *Didn't know. Not what I meant. Nobody has enough money to buy Kat a friend. Not even Bill Gates.*

Evan: *Stop being mean to Kat. Tracie and Ashley, I'm unfriending you.*

There was no response from Tracie or Ashley. I kept staring at his post. Had he actually unfriended them on Facebook, so they couldn't post on his wall anymore?

The private message counter changed on the iPad, going from a one to a two. I clicked on it.

Thanks for sticking up for Kat, Evan had messaged Cipher.

No problem, Skinnyboy. Sometimes I use my barbed tentacles for good.—Cipher.

Cipher's other private message was from Drowningirl. *Things are awful,* it read. *Awful day in an awful week.* It was from two hours ago. According to Facebook, Drowningirl wasn't currently online. A spike of worry and fear stabbed me. It was like being my mom, all of a sudden. Be okay, dgirl. And don't disappear.

Email me, I messaged back to Drowningirl as Cipher. *Or call. 1-800-SUICIDE.*

By the time I glanced back to the main Facebook feed, various other Tracies had piled on. Were they all together somewhere, or was this some test of the emergency Tracies' cell phone network?

Sara: *geez evan they were kidding.*

Lauren: *Partly.*

Right, I posted. *You can say anything as long as you say 'kidding' afterward. Even if you can't capitalize or punctuate and don't have a personality.*

Jenna: *See, Kat dishes 2.* Crap. I'd posted that message as Kat, not Cipher.

Lauren: *Totally, but not funny.*

Sara: *Yah don't take the pity friend thing 2 far evan.*

Evan: *I'm unfriending Sara and Jenna and Lauren along with Tracie and Ashley. Forever.*

Wow. Had he actually done it? There were no more comments from any of the five Tracies. I went to Evan's timeline, and scrolled through his immense list of Facebook friends. It no longer included any of the Tracies—no Tracie, Ashley, Sara, Lauren, or Jenna. Their snark had been fairly mild, to earn a lifetime unfriending. Maybe Evan wanted me to know he was on my side, no matter what. I sat there in a long pause of happy-hopeful stunned. I picked up the iPad, because this might get mushy. As Cipher, I commented. *You are also my hero. Thanks for standing up to those girls for Kat. (*Cipher tucks away her poisonous barbs and wishes she could give Evan a close tentacle hug. He is great.*)*

Evan sent back a private Facebook message to Cipher, *Or maybe someday I could work my way up to at least holding your hand?*

I frowned at the computer screen. Holding hands with Cipher, not the real me, Kat. *With my tentacles*, I messaged back as Cipher, *you'd get covered with sucker marks. Sucker.* Even my flirts, as Cipher, had a drive-by bite to them.

If you also had poisonous fangs, he sent back, *you'd fit right in with some of the girls at my school.*

I hoped he was talking about Tracie and her followers, not me. *Darn. You're already marked with girl wounds? Aren't there any nice girls at your school?*

Thoroughly wounded. There is one great girl, though, who I'm probably crazy about.

For about ten seconds, I went to fantasy dream-park land, and imagined Evan meant me, Kat. But it was a scary topic, while I was flirting with him as Cipher—especially given how into Tracie he'd been last year. I almost certainly did not want to hear him gush about some other random girl at school he liked. *Humph. Skinnyboy, free advice: Never tell a girl you're flirting with that you're crazy about another girl. Tacky.*

Maybe I'm not crazy about another girl. Maybe I'm crazy about you.

Now I got annoyed. It was always so heart-bending when I flirted with Evan as Cipher. What I really wanted was for him to like me as Kat, not go into full-court flirt with Cipher, an imaginary girl he'd never met. *Yeah, right. Me with the poisonous tentacles. Then you're crazy, period. And I don't date the deranged. TTFN, Cipher.* (Ta-ta for now. And, technically, that was (1) game, (2) set, and (3) match, as a drive-by flirt.)

There was a ding of an incoming email. I had Cipher's email open in a different window on the monitor. I clicked over. The new message was from Drowningirl.

Can't take it anymore. On top of everything, BFH is being a total bitch.

BFH is Drowningirl's sister, Brat From Hell. Since my sister Rachel also mostly behaves like a bitch from hell, Drowningirl and I have a lot in common.

God grant me the serenity to accept the things I can't change, Drowningirl went on. *And the self-control not to kill BFH or myself.*

As Cipher, I emailed back and forth with her for twenty minutes, trying to type-talk her down from the ceiling, or maybe even the ledge. She sent a poem.

> *Shrew'ed*
> *An axe whacks, when chopping wood.*
> *The bite of steel into something softer, cut, then broken,*
> *Once alive.*
> *I'm struck, struck, struck by the noise.*
> *Struck, struck, struck.*
> *How like her words.*

Drowningirl finally signed off with *be well*, promising to email again later in the week. I signed off too, as Cipher with *1-800-SUICIDE (784-2433)*. Then, back in my real world identity of Kat, I typed Evan a private message: *Thanks for standing up to the Tracies for me*, less flirty than what I'd sent as Cipher.

I sat, giving the computer monitor a kind of dreamy gaze. I was worried about Drowningirl, but had the warm tingly feeling that Evan—even if just out of pity—had my back. That tingly feeling faded as I thought about the Tracies. They'd been unfriended, by hot, popular awesome musician Evan, for lowly me. Somehow, they'd make me pay.

∽

I hadn't managed to get any actual homework done, so the next morning I peeled off the label from my Yoplait container at breakfast, blotted off the pink strawberry yogurt spillover glop, and stapled that label to a sheet of binder paper. I wrote my name at the top, with the heading *Culture Française*.

In afternoon French class, I set it on Mme Yves' desk. "*Voilà!*"

Mme Yves even looks French—dark-haired and skinny, wearing a belted black dress that made her look like she was headed to a cocktail party instead of serving her latest nine-month sentence with bored high school students. "*Quelle?*" She knitted her brows.

How do you say stroke of genius in French? "*Un coup de brillance!*" I announced. "*Un bon idee, n'est pas?*"

"*C'est quoi?*"

I gave up on French entirely for the rest. I needed to sell this. "Yogurt is cultured milk. And Yoplait is a French name. And the wrapper is thin, a symbol of shallow American consumer culture." I gave her what I hoped was a winning smile. "By comparison."

She crossed her arms and frowned.

"See," I babbled on. "You're essentially French, Mme Y." Although, technically, she was born in Montreal. "And you're looking down on the wrapper right now—that's exactly how the French view American culture and our limited understanding of theirs."

"*Je suis Canadienne.*" She shook her head at my little offering. "*Une grande différence.*"

She lifted the paper, holding it disdainfully with two fingers as if it were still dripping pink yogurt blobs, and dropped it in the trash. "*Zero.*" She pronounced the no credit—or, I guess *pas de credite*—the French way, all gargled in the back of the throat with derision.

Well, *merde.*

Tracie was scowling at me from her seat, like I was trying to deliberately wreck my grade, instead of desperately trying to save it. "*Imbécile,* I'll get you for this," she whispered as I passed.

I stopped and leaned down like I had a secret to tell her. "*Merci, cochon égoïste avec le ballon.*" (Thanks, ball hog.)

She just smiled back, like she had already figured out some payback. Great.

಄

By that night, Beep looked like a zombie from one of his videogames. His lips were the ash-gray color of dust from a vacuum cleaner bag.

He'd spiked a fever of a hundred and three Fahrenheit. Even scarier: Beep, of all people, was too listless to play videogames.

They started an antibiotic drip and made the call to transfer Beep to the PICU. All the ICU beds were full, though, so they scurried around over there, figuring out what kid could be stabilized enough to move out to the step-down unit or the floor to make room.

Probably, when they put the Broviac line in Beep and flushed it with saline, they blew some germs into his chest vein, where there wasn't much immune system waiting, thanks to the blood-cancer. So now he had sepsis—a blood-system-wide bacterial infection. Before the hospital even got serious about poisoning Beep with chemo again, those little germs were spreading, trying to send him home early, in a bag.

It was 7 P.M., and I was visiting, in semi-useless hover mode, trying to keep Mom from destroying medical equipment as she bounced off walls. She called Dad, who—of course—was only now on his way from work.

"Hank!" She barked it with an urgency that made his name an accusation. "Should I threaten to sue, if they don't move Beep this minute?"

Right. This minute. They didn't have a bed to move him into.

I could hear Dad yelling at her, through the phone, even across the room. "*Never* threaten to sue. They're *already* paranoid because I'm a lawyer."

Mom held the phone away from her ear and winced, he yelled so loud. Except when it involves things that cut into his work time, Dad usually lets Mom have her way, because otherwise she'd drive everyone crazy rethinking decisions. For once, though, Dad stood up to her. "Don't even use the word 'sue' at a hospital, except as someone's name."

"Mom," I said, after Dad hung up on her. "Sit down, be quiet, and let the nurses do their job. Or I'm calling hospital security on you, before someone else does." Even Beep looked over at that.

It's possible I was exaggerating, but I doubt it.

5

I was mostly out of it the day after they moved Beep to the PICU, from stress, worry, and lack of sleep. It had been 10 P.M. when they'd finally gotten a bed for him, and even later when we got him settled. Then I'd had to take Muni and BART and then bicycle home, where I'd had trouble falling asleep.

I share second-period Algebra 2 with all five of the Tracies and three of the Tracie-Wannabes. While I yawned—even more than usual—there was whispering and giggling and glancing over when Ms. Clarke turned her back. Why? Giggling wouldn't be the news about my brother's returned cancer making the rounds. Tracie looked over at me with a satisfied smirk. Was she just trying to make me feel worried?

After fourth-period English, Evan met me at my locker. "You, uh, still want to eat lunch together?" He had his scrunched brown paper sack in hand, but for some reason was making eye contact with the locker below mine instead of with me.

"Of course." After carpool that morning, Evan had asked if we could have lunch together. I'd jumped at that, a chance to go back to how things used to be, and a lot less lonely than the end of last year. But now Evan's shoulders were slumped, and he looked unhappy about it. I retrieved my sandwich and fruit from behind my books, with a sinking feeling. I followed him out toward our old spot by the tennis courts. Why did Evan look like he was shuffling to a funeral? "Why? You get a better offer?" It would be just like Tracie to invite him, trying to sink her hooks into him again.

"No. I thought you might not want to, now that you have a boyfriend."

"What?" I stopped. We'd just gone out the back door into the concrete by the steps. Was this some joke? "Who?"

Evan turned around. "I heard you got back together with Curtis Warren—"

"Back? I've never *been* together with Curtis." My mood exploded in a ball of anger. "Wait. You *believed* the slut-shaming fiction Curtis wrote about me?" That wonderfully detailed little note had circulated last year, just before Evan got together with Tracie and abandoned me the first time. Evan opened his mouth to say something, but I kept going. "He even made up half the *spellings*."

"No!" Evan said. "'Course I didn't. But I heard you kissed him . . ."

I put my hands on my hips, one of them holding my now-squished lunch. "I did not—and will not ever—kiss Curtis Warren." I was glaring at Evan so hard, it was amazing that his straight, perfect teeth didn't catch fire. "Who told you that?"

"Ashley said you got back togeth—"

"Ashley. Tracie's friend. Who hates me. Who is mad that you unfriended her and Tracie on Facebook. Who always does what Tracie tells her to do. Hello? She lies."

"Oh," Evan said, like this was the first time he'd thought of that. Guys. So dense. I don't know why we let them run anything when they grow up, let alone whole companies.

Great. This is just what I need. More talk about me and Curtis. "I hope you didn't pass on that wonderful rumor."

"I'd never do that."

"Excuse me?" I was breathing hard, and somehow my eyes were wet at the fresh memory of a sharp hurt. "You did. Last year."

"What?" He gave me a blank stare.

"When you became your own wreck-my-life-media? When— better than telephone and television—the best way to get my snarky comments to everyone was tell-an-Evan?"

"Oh. Right." His shoulders sank. "I don't know why Tracie passed those on—"

"That's what she does, Evan. Getting people excluded is the Tracies' team sport."

"I'm sorry." He looked miserable. "I didn't mean to mess up your life. I know you're mad at me."

It wasn't just that. "I thought I could count on you."

To be my friend. To be my BFF. Or maybe actual boyfriend. Or all of those. I'd thought I was important to Evan. More important, anyway, than holding hands or swapping spit with Tracie. Or even his constant flirts with online Cipher, who he didn't even know.

"You can." Now he was making those big eyes at me. "Count on me."

Humph. I shook my head, thinking about the stupid lies about me and Curtis Warren. "I'm probably the only slut-shamed girl in America who's never even been really kissed full on the lips."

"You've never been kissed?"

"No, Evan," I said tiredly. "Or anything. At least if you don't count a game of spin the bottle in sixth grade, which I don't, because it wasn't exactly romance. Once Curtis lunged at me with his tongue out. But if that counts as a human kiss, I'm dating outside my species."

We shuffled over to our old lunch spot and sat on the bench, but in silence. When I pulled it out, my peanut butter and jam sandwich was mashed so hard from my clutching it through my lunch bag, it was oozing purple jam from four finger-dent wounds.

Evan finally broke the silence. "I have a chocolate bar. You should eat it instead. It has your name on it." He set a Kit Kat bar next to me, a peace offering.

I laughed. That wasn't a cure-all, but it was something. Which was nice, because the day got worse from there.

◌

After lunch, while Evan went off to his class, I was opening my locker when my phone rang. It was Mom, who thinks it's rude to call during the school day, so this was bad. "Beep's doing terribly." Her voice was urgent. Beep was in the PICU, but not responding to the antibiotic. They'd stopped the chemo, to give him a chance to beat the infection before they poisoned him more. One of the docs had told Mom to consider having a priest give Beep last rites, in case. So I should probably go there right after school. Even Dad was on the way, leaving work early.

My locker is outside in a hallway, next to Kayla Southerland's. If it wasn't for my homework holiday, Kayla would be the official screw-up girl of our class. She gets in actual fights, and once showed up with a black eye. I used to think she and I might become friends, but when she gets cranky, I get cranky right back. Now she's especially mean to me, since I'm the only girl who's more of a social outcast than she is. Also, I might have commented a few times on her makeup.

I froze, after hanging up from the call. I couldn't remember what book I was supposed to be pulling out, and I guess my open locker door was in her way. Kayla banged it hard to shut it, but it bounced right back, off my arm.

She glared at me through her hand-trowel makeup. "Move it, Crazy Kat."

"What?" That nickname just never got old. When I turned to her, she must have seen I was crying, but it's probably harder to tell without a smudgy giant river of running mascara.

"What's your problem, freak?" This, from the girl whose look was scary clown.

"My brother's sick with cancer."

"Ooh." She shrank back and wiped the hand she'd used to shove my locker door on her pants, like she'd catch it, from skin contact.

"Cancer's not contagious." I grabbed her by the shirt and stepped so close she flinched. "And it's not like bad manners and bad makeup." I let her go with a push. "You don't already have it."

I closed my locker without getting whatever stupid book I was supposed to grab. Ignoring Kayla's hostile squawks, I walked home, so I could get my bike and go to BART and Muni and UCSF to see Beep. And so I wouldn't beat Kayla stupid. Or more stupid.

Not yet, anyway.

6

With over a hundred copies fluttering around the halls last year and others passed in class for reader comments, almost everyone at my school had had a chance to read the extended slut-shaming fiction about me by Curtis Warren, complete with creative spelling and even more creative description of my supposed moaning.

Here's what really happened:

Freshman year, just before Evan got together with Tracie and before the Evan-and-the-Tracies friendship meltdown when everyone started hating me, I got invited to a party at Cindy Cruller's. I went, because Evan might be there, and I somehow thought it was a good idea to show up to a party he was invited to. Except he never showed up. Being popular, I guess he already knew those things were dull.

The point of parties at Cindy's house, which I didn't know back then, was that her mom's idea of "supervision" was to wander around with a tall glass of vodka, pretending it was water. Then pretend she was still in high school, refill the glass, pretend that she wasn't laughing too loud, pound down a third, and then finally stagger upstairs to hide, embarrassed. Which, for the record, is pathetic.

Evan wasn't there, so while I waited for him to not show up, I talked to Curtis Warren, who was at least sometimes funny. I used to think Curtis and I were in a friendly competition for class clown, about who was funniest (which I totally win, since most of my jokes don't involve fart noises). I also thought Curtis sort of liked me, because of my sense of humor. With some guys, though, when they say they like girls with a sense of humor, they mean they'd like a girl who laughs at their jokes, not tops them. Curtis hunches with his shoulders rolled forward, and his ears stick out so much, they look like they're mounted sideways.

Coupled with his prominent front teeth, the look is skinny gerbil. Not ideal for attracting the ladies, even without the fart jokes, which he managed two of, while we were talking.

Anyway, I was making Curtis laugh, feeling awkward, clutching a red plastic cup of Hawaiian Punch and looking around for Evan. Curtis finished his rum and coke and asked if I wanted to go to the back yard, "to see Cindy's fountain."

That sounded slightly less stupid than craning my neck around her living room, looking for Evan until I pulled a back muscle, so I said sure. On our way out, Curtis stumbled down the back steps, which made me wonder how much he'd had to drink.

Okay—I had never before (or, let's face it, since) been invited to a party at Cindy's. I had no idea—*at all*—that wandering out to the dark back yard was code for being willing to have Curtis try to tickle my tonsils. With his tongue.

We were outside in the semi-dark back yard for fifteen long, awkward minutes of halting conversation, while I came up with various ways to make fun of the gurgling fountain and Curtis got even more fidgety, as if he was nervous or scared. *Was he afraid of the dark?* I wondered. Then I wondered if Evan had arrived at the party and was somewhere in the house behind us, while I was out here babbling bad jokes about fountains. "Uh, should we go back in?" I asked.

"Kat," Curtis said, with stress in his voice. I looked at him, and he grabbed the back of my head, pulled my face down toward his, and tried to kiss me, with his tongue already sticking out. Eww.

I turned my face away, so he mostly got the side of my mouth, with his slimy tongue pressed against my cheek like a slug. I tried to pull away, but he was holding the back of my head and trying to press my face into his, trying to lock lips again, his breath smelling like rum and corn chips. The grabbing, pulling thing crossed over into *way* not okay, and I took a step back, but his hand was tangled in my hair and he was still trying to pull me toward him for the kiss. He got the footwork wrong, so my move pulled him forward and off balance. He tripped and fell.

I took two more steps backward, like I was afraid his tongue would keep slithering after me like a little poisonous snake, then stared down at him, sprawled on the path and in the shrubs.

"Wow, some fountain," I said, before he could pick himself up or I could think of something more appropriate. "It must even have a frog. *Something* tried to catch me with a slimy tongue." Then I fled back into the house.

Not the most thoughtful response.

But not as awful as his, eventually.

When I came back in through the door, people were looking over expectantly, some nudging each other. Then I got it—apparently everyone but me knew that when you disappear to the back yard, it's for the zoning: It's make-out city, protected by darkness and two steps down, so even Cindy's drunken mom can't stumble down to "supervise" you groping each other. Which was a shame, because, at a minimum, Curtis needed some coaching.

A minute later Curtis came in, pink-faced, glaring. His look said *I'll get you for this.*

And by the next Monday, he had. Scattered in the hallways at school were hundreds of photocopies of his two-page description of how he supposedly had sex with me in Cindy's back yard. Later that week, Evan got together with Tracie for the first time.

7

The next day, on a different antibiotic, Beep crawled back from the gray edge of death. Which was great, because it let the hospital get back to the urgent business of nearly killing him with the chemo drugs—so cancer would finally realize he was a bad neighborhood and move out for good.

I dragged myself to the curb for morning carpool. At school, Kayla Southerland was waiting for me by my locker, which was now graffiti-covered, illustrated with a large cartoon cat in black marker and the oversized angular letters "Crazy Kat" below. Payback for yesterday's grab-and-insult?

"Nice." I pulled my World History book out and stuffed my backpack in. I shut my locker.

Kayla continued to slouch there, smirking. She's an art kid, always drawing in the margins of her notebook. And the Crazy Kat writing looked like hers.

"You're really good with drawing." I tilted my head and pretended to admire her cartoon cat—which was nicely done, and definitely crazy-looking. "So I can't figure out why you're so awful with eyeliner and mascara. Really. Your eyes are like little fishbowls of dead rainbow trout."

She frowned, then turned to go. I walked alongside. "What do you call today's look? Stage musical prostitute?"

"No, wait." I snapped my fingers and pointed at her, like I'd just figured it out. "It's 'I'm saving myself for a color-blind guy with a raccoon fetish.'"

"You think you're so funny."

"I just think, Kayla, period. That's why you have trouble keeping up."

She took a left turn where the corridor branched. I kept going straight. "Good luck with Raccoon Boy," I hollered after her. "And have a nice day, scaring children."

Yeah. That went well.

At lunch, Calley Rose and I tried to scrub off the marker, using wet paper towels and liquid hand soap from the girls' bathroom. No luck. It was permanent. "Looks like I'm stuck being crazy forever," I finally said.

Then Mom called with more great news. For some pile of reasons even she couldn't climb over or argue through—Beep had the wrong "allelic ratio" and also had ALL and was too sick from the infection—Beep failed to qualify for the clinical trial we found.

Here's the demented grownup logic: They wouldn't give possibly life-saving cutting-edge treatment to Beep, because, apparently, he was too sick. Really.

What kind of drugs are they taking in these hospitals, to think up things like that?

❦

I'm depressed. It's an official pronouncement and everything. Although Dr. Anne has also hinted about "anger issues" and "anxious depression."

"Depression" *should* mean I get to dress in black, eat chocolate, and lie in bed all day listening to emo bands. I wish. Instead, the symptoms are fun things like inability to concentrate, withdrawal, feelings of worthlessness, and hostility possibly escalating to violence. Basically, I'm miserable and possibly scary, like some parts of life, and can't do homework. Don't flunk me—put my brain chemicals in detention.

The afternoon I heard Beep wouldn't qualify for the clinical trial, I sat in front of the computer, unable to type a single sentence of homework. Somehow I just couldn't. I stared at the assignment of simple questions in a stupor of misery. Ten minutes crawled by in wounded agony, while I felt more frozen and more of a total screw-up.

Then I gave up and went to my cancer blog, because posting about cancer and chemo and barf seemed less depressing. And I might be doing someone else some good, when I couldn't even start a homework assignment for myself.

Then I went on Facebook. Hunter had posted, *Radiation today. I'm cookin' now.*

Beep always said radiation was like being microwaved, so I commented, *Microwave good-bye to blasted leukemia blasts.* Blasts are the immature, mutated, mostly non-working blood cells that blood cancer pumps out.

An incoming email dinged. For Cipher, from Drowningirl. Drowningirl emails from a home she calls Jupiter, where the oppressive gravity is crushing and the atmosphere is poisonous.

D: *I'm at the end. It's too hard.*

Like me, Drowningirl has a sister who's hateful, but unlike me, in some weird Stockholm syndrome, she's grateful for *her* semi-perfect sister because of the help her sister gives her cancer kid brother. As far as I know, her mom is not insane, but worse—unlike me—Drowningirl doesn't get one shred of her parents' love, not even mixed with the little scraps of attention they have left for her.

C: *Less than one year. Then you'll be away at college. The launch date is set. Even on Jupiter, you'll have escape velocity.*

D: *That's too long. Jupiter is so far from the sun, even part of one of my years takes forever. I'd give my life in a minute to make my brother well.*

C: *I don't think that's how it works, dgirl.*

D: *Guess not. But he wants to live, and I don't want to—I hate my life. I think about ending it sometimes, but he's fighting so hard to live, that seems wrong.*

C: *Way wrong. You've got so much ahead of you. What's your phone number? I'll call you.*

D: *Sorry, Cipher. Your phone won't reach Jupiter. We have a weird area code.*

Then she sent me another of her poems.

More
I give and give.
But life demands, More.
There must still be more pain somewhere.

Drowningirl wouldn't give me her phone number, or tell me where she lived. So I just did what I always do. Pasted in the suicide prevention numbers:

C: *1-800-SUICIDE (784-2433) and 1-800-273-TALK (8255).* *They're toll free, dgirl, so you can even call from Jupiter.*

D: *Thanks. If I ever get more bummed (as if) I will. Be well.*

I always send her the hotline numbers, like she'll forget. She always says be well, but I can't remember what well is.

We're the most dysfunctional two-person support group in the world. Or, I guess, even the solar system.

8

A few days later at lunch, Evan and I ended up on the grass at the end of the sports field, looking up at the sky. The top of Evan's head was pressed against the top of mine. Our legs were stretched in opposite directions, so my view of the lumpy clouds was upside down from his.

"It's an exercise," Evan explained. "From drama class. Hey—we should take drama together next year. It'll help you when you're the front singer in our future indie band."

My hair was in a ponytail, and the grass tickled the back of my neck. I wriggled to get more comfortable. "I already have enough drama."

"No offense, but you're not going to carry the world's greatest indie band with just your current guitar skills."

"There's that." We'd have to play songs without the weird jazz chords Evan always noodled with. "Why this exercise, drama boy?"

"We can't see each other. It's supposed to make us open up and talk in a different way."

"I'm not sure I can do this."

"What? Talk and look up at the sky?" He kept his voice light. "Totally easy."

"Talk, period. Let you back into my life." I shifted, which gave me half an inch of distance, but then he pushed his head back against mine. My stomach was weirdly tense.

"Try," he said. "Say something. Not the first things that pop into your head. But something serious."

The first things would be about Beep, and after that about Evan, whose head bumped against mine, and whose absence at the end of last year had mashed my heart so much. "I don't know why Rachel hates me." That just lurched out of my mouth, catching even me by surprise.

"Rachel doesn't hate you. Why would anyone hate you?"

"The Tracies hate me." I tilted my head back slightly to direct the words to Evan, invisible back there. "And Kayla Southerland is working up to it."

"Okay. Tracie does kind of hate you. But you provoke her. How come?"

"Who knows?" My version of the Book of Life is missing the chapter on the popular in-crowd girl thing. "Maybe none of us Monroes know how to get along with girls." Rachel was popular with boys, but didn't have close girl friends. And Dad was so hopelessly confused about females, he'd married Mom. "I don't even know why Rachel's so mean."

"Rachel's probably jealous."

I barked out a laugh. "Of *me*?" Perfect, gorgeous Rachel, with her endless supply of boyfriend-candidates and amazing singing voice. Not exactly. "Did someone hit you on the head with a skateboard?"

"Seriously. She has that dyslexia thing, so she has to study really hard, but you're super-smart, so stuff comes easy."

"Guess again." Like the end of last year, I was already in danger of flunking out, if I didn't either do the homework or come up with a massive make-up project. Which I'd then have to figure out how to actually do.

"Well, weren't she and Beep super tight when he was little? Now you're the one who hangs out with him in the hospital."

When Beep was small, they had been kind of a two-person mutual admiration team. "Rachel doesn't know *how* to hang out at the hospital."

"Maybe it's not that easy. For some people."

"It's not *easy*, it's just not complicated," I said. "Just sit."

"Sit?"

"Yeah. If somebody sick wants to talk, talk. If they don't, let them rest. If they want to play shooter videogames, let them. Even when they're confronting death by shooting zombies, they're not alone. But that chapter is missing in Rachel's book. Maybe with the whole section on getting along with non-boyfriend humans."

Evan laughed, and with a pang, I realized how much I'd missed making him do that. The clouds above us were moving. One looked like a flying ice cream cone, chased by a dragon.

"Rachel always wants to *do* something—entertain Beep, or make things better," I went on. "And wants him to be there for *her* when she graces his room with her gorgeousness. But most times Beep isn't in the mood. Or doesn't have the energy. Or is in videogame gunfire. So she gets frustrated. And Rachel still has sniffles, so Mom makes her wear a surgical mask when she visits."

"See?" Evan said, like that proved something. "Also, this drama exercise is working."

"Humph. Working to make me scared."

"Of what's going on with Beep?"

"That too." I was silent for a long time. "I can't take it if we do the bestie thing again, Evan, and then you disappear."

"I won't."

I thought about that. "Then you're on friend-probation, indie boy."

"I'll be nice." He moved around. There was some light touch on the top of my head, like lips touching my hair. "Now you'll think good thoughts."

What? "Evan, did you just kiss the top of my head?"

"I'm not telling," he said. "I'm on probation, so I have to be careful what I say."

The bell rang.

I was still thinking about the top of my head thing when I got home after school. Probably Evan didn't kiss me. Probably. Why would he kiss me on top of my head? Rachel—who had about eleven thousand times as much experience with guys as me—was sitting at the kitchen table, looking glum with a pile of books spread out in front of her while she typed on her laptop. She didn't even have her music going, so for once she wasn't surrounded by a bleating fog of mainstream pop.

Might as well take advantage of that once-in-a-decade opportunity. I sat down across from her and cleared my throat. "I have a question about a boy thing."

She gave me a long, level gaze. "Is that a dig—how I'm the big expert on boys' things?"

"No." I took a deep breath. Life: so deeply confusing, I was asking Rachel for advice. "I think Evan kissed me, but I'm not sure."

"If you're not sure, then Evan needs lots more practice." But she smiled and closed her laptop, like I'd finally said something interesting after fifteen years.

Lack of kissing practice wasn't Evan's issue, not after last year's Tracie-tongue-tag tournament. "I think he kissed me on the top of my head, but I didn't see it."

"How could you not see . . . ?"

That was too complicated to explain. "If a boy likes you, wouldn't he kiss you somewhere *not* on the top of the head?"

"He's probably scared of getting anywhere close to your mouth," Rachel said. "We all are, because you bite."

"Pffft." Insults. What did I expect? This was like asking advice from the Tracies.

"You've had a massive, obvious crush on Evan forever. He was probably saying that's okay."

"I have not." Also, it's not that obvious.

"Really? Then why were you in a bad mood—for months—after he got together with that Tracie girl from soccer?"

"Because I have to live with you. Also, hello: Beep's cancer."

"Bzzzzt." She made the wrong answer buzzer noise from one of Mom's game shows. "Beep was in remission this summer. When you were total sigh-soundtrack girl."

"Was *not*."

"Oh? Mom and Dad are paying for your therapy because they have extra money?"

That dig was way out of bounds. Mom's crazy, but I'm the one who has to do shrink hour on Tuesdays with Dr. Anne. "Thanks for the reminder. What does it mean, though, if he kissed the top of my head?"

"It means we need to have the condom talk. Because of Evan. With everyone else you can keep using your personality for birth control."

"We don't need to have 'the condom talk.'" This talk was bad enough. "Forget I said anything."

"I'm just trying to help. I think—"

"Help me what? Feel bad about myself? I have that down already." Rachel looked surprised. "No. He . . ."

I stomped upstairs. Me and my pregnancy-prevention personality. I don't know why Rachel hates me so much.

Up in my room, I tried to distract myself from being so annoyed with Rachel that I would break things. So I imagined Evan being my actual boyfriend. For a long, dreamy time. I pictured us sitting in his bedroom, writing a duet. Him watching my lips as I sang about him. Then, I imagined, he leaned over and kissed me with his soft lips.

Then I thought about Evan breaking up with me after that. Which interrupted quality daydream time like a kick in the chest. It probably wouldn't take long. Evan had averaged a week and a half between breakups during his Tracie face-sucking phase. And if I started trooping around school hand-in-hand with Evan, that would draw a thick swarm of Tracies after him, like so many two-legged human flies, their eyes bulging at the sight of hot, awesome musician Evan with lowly Kat. So, after about three weeks, I'd see Tracie or Ashley hauling him away instead, with her arms wrapped around him and his hand in her hair.

At that mental picture, a hot wave of nausea went through me. It was like I'd accidentally gobbled some of Beep's chemo meds.

This was crazy. We'd had a conversation, and Evan touched the top of my head, and now I was actually making myself sick with my imagination. Whatever the touch on the top of the head had been, it was best to decide no kissing had been involved.

My life was already insane enough.

9

Beep begged me to stay overnight in his hospital room that Wednesday, so he could get a break from Mom.

"Please." Beep clutched my hand in both of his, when Mom was in the bathroom. He squeezed almost hard enough to leave bruise marks. "She's driving me crazy. And it's more fun when you hang out."

I was the self-appointed chief morale officer for Beep, in charge of making him laugh, when he was in the mood.

"I'll stay with Beep tonight," I told Mom. "Go home and get some sleep."

On Beep's last two bouts with cancer, he'd stayed at home and gotten his chemo treatments as an outpatient, but with his repeated infections he was stuck in the hospital this time. One family member could stay overnight with him, on the foldout mini-bed that the guest chair turned into. But it was hard to get good sleep there, because every two hours a nurse came in to check vital signs or change a drip bag.

"I can stay," Mom said.

Behind her Beep was shaking his head *no no no*.

Mom looked terrible, with dark circles under her eyes and worry lines on her forehead and around her mouth, as if she'd gotten ten years older in the last month.

"In the morning, you've got a house tour. With clients," I said. "If you don't get some real sleep, you'll scare them. You look like an experiment with raccoon DNA." Mom was a realtor, and on Thursday mornings in Berkeley they have "brokers' opens" where realtors tour the homes that are going to be open houses the next weekend. They can even drag their buyer-couples along, like Mom was supposed to do. She needed a good night's sleep, which she wouldn't get if she stayed in the hospital.

"What about your schoolwork?"

Good question. I nodded toward my backpack on the visitor's chair. "I brought my books." Not that the books would be doing the short-answer questions by themselves. "And a change of clothes." I could shower in Beep's hospital room bathroom before heading back across the Bay on BART in the morning for school.

"You have to be eighteen to stay overnight," Mom said.

"No. I only have to *say* I'm eighteen, if they ask. I'll tell them I look young for my age, and I'm sensitive about it." Which would totally work. The pediatric unit was full of kids with heart defects and lung problems that made them look small for their ages.

I wasn't sure why someone has to stay with Beep all night, because he was surrounded by a hospital full of doctors and nurses, but Mom was convinced that he'd get gobbled up by flesh-eating bacteria or something if one of us wasn't there to press the call button. At least with me guarding him, Mom would be able to sleep, knowing I was on the lookout to make sure they hadn't hauled Beep to the operating room for secret organ harvesting. (Organs full of cancer, probably not high on the must-have spare parts list. But common sense isn't the border of Anxiety Momistan.)

It took twenty minutes of knocking down Mom's objections, one by one, to get her to agree, and in the end, Beep still had to play the cancer card.

"Please, Mom," he said. "Don't make me use my one Make-A-Wish just to get a night to hang out with Kat."

She paused, pressing her lips together, but I knew we had her. "Fine," Mom said. "But you have to call if anything—anything at all—happens."

I promised to text regular updates all evening. Then I physically walked Mom to the door, with my hand on her back, in case I had to literally push her out of the room.

"Whew," Beep said, when we were finally alone. "Thanks." His hair hadn't fallen out yet from the chemo, but he had a buzz cut, so when what was left came out, it wouldn't be in big clumps.

I plopped down on the guest chair, and let out a long breath. "You look good," I said. "Like the world's smallest U.S. Marine. It's weird that you're not doing sit-ups or something."

Beep grinned. "I could do a sit-up. But I'm saving my energy for the dry heaves. They're a better ab exercise. You should try them, to get in shape for soccer."

"I'll keep it in mind." On my current no-homework program, there wasn't much point in conditioning for soccer—dry land, dry heaves, or otherwise—because I wouldn't be eligible. "But maybe you should do a workout video. For cancer kids and bulimics: 'From Sit-Ups to Spit-Ups: Dry Heaves As a Functional Exercise.'"

Beep laughed, which he always did at gross-out humor.

Beep turned off the TV, which had been silently broadcasting some show from the Cartoon Network on mute. "Better call Mom," he said.

"For what?"

"Something 'just happened.' You know—I turned off the TV."

I laughed. "Yeah. I should totally keep her updated. How's it been, in Anxiety Momistan?"

"Gaah," he said. "Insane." He did an impression of Mom's voice. "'Honey, should I try to get them to increase your dose of Zofran? Have some water. Don't get dehydrated. Let me adjust your pillow. Don't rub your eyes—you can get germs that way. You really should use the hand sanitizer again. Eat something, honey.' Yeah—something pretty, because I'll see it again."

He flopped back on his bed. "Was Mom always this bad? And I just didn't notice cause it wasn't focused on me?"

Not really. Her anxiety had gotten worse, but I didn't want Beep blaming himself or his cancer on how whacked-out Mom was. "Pretty much. She just freaked out over smaller things, so it was even weirder."

"Smaller than—"

"You know, cancer. It's like the woman thinks you have a serious condition," I said. "Crazy bitch."

I got a shock laugh out of Beep with that, which was the goal, but he couldn't stop laughing, and then the laughs turned into coughing. I got up to pat him on the back, but before I could he leaned over the side of his bed where the spit-basin was, and threw up with a watery splat. And then another.

I felt awful. "Sorry, sorry." I grabbed the pink basin he'd barfed into and carried it into the bathroom to get the acid-retch smell away from him, and set out a clean plastic basin to replace it. Then I gave him a warm wet washcloth for his face and gave him a peppermint candy to get rid of the puke taste. "I'm really sorry."

"Don't be," he said. "It was going to come back anyway. That's the most fun barfing I've had all week. You should come entertain me all the time."

"Nah. You're already sick of my jokes."

That made him laugh again, so I clapped him on the back.

"I'll rub your back," I told him. He rolled over onto his side, so he wouldn't mash the snaking Broviac line in his chest. I rubbed his back, keeping it gentle so he wouldn't bruise. He was already bony again. I could feel each of his little ribs. *Get well*, I thought with every circular rub across the tops of his shoulder blades. *Get healthy*. I wished his cancer hadn't come back, and that it would have waited until he was bigger and stronger.

"You give the best back rubs," he said after a while.

"Don't tell Rachel. She'll get jealous."

"Yeah," Beep said. I'd been joking, but he sounded serious.

"She's bummed that she can't visit you more," I said. "Because of her cold and Mom's paranoia." Rachel hadn't actually said that to me, but I assumed that she would have, if we still talked, like normal sisters.

It was totally worth it, but it was a long night. Every two hours a nurse came in to check on Beep and take his vitals, waking me up, and the blood-draw lady came before 6 A.M., when it was time for me to get moving. But it had been fun, chatting with Beep, and at least Mom got some sleep. In the morning I headed back across the Bay to spend the day yawning and dozing in school, unaccompanied by finished homework.

10

I was doubled over in P.E. on Friday, after running the mile for time, gasping for breath, while my stomach tried to decide if it was going to start Beep's dry-heaves-as-exercise program. I was definitely not in soccer shape, but I'd gone for it anyway. Coach Paulsen had said this run affected our P.E. grade, and she's old-school, always-give-a-hundred-and-ten-percent.

"Nice hustle, Kat." Coach Paulsen walked over. She's also the varsity soccer coach, so she knows me. She's tall, with short blonde hair, an angular face, and that athlete-for-life lean look even in her thirties. "You'll get more air if you straighten up."

I knew that, but I wasn't sure if I was going to spit up. I straightened anyway. I figured she was going to hassle me for being out of shape.

"We need you out there this year. Playing center mid," she said.

Ah. About soccer and my grades. Deep breath in. Slow breath out.

"The other girls play harder when you're on the field," she said. "Scrimmage harder, too."

I'd never thought about that. I play aggressively on defense, all about the slide tackle, even in practice. I play clean, but intense. I'm that girl that the other team starts fouling before the first half ends.

"So you need to get your grades up," she finished.

"I'll do what I can," I said, which in most of my other classes so far hadn't included finishing homework.

"Good. We need you."

No pressure, or anything.

11

The first time Beep temporarily died, he picked an inconvenient night. It was the evening in October when I was supposed to put together the final PowerPoint for our World History group presentation and email it to Kayla and Ashley and Jamaal, so they could practice it before morning. Instead, I saw Beep go into cardiac arrest and stop breathing for a while.

Beep had been pretty thrashed coming off radiation treatments, and they'd put him on an even more barf-o-matic chemo cocktail than usual, which made him throw up so much that his esophagus ruptured and started bleeding, as he weakly puked red streams. With a lot of blood cancers—including Beep's—bleeding isn't good: Your blood is so messed up it doesn't clot; once it starts pouring out, it won't stop.

The whole family had been visiting Beep when he started the red spit business. Mom freaked out, which, for once, was totally appropriate. She put half the hospital staff in headlocks until they'd come look at Beep. Pretty soon the room was crowded with scrubs. Beep's vital signs crashed and he stopped breathing, and his heart stopped. At that point, they semi-threw us out. Mom, wanting us out of the way of the medical staff, herded the family to the waiting room to sit, terrified.

I get why you push the family out, so they aren't in the way, when you're trying to save a kid's life. Still, the waiting room? Where we can't even hear what's going on? While my brother might be dying? It was partly Mom's doing, but that was bull manure piled so deep it could drown short people.

Mom, Dad, and Rachel were sitting in the waiting room clutching each other looking frozen—except Dad, who was trying, but failing, to look *not* scared, which was somehow scarier. I said I was going to the bathroom, and instead marched toward the ICU. Dad made sputtering Dad noises, but Mom shouted after me, "Report back."

Sneaking into the ICU is easy—just don't skulk. Stride down the hall like you belong or even actually own the hospital wing because of some huge charity donation. It's not hard, because (1) any hospital floor has dozens of rooms screened off by curtains, with plenty of places to duck into, (2) during a code involving your brother, with his heart and breathing stopped, the scrubs-people have plenty to do other than keeping you out of the room next door, and (3) I did belong. By then I'd logged more hours in the ICU than most bone marrow kids.

So I strode back to the room next to Beep's. The kid in there was a frightened ten-year-old named Nathan with ALL, who stared at me with wide eyes. His mom had stepped away for all of fifteen minutes to the cafeteria, leaving the poor guy to overhear a nearby cardiac arrest after chemo.

"Don't worry, he's fine," I lied confidently. "And his kind of cancer is different from yours." But not being able to see what was going on ramped up my anxiety. "I'll check on him, though, to make sure."

I scuttled over into Beep's room and slid into a corner, like I was invisible. The nurses and the doc working on Beep were matter-of-fact about it, which was slightly reassuring. Nurse Chestopher was doing Beep's breathing for him, holding a plastic balloon up to Beep's face. It's called hand-bagging, which sounds like hitting someone with a purse but was totally different. He squeezed it to force air into Beep's lungs. At the same time, Nurse Adrienne was next to the bed, mashing on Beep's chest to keep his blood flowing. She was also watching the red LED readout on the monitor. At short breaks, she'd stop her mashing and say, "No pulse. No breathing."

Beep sat up during one of those, stunning everyone. Chestopher pulled the bag away from his face. "I'm not ready to go," Beep said in a clear voice. He didn't even open his eyes. "I'm just *twelve*."

I got excited about that. But then he flopped back down.

After a shocked moment, while a couple of people looked at each other, they went back to shoving on his chest, and Adrienne said, "No pulse."

Beep. Come back. Please please please.

Chestopher spotted me and switched off with someone else, who started hand-bagging Beep instead. "Kat, you don't need to see this."

I moved, as he came over, like I'd dodge his long arms if he tried pushing me out. "I'm staying."

"Then let me explain," Chestopher's voice was quiet, like how you talk to an animal you don't want to frighten. He talked me through the rest of the drama. They gave Beep drugs to sedate him and partly paralyze him so they could "intubate" him, which is to stick a plastic hose down his throat into his lungs to have a machine breathe for him. Once they had that going, they'd shock his heart, to restart it.

Someone yelled "clear," and they slammed electricity through the paddles. Beep bounced about a foot off the bed. It didn't work. They did it again. Then Beep's heart decided that was exactly enough electric-shock torture, and started beating on its own.

They just tidied up after that, putting more blood products in him and stopping the potentially fatal bleeding. Piece of cake. My hands shook for forty minutes after they said he'd be fine.

൭൦

The leading book for leukemia patients warns about chemo drugs: "Heart failure can also occur, but is rare, mild, and usually successfully treated."

Really. That's a sentence from an actual book, from an actual hospital, called *Johns Hopkins Patients' Guide to Leukemia.* Coming at us with more spin than a world-class Ping-Pong serve. No wonder Mom has an anxiety disorder, when even the freaking hospitals are so obviously lying about important stuff.

How can they get away with calling heart failure "mild"? ("Sure. The kid's heart stopped and he died. But it wasn't, you know, *spicy*.") There was nothing mild about the terrifying procedure that yanked Beep out of the revolving door next to the pearly gates. But I posted a quick Facebook update on Beep's adventure anyway, in Mom Calmese:

A little scare with Beep tonight. Some trouble stopping bleeding. After great work from our wonderful medical team (and lots of bags of blood) Beep's stable, and fine, and sleeping well. Remember, donate blood! Our cancer kids need it. Thanks again to the great team at UCSF.

"Sleeping well," really meant sedated out of his bald little head. While they were at it, the docs should have given Mom a shot too. If the bags under her eyes got any bigger, she'd mistake one for her purse, and we'd never find the car keys.

෧෨

With Beep briefly dying, and my hands shaking, and then my sitting there staring at Beep while he was sleeping, I didn't finish the PowerPoint slides for our group project and email them until the next morning. That is, the same morning we had to present, first period.

It was harder than it sounds to pull together, because I had to revise what everyone sent me and put it into bullet points, especially difficult with Kayla Southerland. She uses words like she uses makeup—too much, badly, and not in the right place. And after Beep's cardiac arrest, somehow I had trouble concentrating.

The kids in my presenting group—especially Kayla and Ashley— were furious, like I'd single-handedly wrecked everybody's academic record and choice of colleges. Even though I'm not sure Kayla Southerland needs a good World History grade to get into remedial beauty school, where she should probably go to adjust her makeup before going outside, let alone off to college.

I cut short the group rag-on-Kat session at the start of class by saying I'd talk to Mrs. Miller, explain about Beep's heart stoppage, and get us put over to the next day. There were other groups presenting, and they always run over anyway.

So I tromped up to Mrs. Miller, barricaded behind her big gray desk, bathed in the scent of dry erase marker and too much floral perfume. As soon as I started explaining, she folded her flabby arms across her chest and cut me off. "I told everyone at the beginning that deadlines are deadlines, and the point of working in groups is that if you run into problems, rely on the people in your group. I'm sick of student excuses."

I stared at her. I was pretty sick of my brother having cancer, but watching him temporarily die really did cut into quality homework time. I tried to explain again, about how Beep had his heart stop, and how they had to bring him back with electric paddles.

She closed her eyes briefly. "Hold on. Beep Monroe is his name?"

I nodded.

She pulled out her phone, and started thumb-clicking away. Students weren't supposed to use our phones in class, but maybe teachers could get away with setting a bad example.

"Well." She gave me an exasperated look, like she was disappointed, but not surprised. "According to his Facebook page, it didn't sound dire, since it was just 'a little scare.' I've had it with exaggerations and alibis. Your group will present first."

I couldn't believe it. I was getting slammed for successfully downplaying Beep's temporary death in Mom Calmese.

Our group got a D-plus on the presentation, a grade that included massive additional points taken off because of my so-called "insolence" when I tried to argue more about our presenting first.

Then, in a really amazing coincidence, the next morning the cartoon cat on my locker sprouted enormous permanent-marker male genitals, with an arrow pointing at them and lettering that shouted "Kat Likes." The handwriting looked like Kayla's. My life kept getting better and better.

☺

"Kat, could you stay for a moment?" Mr. Brillson asked at the end of English class the next Friday, looming over my desk. "I'd like to talk to you about your assignments."

My stomach dropped. I'd been expecting this for weeks.

The bell rang. Tracie shot me a poisonous glare of tight-lipped disgust on her way out the door that said *great—you're screwing up in another class.*

Since the beginning of the quarter, instead of doing the essays and short writing, I'd been handing in reworked pieces from my cancer blog. The first couple had been vaguely related to the assignments, but now I was handing in stuff about cancer and the language of Mom Calmese and the side effects of chemo that had zip to do with the work assigned. And my papers kept coming back from Mr. Brillson marked, *Please see me*, which so far I hadn't.

Everyone else gathered up their stuff and shuffled out to the noisy hallway, while I pretended as if it took me forever to gather up my book and notepaper. Then, when the room was empty except for Mr. Brillson at the front, I walked to his desk.

"Do you want to sit down?" he asked.

I crossed my arms, holding my English book over my chest, like it would protect me. "No, I'm fine." I thought about Evan, who'd be waiting for me to have lunch with him and looked toward the door.

"I'll only keep you a few minutes." Mr. Brillson pushed my latest paper across his desk. It was marked with corrections and a red A–, even though it had exactly nothing to do with *Julius Caesar*, which we were supposedly studying.

What?

"Your writing is excellent," he said. "But always on a different topic than the one I assign."

I didn't deserve an A–. "I have trouble thinking about anything except that my brother's cancer is back."

He nodded.

I looked down at his gray teacher's desk and my paper perched there. "And I'm having a hard time." Mr. Brillson's class is the one I have to skip once a week to go to my therapy sessions.

"I'm so sorry." His voice was gentle. "But you've been identified as a 'student of concern' by your counselor. For academic progress. Because of missing assignments in other classes."

Meaning my almost total lack of finished homework.

"And I understand you handed in a yogurt label for 'French culture'?" The ghost of a smile tugged at the corner of his lips.

"I totally should have got credit for that," I said. "And I might have, if I'd only included a footnote, explaining the cultural significance." In Mr. Brillson's class, we'd just talked about footnotes.

"Well," he said. "I'm happy to continue accepting your writing from your cancer blog instead of my assignments. And I've talked to a couple of your other teachers, about whether they'll give you extra credit for longer papers on the cancer treatments, to make up for some of your other missing work. Perhaps in Biology and World History?"

I blinked at him. "What does cancer have to do with history?"

"Disease does," he said. "The plague. Influenza and smallpox—part of the reason European people successfully invaded the Americas. Besides, it's not just the subject matter you're learning. It's how to think critically and organize your thoughts and understand the past and how it affects us. And if you write about what happened this year, it's history."

I blinked at him again. I'd thought World History was just trivial pursuit on steroids, about long-dead white guys. At least so far.

Mr. Brillson leaned back in his chair. "I could talk to Ms. Tang and Mrs. Miller about it."

It was widely rumored that Mrs. Miller had a giddy crush on Mr. Brillson, who was cute and maybe fifteen years younger than she was. "Uh, wow. That would be great."

"I think it's probably too late for this grading period, though," he said.

I thought so too.

"But maybe we could work out something going forward."

⚬⚬

Out in the hallway, I texted Evan. *Teacher meeting. See you in 3.* Meaning five or six minutes, really, after I hit the bathroom and my locker, but I wanted him to know I was on my way, not ditching him.

When I found Evan at our usual spot on the concrete steps looking out at the grass and the tennis courts, he was surrounded. My former friend Amber was on one side, and my former friend Elizabeth was on the other. She was sitting really close to Evan, with her lunch tray in her lap.

"Hey," I said.

Evan smiled. "Hi."

"Hey," Amber said. She looked embarrassed, maybe about how they'd boxed Evan in.

"It's kind of cold out here," Elizabeth said, without even "hi" to me. "Let's go inside." She looked brightly at Evan. "Want to come?"

Evan looked at me. I gave him the tiniest shake of my head. I'd rather talk to him out here about the latest Mr. Brillson intervention.

"No, I'm good," he said.

"Maybe some other time." Elizabeth stood and patted his arm.

Amber waved bye to me, and I waved to her. Elizabeth acted like she hadn't noticed I was there at all, which felt like a claw shoved between my ribs. She'd been one of my best friends.

Evan and I watched Amber and Elizabeth head back inside, then I sat next to Evan and pulled my sandwich and apple out of my brown bag. "Sorry. Brillson kept me late."

"What's up?" he asked.

"Apparently, I'm a 'student of concern,' counselor-speak for about to flunk out. Brillson wants to help." I was kind of stunned about that. Ever since Beep got sick, it was unusual that someone was going out of his way to try to take care of *me*. I told Evan about the conversation.

"You're exaggerating, right?" he asked at the end. "About the flunking-out part?"

I shook my head. "No. Apparently, there's some weird notion around here that we have to do the homework."

"You want to study French together?"

"Is that a euphemism for tongue-tag?" my mouth said, before I could stop it.

He laughed. "No. Unless you want it to be?"

Dangerous territory, and after a heart-flutter, I could feel myself closing up. "It's not fair, Evan, when you flirt with multiple girls like this. Gives us the wrong idea." I waved my sandwich in the direction of the disappeared Amber and Elizabeth, then took a bite.

"Who says I flirt with multiple girls?"

"My online friend Cipher says you flirt with her outrageously." Which he totally did.

"That's different," he said.

"Because I know about it?"

"No." He didn't elaborate.

And I didn't really want to talk about Cipher, because I didn't want anything to slip that suggested Cipher was my secret identity. Cipher flirted outrageously with Evan, too. Instead, I blurted out, "Tracie claims she could have you back at the snap of her finger."

"Well, she can't." Evan's voice was steely.

Good. "Then don't tell me what other body parts Tracie would have to use, and how, to get you back."

He laughed again. "There's zero chance I'll *ever* get back together with Tracie. You know why she broke up with me? The third time?"

I sighed. Great. Here we were, talking about Evan and Tracie's relationship, my least favorite topic.

"Because I was about to break up with her," Evan said. "That girl has *issues*. She has to be the one to break up with the guy first."

Evan looked earnest, like always, but the reason for their third breakup was news to me. Both prior times Tracie had broken up with him, Evan had been a crushed mess of moaning romantic angst. For weeks. By the time of his final breakup last year, I hadn't been talking to him anymore. I figured he'd cried on some other girl's shoulder—there would have been lots of volunteers, including my former friend Elizabeth—or done the guy thing and obsessively played videogames, or the musician thing, writing a bunch of angry emo songs to channel the tears.

"If we ever do write songs together again," I said, "don't even *try* to get me to help you write an 'I'm so sad after my breakup with Tracie.' I'll throw up my entire head."

Evan laughed again, which made me three for three. Score. Then he turned serious. "You and I could write songs. About something else. We could hang out at my house. Or yours." He casually leaned back and put his arm on the step behind me, so it was almost around me.

It would be so nice to lean back onto that arm. And so scary. I had almost no other friends anymore. Instead of leaning back, I hunched forward, and wrapped my arms around myself, across my chest. "I'm barely holding together, Evan."

"What?"

The concrete in front of us was marked by black dirt spots of ancient gum. "Sometimes it feels like all it would take is one more tap, and I'll break into a hundred pieces." I didn't want him to be that hammer tap.

"Oh," he said.

I put my head in my hands, and rocked forward and back, like that was somehow going to comfort me. "I'm pretty messed up."

"No you're not," Evan said. "You're just dealing with hard stuff."

That made me want to hug him, and there were sudden tears in my eyes.

"So why don't we study French together?" he said. "I can help. A little."

That was complicated. Mom had rules about no boys over at our house without "adult supervision" and with Beep and Mom at the hospital and Dad at work all the time, there was no supervision. And if I went to Evan's house, he'd eventually pull out his guitar and try to make me write songs with him again. Which I didn't feel ready for, and besides—I didn't want to be just the girl who was good at helping write Evan's songs. I jammed my forehead into my hands.

"Tuesday nights," I said. "At Tyler's. His mom feeds me dinner." That was the new arrangement, for as long as Beep was back in the hospital. Rachel was eating dinner on Tuesday with her boyfriend Brian and his parents, which seemed weird to me. Supposedly she and Brian would spend the rest of the evening "studying" together. Rachel still had the sniffles, so Mom had accused her of passing a cold back and forth with Brian.

"What?" Evan said.

"I spend Tuesdays at Tyler's. Welcome to cancer world," I said. "Where nothing makes sense."

"You spend the night at Tyler's house?" Evan looked alarmed, which was flat annoying.

"*No.* Jeez. I spend *dinner time* there. But if you came over, you and I could study French, while Tyler plays his videogames." Which is what Tyler always did.

"Okay," Evan said. "We'll study French." He was friends with Tyler, so he could totally go there to study.

"Thanks," I said. It was probably too late to save my grade in this quarter, but it would help for the next one. And Evan was taking Algebra 2 with the same teacher, just a different period, so we could probably study that together too. I started crying, only partly out of relief. "I'm so scared." Scared about Beep, scared about flunking. Scared about Evan. Scared about everything.

Evan wrapped his arms around me, in a warm, perfect hug, and I dropped my sandwich on the concrete steps and hugged him back. It was the world's greatest hug, and long, and it felt so good that it made me even more scared, while he wrapped himself around me, trying to hold me together.

∽

When I got home that day, there was no sign of Rachel. I took Skippy for a long walk, and when I got back, the house felt even emptier, with just Skippy and me wandering around in it, as if it would echo forever when Skippy barked. I brought Skippy up to my room and fed him four liver treats, one by one, then rubbed his belly. He wriggled with joy. It's nice that it's easy to make someone happy. I looked over at my Stratocaster, sitting lonely in its stand under a layer of dust, and thought, *I should play guitar.* But I didn't. I just thought about Evan, and how I'd sort of friend-zoned him for my own protection, but his hug had felt so good he'd nearly snuck right back out of the friend zone. I had a freaking zombie crush on Evan—every time I thought I'd killed it, it came back.

I turned on my computer and opened a new, blank Word document. Maybe, with the lift from Mr. Brillson's extra-credit idea, I could actually get some homework done. But instead of typing the World History assignment on the ancient Greeks, I just stared at the screen. *If I just get started,* I told myself, *I'll be on a roll and can keep going.* Yeah, right. The heaviness of all the other assignments I hadn't done weighed down my arms. What happened to kids who flunked out? Besides almost fatally disappointing their parents? I thought of a future of wearing a paper hat, asking people if they wanted fries with that.

Ten self-punishing minutes of non-productivity later, I gave up and went on Facebook. Drowningirl wasn't online, but Hunter was. I shot him a private message.

Kat: *Do you ever have trouble keeping girls in the friend zone?*

Hunter: *Not so much. I just get cancer and lose all my hair, which kills their romantic interest.*

I didn't believe that for a minute. Hunter was really cute, even with no hair.

Kat: *Ha. My brother Beep is adorable with no hair. Super cute.*

Hunter: *Well. If you don't mind a lack of hair, then maybe you should get a long-distance boyfriend to keep your local guys trapped in the friend zone. I know just the shiny-headed dude for the job.*

I thought about that. He was cute, and funny, and he really liked my jokes. In a way, a crush on Hunter was less scary than a crush on Evan.

Kat: *As soon as I'm taking applications, I'll let you know.*

Hunter: *Don't wait too long. I'm funnier and more charming while I'm still alive.*

Okay, maybe Hunter wasn't completely ideal, either.

12

The next Tuesday, Mom picked me up in the middle of school, to drag me to my weekly depression session with Dr. Anne. It's mortifying, skipping English class once a week to get whisked away by Mom during the passing period, when everyone else is walking to class. They can all see me standing at the curb waiting. About the time Evan got together with Tracie last year, the word got out that the reason I'm not in class this hour every week is that I'm at an I-must-be-a-crazy-person appointment. So, as usual, I rode the whole way in Mom's car in grumpy silence, with my arms crossed over my chest.

Mom and Dad have basically contracted out to Dr. Anne the job of having any idea what's really going on with me, which I guess is good, because they and I have no clue, and *someone* should figure it out.

Dr. Anne's office is in Kensington Circle, upstairs in a two-story building. She sits in a leather chair, behind her big frame glasses and little notebook, surrounded by so many ferns and plants it's practically a forest. She has an actual couch, like shrinks do in cartoons, but I just sit on it, I don't lie down. I start talking about something, and then we sort of blunder our way into other topics. By the end, I'm supposed to have more of a clue about what's going on in my head, to partly make up for the weekly humiliation.

I wanted Dr. Anne to explain the reason that I couldn't get any of the homework done, but, as usual, it didn't work that way. Instead, she asked me questions—like I'm supposed to explain it to her—and we went off on tangents. About halfway through, she asked, "How does Beep's having cancer again make you feel?"

I gave her a look. For this, Mom pays the woman one hundred and twenty dollars an *hour*? Which Dr. Anne always ends ten minutes early, so she can do shrink-yoga between patients. "I'm going with 'bad.'"

She waited, perched there behind her glasses and notebook, until the silence got so big I had to fill it with something. "I'm afraid. For Beep. Worried. He nearly died. I want him to get well. I want to *save* him, with my bone marrow. But everything in our family just orbits around his cancer and his blood tests. It's like cancer is the sun, and we're all just little separate planets being pulled around. Except Dad. He's the comet that whooshes into our family solar system and then goes back out, into work-space."

"Which planet do you feel like?"

"Mars. The angry little red one way out in the cold. Alone." I picked at the couch. Familiar, but alien and lonely. "Mad."

"Besides Beep's cancer, what makes you mad?"

"I used to get along with Rachel, but now she hates me." I swallowed and stopped talking for a while. Mom's anxiety used to be something that united Rachel with me, against a common enemy. "Mom used to burp out some wacky new rule, like we had to wear sweaters when we went outside in a breeze, and I'd take Mom on, arguing with her insane grownup logic, while Rachel snuck out without a sweater. And Rachel helped explain Mom to me. And explain Dad, who's kind of removed. We had a good team thing going until Beep got sick. Now Rachel hates on me full-time. And I get pissy with her."

"Pissy?"

"Sarcastic."

"Really?" Dr. Anne smiled.

"Hey. *I'm* the sarcastic one. Also, I have almost no friends anymore, and I'm mad at my ex-friends for abandoning me last time Beep was sick." When I needed them. I looked down at her tangled vine-design carpet, in greens and gold.

"Do you want to reconnect with them?"

"Yeah," I said. But then wasn't completely sure. "Except that I already apologized. For my jokes about them. *They* should apologize for abandoning *me*. What if they do that again?"

"So you want to connect, but you're afraid, and you haven't forgiven them."

We sat in silence for a while. The clock said we still had over ten minutes. "You make it sound like it's my fault."

"Not necessarily. But if you keep finding yourself in situations you don't like, could you do anything to change that?"

"Beep has cancer—not my fault. Mom is crazy, crazy—probably not my fault. Rachel is boy-crazy—definitely not my fault, and I have no idea why she hates me so much."

"You feel powerless?"

I didn't say anything.

"Why do you say your mom is crazy?"

"Fine. She has 'anxiety disorder.'" Beep's bruises turning out to be life-threatening cancer wasn't the best thing for Mom's anxiety. "Beep's cancer coming back is hard on everyone. It even interferes with Dad's *work schedule*. He almost had to give me a ride home from the hospital one night."

"Why do you think he's always at work?"

"Because they pay him?" His old law firm went out of business and into bankruptcy. He only got his job now because he brought over this big patent case, and that meant he could get his whole "trial team" jobs with his new firm. "We get our health insurance through Dad's work, which is pretty key."

"Umm hmm." Dr. Anne made that sound like therapist-code for horse droppings. "Do you think he might have trouble being present? Because of Beep's illness?"

I frowned at her and crinkled my eyebrows. "Mom's in charge of being crazy, in our family. Don't get people's roles confused. Dad's just in charge of work."

"What's your role?"

I was the smart, funny one. The soccer player. But that had changed since Beep got sick and I went on academic probation. "I'm the one who can deal. Maybe the only."

"Deal?"

"Yeah. Mom totally can't deal." It was hard to explain. "I can just sit with Beep. In the hospital. Hang out. Talk if he wants to, or not if he doesn't. Mom endlessly futzes with him, trying to make him more *comfortable*, until he rolls his eyes into a please-jab-that-woman-with-a-syringe look, and I have to lunge in with a sarcasm strike to get her to stop. Or Dad, who can play videogames—but can't just *be*. Or even Rachel, who wants Beep to be there for her, when she graces his room with her surgical-mask-over-snotdrip self."

"So you can deal, in the hospital. But have trouble dealing with homework."

I'm getting treated for depression, but Dr. Anne always brings us back to the most depressing topics. At school things weren't getting much better. It looked like I was sliding down the porcelain passageway toward flunking out. "I can't even do the easy assignments. I don't know why."

"Maybe you don't want to be the person who always deals?"

I shook my head. "Maybe I'm not wild about being me, period."

Evan was waiting curb-side, with his lunch, when Mom dropped me off after the end of the Doctor Anne session.

"Hey," he said. We fell into step, headed toward our usual lunch spot over by the tennis courts. "You gonna make it to my show at the Gilman tomorrow night?"

The Gilman is a local club, where Green Day got its start. Evan, playing solo, was on the bill with a couple of other bands and some super-secret awesome guest appearance. "No." I looked down at gum on the sidewalk. "I'm really sorry." I was supposed to stay with Beep.

Rachel couldn't, because her nose was still a running snot hose. "Wish I could."

"Me too," Evan's voice was glum. "How was your, uh, meeting?" Someday we'll run out of euphemisms for my weekly shrink-rap. But not yet.

"Weird. Apparently, I discussed being from Mars with my therapist."

"I thought boys were from Mars and girls were from Venus."

"You were *so* asleep in health class when they explained *that* process. 'When a mommy and a daddy like each other very much . . .' Thought you got a refresher course, though, last year with Tracie."

Evan's ears pinked. "I try to forget my worst mistakes."

"Good thing you're not me. Life would be like having amnesia."

"What mistakes have you ever made?" he asked.

"Missing your show, tomorrow. Opening my mouth, constantly. Being born, almost sixteen years ago, but if my bone marrow gets used, I might make up for that one."

Evan scuffed the ground with his running shoe. "Why do you say stuff like that?"

"Because if we get the kind of life we deserve, I must be horrible."

"You don't like having lunch with me?"

I approximately loved having lunch with Evan. So much it scared me. What if that stopped again? "You're a bright spot, indie-boy. So I'm lucky you're not on a PET scan, because then you'd be a massive tumor."

"I love it when you compare me to having cancer. It makes me feel all—" He looked up, then shook his head. "Not great."

"Then hang out with me more," I said. "Life vaporizes my self-esteem. Inhale some."

He leaned toward me and put his face right in my neck. *Was he going to kiss me?* Evan made a big show of breathing in, like he was smelling perfume. I could feel the air pulled along my skin. My knees felt weak.

"Wow," he said. "You're right. I suddenly feel awesome."

I was feeling all woogly from him sniffing my neck and from thinking he'd kiss me. "Good. One of us should model that. Go, indie-boy, you rock." I was just babbling. "But indie-style, not with mainstream predictability."

"If I liked it predictable, instead of weird, how could we have conversations?"

"On that subject—" My session with Dr. Anne had actually worried me. Mom saw some kind of psychiatrist once in a while, but I was the only person in my family doing every-week shrink sessions, I couldn't do homework, and I couldn't even control myself enough to stop spraying Kayla and the Tracies with sarcasm. Or to stop arguing with Mrs. Miller, digging myself in deeper. "Do you think I'm not just bummed out and cranky—that I'm crazy, crazy?"

"Why would you ask that?"

"Being from my family hasn't super-prepared me for recognizing *not* crazy. They're all crazy, except Beep, and we're having him chemically poisoned. So—am I? Crazy?"

"Uh," Evan paused. "No, I wouldn't say that." But it took him so long, that pretty much meant yes.

"Least convincing 'No' in history."

"Well, you're strung kind of tight."

"Strung tight?

"Yeah. Strung so tight, if I patted your butt, dogs would howl."

"Cute. For now, Evan, please stick to actual stringed instruments and keyboards."

"We'll also need a drummer," he said. "For our future indie band."

"Not who drums on my butt. We don't want dogs howling over our great vocals. What do you mean, 'strung tight'?"

"You don't let things go. And you always say the funny thing, to block stuff that hurts. You work so hard." He looked down at his feet. "To keep things from getting to you."

I just sat there. For once, I had absolutely nothing to say.

"But—" He looked over, guilty. "Not *crazy* crazy."

13

The next night—during Evan's gig at the Gilman—I was back to my by-then-usual schedule of spending Wednesdays in Beep's hospital room, on the visitor's chair that turns into a foldout bed. Mom spent most other nights there, except for Saturdays, when Dad spent the overnights so she could prep for her Sunday open houses.

Mom would only get rest at home if someone else in our family slept in Beep's room, poised to wrestle the angel of death away.

I tried to get out of it, because of Evan's show—he was even playing the four songs we wrote together last year. But Rachel was still under quarantine with continuing post-nasal drip that made her cough. When Rachel did make her five-minute visits, Mom made her put on hospital gloves and wear a surgical germ-mask across her face, so Rachel looked like some hot young doctor from a daytime TV show who had stopped by to replace a kidney. And Dad was out of town because of some "expert deposition," so no dice. When this cancer thing was finally over and Beep was well, my family was seriously going to owe me.

"Want some apple juice?" Beep asked, pointing to the little pitcher of his urine sample. "It's recycled."

I rolled my eyes. He'd also recycled that joke. Because of the chemo, the pitcher was marked with the curving six-horned symbol for bio-hazardous waste. Beep wasn't even allowed to pour his pee, with its poisonous chemical leftovers, into the toilet. "Save it for Rachel. Yellow goes with her hair."

"Nah. Rachel's like Dad. Doesn't come around enough."

"When she does, notice her more," I said. "With her looks, she's used to getting attention, so it's weird to her that you just keep playing videogames."

Beep grimaced, and pushed around some of the hospital "food" on his tray, left from dinner. "Something's wrong with Rachel."

"No kidding. She's stuck-up, but unlike blood cancer, its not curable."

"It's not that. Last time she was here, she spent half the time out in the hall, crying, on her phone with her boyfriend."

I rolled my eyes. "Boyfriend problems."

"Nah," Beep shook his head. "Something serious. Can you find out?"

An uneasy thought nagged at me, just out of reach. It had to do with her boyfriend. Then worry. Something *was* wrong with Rachel. Didn't she know, though, with Beep sick, the rule for the rest of us was don't create any more family drama? "I'll ask, but Rachel doesn't really talk to me anymore."

Beep nodded, like we'd made a deal. He had only eaten the dessert part of his hospital "dinner" and just pushed the rest around on his tray. "And can you work the nurses for more Jell-O? Tell them the Make-A-Wish lady says I can have as much as I want."

"Sure." I had money to buy him some in the cafeteria, but Beep's neutrophil count was so low now that they'd only let him eat stuff that came directly from the kitchen, wrapped in plastic, so no germ colony had dropped in on an air current.

"Tell 'em I want two," Beep said. "In different colors. So when I barf, it's art."

Gross. "Be sure to sign it then, and give it to Rachel. Tell her you want her to keep it always."

He giggled. "You're a bad influence."

"I try." I went out to the nurses' station. My favorite nurse, Chestopher, was there. He's a tall, gentle African-American man with gorgeous long eyelashes and an earring. He's a Buddhist, so I asked him if some Jell-O for Beep could be in the present moment, and earned a smile.

When the Jell-O arrived twenty minutes later, Beep even ate some.

"How are you feeling?" I asked.

"Like microwaved dog crap." Beep pushed away the swinging tray with its quivering gelatin remains. "So—better than yesterday."

I changed into sweatpants and a long tee shirt in the bathroom, then came back out and unfolded the visitors' chair.

"Can we talk, after lights out?" Beep asked.

"Sure." Sometimes Beep liked chatting in the dark. I liked it too. It was like a girl sleepover then, from back in the days when I had multiple friends.

I put the sheets from home on top of the foldout bed, and set out my earplugs and sleep eye mask. Even in the middle of the night, nurses come in and out to monitor blood pressure and replace drip bags. The sleep mask sort of defeated the purpose of lying in wait for the angel of death, but I could count on Nurse Chestopher to play backup. I flipped off the light and lay down on my little foldout bed, breathing through my mouth to avoid the faint mouthwash-truck-hit-pine-forest hospital smell of disinfectant that didn't quite cover the ghost scent of stomach acid from an earlier barf.

"You know when my heart stopped and they shocked me with the paddles to restart?" Beep's voice came out of the darkness from under the red glow of the LED readouts of his heart rate and blood pressure.

"Yeah. That night somehow sticks in my mind."

"I floated up out of my body. I could see everything. Mom pushed you guys out the door. Dr. Manning told everyone what drugs to get. Nurse Adrienne was pushing on my chest, and Chestopher was squeezing a plastic bag to put air in me."

That was actually a good description of the code, when they were hand-ventilating him. Had someone told Beep about it?

"I drifted out into the hallway, and saw you coming back, but you went into Nathan's room instead. You told him I'd be all right, then came to my room, into the corner."

I don't know how Beep could have known that. None of the nurses were paying attention to me then, so he didn't hear it from them.

"Then I floated through the wall out past the nurses' station, where they were bringing that cart in, and went out, along the ceiling, to where Mom and Dad were sitting across from Rachel. Mom spilled everything in her purse. Dad was patting her arm, but he was scared, and Rachel started grabbing everything that dumped out, including a quarter that rolled into the corner." Beep was quiet for a while. "I went up this long tunnel, and it was like I could see my whole life, in fast forward. I went toward this ball of light. Like a star, out in space, a ball of light in the darkness. Except it was alive. I think it was God."

I lay there in the dark, in rapt attention.

"It was love. Complete love. The ball of light. And it felt *so* good. Like being home, but perfect. Like it loved me, even the bad parts. All of me. It was . . ." He trailed off. "Great. But hard to explain to people who haven't seen it."

Goosebumps. I shivered. If that was death, I guess I'd get there eventually. In the meantime, I'm not doing the original research, even for a make-up paper. Still, it felt holy, hearing about it.

"It asked, in my head, about whether I wanted to stay there, or go back. To my body." Beep's voice was quiet. "I thought about how you looked, and Mom and Dad and Rachel. I wasn't ready to go. So I said I wanted to come back. Even though it would hurt. I was sad to leave, but then I whooshed away, and snapped back into my body. They were giving me that shock, and my heart started again."

"Before that, you sat up. Said, 'I'm not ready. I'm just twelve.'"

"I was talking to the ball of light. It was beautiful. And perfect. There."

It might make Mom feel better to hear this. "Did you tell Mom?"

"Tried to. She changed the subject."

"Go figure. Talking about her son dying."

"Yeah," Beep laughed. "Mom's weird that way." He paused. "Could you tell her?"

"She'll try to shush me, too."

"You don't let people shush you. It's not your deal."

True enough. Even *I* couldn't shush me. "Sure. I'll try."

14

The next morning, I didn't have any school homework done, but I did start on one of my assignments from Beep. I got up in the dark, even before the 6 A.M. blood-draw lady came around. Instead of heading to school on my bike from the El Cerrito BART station, I pedaled home. Mom was off meeting house-buyer clients for coffee before the morning "brokers' open" house tour, so I figured it would be a good time to ambush Rachel and ask her questions. About what was wrong.

I went through my list of suspicions. Rachel was off with her boyfriend all the time. When I said Evan might have kissed me on the top of the head, Rachel said we should have the "condom talk." And mentioned my "pregnancy-preventing personality." She was cranky in the morning, always insisting on getting into the bathroom by her appointed minute. Maybe because she was rushing in to throw up?

When I got upstairs, by then seriously worried, Rachel was in her room and had finished in the bathroom. It was still shower-steamy. I scuttled in to search for clues. I bent down and used the plastic hanger she left on the door to poke through the trash-can. There wasn't any discarded stick from a pregnancy test kit, but even blonde Rachel probably wasn't dumb enough to leave that evidence around. I looked at the toilet. If Rachel had thrown up in it, there'd probably still be that faint acid barf smell, even after a flush. I couldn't smell anything from up here, so—eww—I knelt down by the bowl. The tiniest, gross experimental sniff. No vomit smell.

"*What* are you doing?"

I startled at the sound of Rachel's voice and banged my head on the sink. "Ow. No idea."

"Why are you here?" Her voice was sharp. "Why aren't you on your way to school?"

I rubbed the back of my head, where I'd sink-smacked it. "I don't have my assignment done for World History. So I'm skipping. I'll try to get Mom to write me an excused absence." Not that I'd probably have the assignment done tomorrow, either.

"Were you throwing up?" Her perfect eyebrows scrunched together. "Or sniffing the toilet?"

"Rachel, are you okay? I mean, is anything wrong? With you? I'm worried about you." I was.

She crossed her arms. "I'm not the one snorting toilet seats." But there was something uncertain about her expression. Like, if I asked about the right thing, she might open up.

"Like, for example, are you pregnant?"

Whatever the right question was, that wasn't it. Her face closed and she pressed her lips into a white line. "You're the worst. Just because I have a boyfriend." She sputtered to a stop and then blew out her breath in a disgusted snort.

"Well is there anything else?" I asked. "That you should say to someone?"

She looked from me to the toilet seat. "Yeah. Try not to be so weird and annoying, Kat. If you do donate bone marrow, I don't want Beep catching that from you."

She muttered all the way down the hall to her room.

But she never actually said she wasn't pregnant.

⟲

I made it to school after first-period World History, and at least had lunch with Evan to look forward to. But that didn't start well either. Evan, it turned out, had invited Elizabeth and Amber and Calley Rose to join us for lunch outside. They brought their lunch trays and all gushed endlessly about Evan's show, which was, apparently, the most amazing experience in the history of sound. After his set, which was incredible, the hottest local band ever, Tranq Girl Reunion, played. (They've opened on tour with The Matches and for OZoNation. Yes, really.) Then, for their encore, TGR invited Evan back onstage, and he played two songs with them. Which makes him, officially, third-hand famous.

I apologized a bunch for missing the best gig ever, especially since Evan had dedicated his set to Beep. But mostly I sat there—not just a fifth wheel, but more like a pointless weather vane strapped to the top of a car. All the other wheels were moving the same way, pointed the same direction, going on about something impressive, while I wobbled silently, looking out of place.

"How was the night with Beep?" Evan finally asked.

I told them about Beep's description of his near-death experience.

"Wow," Evan said.

"Anywho—" Elizabeth tugged on his sleeve. "Back to the Gilman. What was it like being onstage with Tranq Girl? Are you going to play with them again?"

Evan raised his eyebrows at me, like he was asking if there was more.

Well, yeah. "Now Beep wants me to tell Mom everything he told me. Because when he tries to tell her, she keeps shushing him."

That led to general silence, the first of our lunch hour. I'd now successfully bummed everyone out.

"Parents are weird-wired," Evan said. "About their kid dying. It makes them go temporarily insane."

Where did *that* come from? Was Evan now the boy expert on everything, holding court to us cute-musician-struck girls, telling us how the world works? Plus, my mom's *always* been insane.

"You should write a song about that," Elizabeth said to Evan. "'Temporary Insanity' is a great title." She grabbed his arm with both hands. The gesture was somehow *this guy is mine.*

Oh. Got it. That's why Elizabeth was here, Amber in tow. Why Evan had invited her to our lunch. Why they were gushing over their time together at the gig. So amazingly amazing and also especially special. I'd been the one who used to write songs with Evan.

It was too much, and I wasn't going to sit and watch her drag him away in front of me or get teary about it in front of everyone else. "I have to go to the bathroom." I brushed crumbs out of my lap. "Be sure to rely on Elizabeth's musical sensibilities while I'm away."

"I can come too," Calley Rose offered.

Right. To leave the love-birds alone.

I just fled, though, toward the baseball field, which, technically, was not in the direction of any bathrooms. I was striding so fast, I'd already reached the grass before Evan caught up with me.

"Hey." He tugged my elbow.

I stopped and turned around.

"Your eyes are watering."

"I'm allergic to my life." I wiped them with my hand. "It's a problem."

"What's wrong?"

"I'm not sure." Was he already *together*, together with Elizabeth? "When I get it figured out, I'll let you know." I looked down. "I'm glad your show was great. And really sorry I missed it."

"For a little thing like talking to Beep about dying."

But I had missed Evan's gig. And if I was an actual friend instead of a bad person, I'd be excited about him having a girlfriend who wasn't one of the evil Tracies. "I'm a bad friend, Evan. Maybe you should go talk to your other ones. Who go to your shows and hang on your arm. Who you invited." To our lunch. When I really wanted to talk to Evan.

"What do you *want* from me?" He kicked the ground. "I invited Amber and Elizabeth so you guys could hang out. Like you used to. Before I wrecked your life."

"You didn't wreck my life, Evan. My life was pre-wrecked. I wrecked my life. The worst you ever did was get in the way of a tow truck."

"Then why are you mad at me?"

"I'm not mad at you, I'm just mad." Okay, that wasn't completely true. "If Elizabeth drags you off to go make out, and you stop eating lunch with me, I'll puke on you both."

"Why would Elizabeth—"

"Hate to spoil the surprise, Evan, but girls think you're cute." Apparently, even Tranq Girls.

"'Girls' think I'm cute?"

"Yes," I said. "We do. It's your beautiful brown-eyed burden, indie-boy. But just because you're too shy to ask anyone out, doesn't mean you should let the first one who comes along drag you away by the hand. Or arm. Or the anything else."

"Well, 'guys' think you're cute."

"This isn't compliment tag." I looked up at the side of the gym in exasperation. "You don't give me one back just because I gave you one. And at least make it believable—I'm funny."

"You're frustrating."

"Glad we could agree on a compromise. Bargained that pretty far down from cute."

Evan crinkled his eyebrows. "You didn't answer. What do you want from me?"

Everything. And not to be afraid of losing it. "I don't know."

"Guess."

"I want . . ." Now it was my turn to kick something. I booted the fence so hard it rattled. "Ouch. Just don't let me scare you away."

"You want me not to be scared?" He raised an eyebrow. "Don't kick things."

So I punched the chain link fence instead. Evan winced. I shook my hand out. Dang. "Everyone's scared, indie-boy. Just don't get scared *away*."

"So I can be scared of you, just not away."

"Exactly," I said. "That would be great."

"For the record, you were the one who ran away. Again."

"I told you. I have allergies. Also." I flung out a hand theatrically, and put the other one to my forehead, movie-star-doing-an-interview style. "This is a very emotional time for me."

"Do you know what my best songs are?"

Oh good. We were back to talking about the important thing—Evan's music. "No. The suspense is killing me."

"The five I wrote with you. Last year. They're still the best."

"We only wrote four." Although one of them, "Front Singer with a Tambourine," is the funniest and most awesome song ever.

"I used your lyrics for the bridge of 'Hang On.'"

"After you changed them."

"To fit the changed rhythm. You're better with lyrics." He looked down at his hands. "Better with words, period."

"I'm *terrible* with words, Evan. I use them like sharp sticks, jabbing people. And I don't know how to stop."

"You wake people up." He looked at me earnestly.

"That's an upgrade from 'frustrating'?"

"It's a compliment."

"And you claim other people have a better way with words."

"See?" he said. "That's exactly what I mean."

"No. That's exactly how *I'm* mean."

"I wish . . ." He trailed off.

"Wish what?"

"You fill it in." He shook his head, tossing that cute, fine hair. "You're good with words."

"I wish Beep would get all better."

"Hear, hear."

"We should go back to our alleged friends." I looked over at them, the little clot of three girls, looking our way. Calley Rose was standing, and it looked like she'd taken a step in our direction. "On the way, let's come up with some explanation for my apparent psychotic break."

"Nah," he said. "Leave 'em with a sense of mystery." We started walking over. "Would you write songs with me again?"

"Sure. As soon as you've completed your friend probation."

"When is that?"

"Depends," I said. "On how much credit you earn for good behavior. Somewhere between weeks and years."

"Great. Your plan to end loneliness is to drive *me* crazy."

ᏆᎧ

For my other assignment from Beep I got help from the Berkeley Public Library. They had a pile of books about near-death experiences. (Even one called *The Complete Idiot's Guide to Near-Death Experiences*, which—with the bone-headed things I did this year—was pitched right for me.) The same thing, it turned out, happens to lots of people when their hearts stop: They leave their bodies and go through a tunnel to a ball of light. There were arguments over whether these are real glimpses of an afterlife or just a hallucination caused by lack of oxygen and expiring brain chemicals. But the only people who knew for sure weren't telling—at least until any zombie apocalypse.

I dumped the books onto the coffee table in front of Mom.

"What're those?" She scooted her chair back when she saw *Toward the Light* on top.

"Books, Mom. Did Beep tell you about what he saw when his heart stopped?"

"I don't want to discuss—"

"You don't have to. Just listen." And I launched into what Beep told me, powering right through her three attempted interruptions.

"Honey," she finally said. "I really do need to get ready for a call, with a couple who want to buy a home—"

"Nope. The I-have-a-work-thing excuse is taken. It's Dad's. Did you spill your purse? While I was in with Beep during the code?"

"Yes." It was like I pulled the word out of her. "And Rachel did get the quarter. That rolled into the corner."

Somehow, that was a huge relief. "Great." I pushed all the books at her.

"Why?"

"Set a good example." I picked up my empty backpack. "Like you always tell me: Even if you can't do the homework, at least do the reading."

15

"I can't believe you're ineligible for soccer," Mom said, yet again. We were standing outside the closed door to the counselors' offices after school, and Mom was fussing with the buttons on her jacket like they were worry beads. From around the corner, someone slammed a locker, and the noise echoed in the empty, tiled halls.

"You *need* soccer," Mom went on. "It's an outlet for your anger."

What I really needed was an outlet for depression, but this meeting would probably depress me more. My first quarter's grades were an ugly puddle of Ds and Fs, except for English and P.E. And apparently the consequences of completely whiffing on homework were worse than being ineligible for soccer. So bad that Mom and I were summoned to a meeting about them.

Mr. Brillson opened the door and ushered us in.

The conference room was small for five people. Vice Principal Janey Fitzgerald, Mr. Brillson, and my counselor, Sheila Martin, sat across a table from Mom and me. Behind them, the white board had "Goals" and "Action Steps" lettered in smudged green marker.

After greetings, Vice Principal Fitzgerald leaned forward, with a grim expression on her lined face. She had gray hair that's so curly the kids in school call her "the Fritz," but she radiated so much no-nonsense seriousness, I couldn't imagine anyone calling her that to her face.

"If the situation does not improve," she said, "you will not pass your classes, Kat. You will have to retake most of them next year, and you will not graduate on schedule."

I sat stunned in the long silence that followed.

Counselor Sheila opened a folder in front of her. She was a small, nervous-looking woman whose dark hair swung as she bobbed her head, looking between the notes in her folder and my mom. She rattled off a bunch of "requirements to advance and graduate." I couldn't take Chemistry next year without getting at least a C in Biology. Without a passing grade in Biology, I wouldn't graduate. I couldn't take the next installment of French, unless I got at least a B– in my current French class. Unless I got at least a C in Algebra 2 this year, I couldn't take precalculus or any of the higher math classes for the rest of high school. And I needed a passing grade in World History to graduate. Which I currently didn't have.

I sat in a stunned fog, having trouble hanging on to the specifics, even after Mom asked questions about graduation.

The bottom line was that unless I got my grades up, next year I'd have to repeat almost every class I was in. I'd have to sit through them again while a bunch of former freshman gazed at me in pity and disgust, knowing I was S-L-O-W. If I did ever apply to college after that, they might as well stamp my high school transcript LOSER before sending it off.

I tuned back in to the end of Mom's wide-eyed rejection of several alternatives.

"No," she said. "If Kat can't finish her homework, independent study—doing her homework outside school and handing it in once a week—won't work either."

No kidding.

Mr. Brillson cleared his throat. "I've spoken with Ms. Tang and Mrs. Miller, Kat's teachers in Biology and World History. They and I are willing to accept papers about her brother's cancer in place of assigned homework. Kat would still have to take and pass tests and quizzes, but she could hand in short papers along the way, with a much longer paper at the end."

We all looked at him. Especially me, because he was outlining what might be the only escape plan from a horrible fate.

"Kat writes well," he said. "And I've seen her cancer blog. The writing on it she did this quarter was more than I would expect of a student in three classes."

After that, we worked out the details of my plea bargain, a massive make-up paper, delivered in installments, to avoid one-year re-incarceration in all my classes.

I'd better not screw that up.

16

"I don't think growing up is such a big deal," Beep said, a few weeks later, near the end of his last pre-transplant stay in the hospital. He was playing Xbox in his room, and I was watching him, to avoid having to work on my make-up paper, which was starting to look harder than the homework it replaced. How was I going to finish it if I couldn't even do one-page assignments?

"That's what kids here are supposed to do." Beep shrugged a general reference to the PICU, without taking his thumbs off the controller, which he was using to kill endless numbers of battle droids in *Star Wars Battlefront* Roman-numeral-something-way-too-much. "Get well. Become *grownups*." He said it with scorn.

"So?"

"Grownups are messed up. And unhappy. Look at Mom."

"Mom's a special case." I'm good with understatements. I got a tight feeling in my stomach, though, over where this conversation was headed.

"Then look at Dad—he makes enough money to buy an Xbox, a Kinect, a Wii game system, a *beast* gaming computer, a PlayStation, and every cool game ever made, but he doesn't."

"Maybe he doesn't want those things. Or have time to play them."

"Exactly." With a thumb jab to the controller, Beep slashed a robot tank into exploding scraps. "Something wrecks grownups' brains. They don't even *want* to have fun anymore." He sounded certain, like he'd worked it out over time.

"Rules." That was my theory. "Once you follow a thousand pointless rules, your brain shuts off."

"Maybe, but it doesn't happen to everyone. Not pro snowboarders or people who make videogames. Some escape." Beep paused for a couple of seconds, to get through a packed crowd of fighting robots. "It's like the zombie virus in *Left 4 Dead*." A videogame series. His voice went quiet. "I might not be around to catch the grownup virus."

I swallowed. A lump in my throat kept me from talking. That week we got back the report that the cancer wasn't gone. His blast count just wouldn't shrink to zero.

"They don't even eat dessert first," Beep's eyes were still on the screen. "Grownups can do whatever they want, but still don't eat dessert first. Ever."

"Tragic," I agreed. "Think of all the people who choke to death every year on food. Their last taste is the Brussels sprouts blocking their airway. They never got to the good stuff. Their parents can't even say, 'Well, at least she ate that great strawberry pie before the end.'"

"I think if you eat dessert first, it *prevents* grownup brain damage." Beep blew up another robot tank for emphasis. He was the one who'd been to the ball of light. For all I knew, they really did pass out secret dietary knowledge up there. Beep froze the game. "I'm worried about *you*, Kat." He put down the controller and turned to me in the visitor's chair. "Promise me you won't get grownup brain lock. For real. Promise you'll always have fun and eat dessert first."

So I raised my hand, like a Boy Scout. "I promise not to let my brain turn into gray grownup jelly. And to eat dessert first."

"Excellent." Beep nodded seriously, then broke into a smile, like he'd accomplished something huge, and went back to blasting droids on the Xbox.

The next morning as I was getting dropped off at school, Mom called, anxious because she had a meeting with homebuyers and wouldn't be at the hospital to get Beep's latest blood count.

"Have Beep text them." Whether or not Mom got them instantly, the results would be the same. "Remind him, though, it's not the kind of thing he should joke about." Beep got bored, but messing with Mom over blood counts for the recreational value was a bad idea.

"Does he know how to text?"

"Yeah, Mom. Really well. He's not over forty."

Evan was waiting patiently for me, to walk into school together. While I was trying to talk Mom into joining the rest of us in the rational universe, I wandered to the right, so I could watch Evan's cute butt in his snug jeans during the conversation, making it less painful.

"Sorry," I apologized to Evan after hanging up. "It must be hard for you to understand my life, since your parents aren't insane."

"You'd be surprised."

"Okay, fine," I said. "Because you don't have parents who are even more insane than usual, because they have a son sick enough he might die."

"Guess again."

"What?" A jolt of terror went through me. Was there something wrong with Evan? Potentially fatal? He was an only child. "Are you sick?"

"I'm fine." At my expression, he laughed. "It's not that. I'll tell you someday, though."

"Tell me what?"

The bell rang, he shrugged, and we strode off to our separate first-period classes. Maybe everyone's family was a little weird.

❦

The next Saturday, our neighbor Mrs. Umbriss ambushed Mom and me during our weekly shopping in Andronico's market. We'd just innocently turned the corner from frozen foods to the deli counter, and there she was, lurking under piled-up hair in a muumuu dress.

"How is Beemer?" she asked, leaning forward.

"Beep," I said into my hand, like I was coughing. *He's not a car.*

"We're preparing for a bone marrow transplant," Mom said. Because they couldn't get him into remission.

"That's great." Mrs. Umbriss beamed, like a transplant was one-stop shopping for perfect health. She lowered her voice dramatically. "We're praying for you."

My face froze into an expression I hoped resembled a smile. When Beep had first been diagnosed, Mrs. Umbriss had said the most awful, clueless things. I wasn't a fan. And prayers are good, but almost everyone else on the block was also providing periodic casseroles, even through compassion fatigue. I was still even going to Tyler's once a week, to get fed dinner by his parents, and Evan was putting in study time with me there, to resuscitate my French and Algebra 2 grades.

"Thanks," Mom said. "Things have been tough for the whole family." She glanced over at me.

Mrs. Umbriss clasped her hands together. "Well, God never gives you more than you can handle."

"Excuse me?" I stepped between her and Mom. "I'm not sure why Beep has cancer, but it's not because our family *is good at handling stuff.*"

"Kat." Mom's voice was a warning.

I took another step, as if crowding Mrs. Umbriss in a soccer game. "And I doubt God takes personal charge of dealing out the cancer card. To little kids. Even the assistant manager at McDonald's delegates the really crummy jobs."

"Oh." Mrs. Umbriss raised her puffy hands. "My."

"Kat!" Mom grabbed my shoulder. "Go get sprouts for your sister."

As soon as we were out of earshot and Mrs. Umbriss was in lurching retreat toward the meat counter, Mom started on me. "That was rude, and you are *never* to talk to our neighbors—or any adult—that way."

"She started it," I was fuming, almost shaking with anger. Our family definitely attracted cancer because we *handle* things: Mom has an anxiety disorder, Dad hides at work, Rachel hides in boyfriend-land, and I can't even turn in homework that gets completed by high school stoners. "She's lucky I didn't slide tackle her in the cracker aisle, because God thought she could *handle* it."

We walked in silence for a long time except for the faint squeaking of one of the grocery cart wheels. Mom finally squeezed my arm. "I suppose. Let's count our blessings."

Every minor triumph of self-control should be congratulated.

☍

Evan was off at one of the part-time dog-walking jobs he does for amplifier money, and his cell phone was on the counter at home, getting charged—or so his mom said, when she answered it. So instead of complaining to Evan after I got home, I ended up emailing Hunter about getting Umbrissed.

K: *Grownups say the most clueless things about cancer. When you get well, if I commit assault, would you write to me in prison?*

H: *I'll even send flowers and a hacksaw.*

I described our run-in with Mrs. Umbriss, then went on to list her earlier insensitivity crimes, when Beep first got diagnosed, the slew of questions she'd asked, like it had to be Mom's fault:

K: *Did you drink a lot of alcohol when you were pregnant with Beep? (No, but if you ask Mom again, while I'm around, you'll need a drink.) Is your house near a power line? (Not especially. And, by the way, Mom's a realtor, so definitely tell her that he got leukemia from her choice of house.) Does anyone in your family smoke? (No. That's steam coming out of my ears. In the future, though, we'll set people like you who ask that question on fire.)*

H: *LOL. Wish I could sic you on everyone who hassles my mom. My favorite was the people who asked if I ever took steroids for basketball, to bring it on.*

K: *It's like the cancer diagnosis comes with a portable stupidity field, which moronifies every grownup.*

H: *They're afraid. You know—some people think blood cancer is scary.*

K: *Yeah. Wimps. Maybe it makes them feel less scared if the cancer is somehow your fault. Or they tell you "Google vitamin D and cancer" because, you know, the cure for cancer must be just a mouse click and two million search results away.*

H: *It's hard to accept something as unfair as fatal cancer.*

K: Potentially *fatal. Let's split hairs here, cute bald guy. But, yeah. I don't know why people keep saying I have anger issues, when really life has will-make-people-paying-attention-angry issues.*

H: *You have anger issues?*

K: *Yeah, but they should go into remission as soon as Beep gets well.*

I stared at the screen for a long time, and thought about grownups being scared, then added some more.

K: *Actually, I'm afraid. Since they couldn't get Beep into remission, my bone marrow might be his last shot.*

H: *Beep's lucky to have you for a sister. And also lucky you're a pretty close match.*

Eight out of 10 HLA match. It was sweet of Hunter to put it that way. I hoped that was close enough.

17

Mom met with the medical team to work out a treatment plan to get Beep well enough to get a transplant. The docs were afraid they'd croak him, not just his bone marrow, when they upped the chemo and radiation. After the meeting, Mom went off to the bathroom to pull herself together and to get rid of the tear marks—you know, so Beep wouldn't *worry*.

So I talked to Beep. "For the transplant, you have to get better."

"Right. So they can almost kill me with radiation and chemo again, then maybe kill me with the transplant."

"Don't sugar coat it, Beepster. It might not *all* be fun."

"Probably not." He shook his head. "Tell Mom I'm holding out for whatever videogames I want. The chemo would only be two weeks, right?" He'd had courses of chemo that had lasted months.

"Just two. But bad." And then months of isolation in the bone marrow unit, if it worked.

"Imagine. Bad freaking chemo." He closed his eyes and rested between words. "Did you ever figure out what's up with Rachel?"

"No." I'd seen Rachel's tampons in the bathroom trash can again, so if it was a pregnancy scare, it was over. "Don't change the subject. Can you get better, for the transplant?"

"Maybe. Sure. But that's it. If the transplant doesn't work, no more chemo. I'm done. You have to back me up on that, with Mom."

I swallowed, then nodded. Of course, if the transplant didn't work, he wouldn't be around for more.

Mom and I wedged ourselves into the visitors' chairs of Doc Hanfield's small office, surrounded by her looming bookcases, to go over the "known risks" of being a transplant donor.

Doc Hanfield, in a white coat, sat behind her desk. She was a tall, light-haired woman older than Mom, with round glasses and a long face even when she was being cheerful. Mom was holding—clutching, really—my hand, while Doc Hanfield explained they'd give me Filgrastim, a drug that would produce lots of stem cells and make them run extra laps around my bloodstream.

"You may get headaches and joint pain for four days," she looked at me over her clipboard. The brochure had said there was an over ninety percent chance of that. Fun. She went on to cover the incredibly unlikely "standard" risks of any kind of donation, which happen a tiny part of one percent of the time, like continuing bleeding or lingering pain.

"Mom," I interrupted. "You're squeezing my hand too hard."

"Sorry."

Doc Hanfield leaned forward and explained the process, tapping the folder on her desk with a pen for emphasis. In an old-school bone marrow transplant, I would have gone to the hospital, had anesthesia, and then they'd suck goop out of my hip bone with a needle while I snoozed. I would have had a sore hip for a day or two, but I probably could have milked that for a whole extra week, pretending to limp nobly everywhere and making a delicate brave wince whenever I sat down, like it was as painful as fifty minutes of Algebra 2.

No such luck.

UCSF Benioff Children's was running a clinical trial of a more advanced approach, called peripheral blood stem cell donation. My stem cells were supposed to find their way where Beep's nonexistent marrow was and take over there, making all his blood cells after that. Stem cell donation was supposed to reduce the risk of rejection and of graft-versus-host disease, because they'd take some of the parts out that didn't match Beep as well.

"Mom," I interrupted. "You're *still* squishing my hand."

Doc Hanfield sat up straighter and explained they'd start killing Beep's marrow completely, which would take two weeks. Five days before they finished, I'd get the Filgrastim. Then, on the day of the donation, they'd "harvest" my stem cells (making it sound like tiny wet wheat) in a glorified blood donation. Then they'd stick those in Beep, so he wouldn't die. Because once they killed Beep's marrow, he would have no other way to make blood cells unless my stem cells became his new marrow. Behind Doctor Hanfield, hiding among the other books on pediatric oncology, was a big gray volume with large blue letters on the spine. *End-of-Life Care.*

I swallowed.

"Your cells will fix him," Mom said brightly. "They'll fight his cancer. And win."

"Actually, Beep's body has to fight the cancer," Doc Hanfield said. "But your cells will give him another tool to use."

After all the other tools had failed. I squirmed. My hand was damp, in Mom's grip.

"So Beep will beat the cancer, with your cells," Mom said.

Doc Hanfield looked over at Mom, then back at me. "There are no guarantees."

No kidding. I'd had to read all the way to the very last page of the colorful *You're a Match!* booklet from the National Marrow Donor Program, to find a word about Beep's odds: The two-year survival rate for transplant recipients was "30 to 60 percent."

"I'm feeling good about this," Mom wore her determined cancer mom expression, chin raised. She squeezed my hand even harder.

Even though it was my hand getting crushed, Doc Hanfield wore a pained expression. She opened her mouth again, but I waved her off.

"I got it." I nodded toward Mom. "I'm good with thinking my cells will totally fix Beep, even if there's no guarantee. I'm good to go."

"Do you have any questions?" Doc Hanfield asked.

It felt like there wasn't enough air in the little office, probably from Mom's breathing so fast. "Yeah. Could you give my mom a Valium? She's *still* squeezing my hand too hard."

Unfortunately, the answer to that was no. Hospitals, it turned out, have rules about access to drugs, and don't allow random family members to gobble anxiety meds off passing carts. No matter how much they need them.

So I signed my "informed consent" and Mom let go of my squished hand to sign too, because I could donate stem cells to save my brother's life but, as someone under seventeen, couldn't be trusted legally to understand what I was signing, so my crazy mom also had to scribble on the form.

18

If you distilled human despair and drank it in the dark while emo bands played funeral music, the result would be more cheerful than Drowningirl's poetry. That night, Drowningirl sent some to my online alias Cipher. If her high school has a literary magazine, the editors are probably organizing an intervention.

Pleading
He kisses my wrists,
Tells me
They're perfect how they are,
Covered with unbroken skin.
Tries to hold me with his frightened eyes.
Please, they plead. Don't reach for the razor again.
Please.
My eyes can't promise back.
I look away, can't bear reflected pain.
Be well, I whisper to myself,
But don't know what that means.

BFH—
Perfect retorts
Perfectly hostile
Perfectly horrible to me.
Perfect everything, except teeth.
But how would you put braces on a chainsaw?

They're heartbreaking, but beautiful. She says she only sends them to me, in my secret identity, Cipher. Maybe she's afraid that if she shared them with someone who knew her in the real world, she'd get herself locked up, as a danger to herself.

I worry about her.

19

They stabbed me with the Filgrastim shot in the left buttock, as they say in hospital-speak, and the sting of the needle was nothing compared to the pain-in-the-butt side effects. The headaches and joint pain showed up the next day, right on time, promising four days of increasing agony before the harvest.

For once I had a real excuse for not doing homework or going to school—a massive throbbing headache from trying to save my brother's life—so I worked it. Added to the headache of dealing with the Tracies? Too much to bear.

Mom didn't want me in school anyway, in case some kid coughed flu germs on me before my cells went into Beep. Beep was busy across the Bay at UCSF, having his bone marrow killed, leaving him with no immune system; the last thing he needed was a potentially fatal virus hitchhiker with his last shot at life, my borrowed cells.

The afternoon before I was supposed to donate, after I'd missed three days of school to be bored lying in a dark room, posting blog whines about Filgrastim aches, Evan called to see how I was.

"I have a headache as big as Rachel," I said. "She's a huge pain."

"Why don't I come over and distract you?" It was after school for Evan, and I was home alone.

"I don't know." I stalled. Technically, it was against the rules to have a boy over when there was no "parent supervision," but Rachel had bent that house rule so many times, it was pretzel-shaped. "Probably because I'm almost bored out of my skull, and if that actually happens, my headache might stop."

"I can be boring."

"No, your sense of humor is too good." Don't I get adventurous when my head hurts too much to retreat into my shell.

"I could bring brownies."

"You have brownies? Now we're talking."

"I have a box of mix to make them. They're a headache cure."

"They are not."

"Well, it hasn't been completely tested. We're doing a phase II clinical trial. Ford and Monroe, 'Chocolate brownies as palliative care for Filgrastim side effects in stem cell donors.' Are you in?"

He had the language down, from our clinical trial scavenger hunt. "Not unless you put my name first. I'm the test subject, so I outrank you."

"Fine, but you have to follow the test protocol. First, invite me over. Then, I make brownies, then you eat them."

"In the interest of science," I said, "okay."

Five minutes later, Evan was at the door. Skippy barked to announce him, then tail-wagged himself into a frenzy when he saw it was Evan. I opened the regular door, but kept the screen door closed, with Skippy jumping against it, while I made Evan confirm he had no cold, sniffles, fever, headache, swollen lymph nodes, or any other kind of sick.

"I don't even have athlete's foot," he said. "That's Tyler. I only have boredom, from three days without you."

I missed Evan, too, although I wasn't brave enough to say that. But I have plenty of boredom antibodies, from sitting through high school classes, so I let him in. He brought the box of brownie mix and ice cream in a fabric grocery bag, along with the other ingredients, milk and eggs. And Tylenol, which he said he researched and could be used on top of ibuprofen to fight headache and joint pain.

"Wow. Remind me some time that you're awesome."

"I'm awesome," he said. "And you haven't even tasted my brownies."

After I gobbled two Tylenols, I hunted down a bowl and a square baking dish, and we preheated the oven to 350, like it said on the box. Along with headache medicine and the brownie ingredients, he brought a dark washcloth. He rolled it up, got it wet, and put it on my forehead while I flopped down onto pillows on the cool kitchen floor to watch him make brownies. Skippy dashed between us, nudging Evan to persuade him to drop ingredients, then dog-snuggling me on the floor.

"This isn't right," I said. "You'll make me feel worthwhile—that'll leave me confused."

He stopped mixing ingredients. "Are you fishing for a compliment? Like, for example, I think you're great—and cute. When you're not headache-scrunching your face."

Did that mean he thought I was cute? Or was that just an example of a compliment I'd fish for? If he *did* think I was cute, how come he hadn't resisted the year before, when Tracie had dragged him away, time after time? I couldn't untangle that snarl while I had a headache. It would give me a bigger one. "No. If I want a compliment, I'll ask. Like, for instance, tell me I'm brave and noble and this will make Beep well."

"You're brave, and noble, and I hope this makes Beep well."

"Hope? Skinn . . ." Oops. I almost called Evan Skinnyboy, which I only call him when I'm Cipher. My headache was making me stupid. "Even if it's by the skin of his teeth, this *better* make Beep well. Give me a guarantee here, Evan."

"Sorry. No guarantees." He finished mixing ingredients. Before, I'd shared with him the real odds. "I'm not going to lie."

"Then double crap, there goes that. I also wanted you to tell me I'm funny."

"You are funny, but only when you're not running yourself down. Why do you do that?"

"Saves time. I like to get it in, before the Tracies do. Also, to get rejection out of my system, before Beep gets my stem cells."

"How about you go easier on yourself?"

"Sorry, can't understand you. Did you lapse into French?"

Evan made a frustrated noise, and poured the ingredients into the baking dish.

"Make sure it's fully cooked," I said. "It's got eggs, so if you don't cook it all the way, it could kill Beep."

"I'll cook it all the way," he said, cranky. "My *brownies*, in you, won't kill Beep."

Right. "They won't." Evan was being great to me, and I was being a jerk. "I'm afraid my stem cells will. Kill Beep. Or not save him. Which is the same." At his concerned look, I went on. "Sorry. I have a headache, and I'm worried. That I'll kill my brother with my cells. I'm not real entertaining."

"Lie down on the couch. You're not supposed to entertain. I'll rub your forehead."

"You don't have to do that." Butterflies. With little hammers. Attached to their wings.

"It's part of the clinical trial. Headache cure." He put the brownies in the oven and set the timer. I lay down on my back on the long couch in the front room, bending my legs so there was some couch left for Evan. He put the cold, rolled-up washcloth back on my forehead. He sat next to me on the couch and started rubbing my head on the sides, little circles with the tips of his fingers, on my temples.

"Evan." My headache was actually less, and I couldn't feel any ankle or knee or wrist pain anymore. Instead I felt tingly. "I owe you a Massive Lifetime Favor. You can call it in anytime."

"Well—" he said.

"For anything except making me write songs with you, before the end of your friend-probation."

He sighed, a long one. But he kept rubbing my temples. Then he started stroking my hair, running his hand over it, then combing through it with his fingers. Wow. Wow. Wow.

I wanted to lie there forever like that. I wanted to push my head further into his hands. I shifted.

"Relax. It's part of the protocol."

I tried to. "It's good I have a headache. Otherwise this would be too nice."

"Why?"

"I don't know." It was hard to explain, even to myself. Because Beep had cancer. Because Evan might get dragged off again by some other girl. Because it didn't fit my life. Because he flirted so much with Cipher online, I couldn't trust him. Or because it could lead to other things, or all of the above. "But it's mmmmmmmmmm." I snuggled toward him. The smell of baking brownies was filling the house, warm and wonderful.

"I even make follow-up house calls."

I was silent, enjoying him stroking my hair. Then my mind went off in a different direction, worried about the transplant. "This is Beep's last shot. What if it doesn't work?"

He stopped. I guess that was too serious for him, too. "You'll know you did your best."

No. I'll know my best wasn't good enough. But I didn't say that to Evan. I might suffer from depression, but I don't want it to be contagious.

Evan leaned over. He was moving his face toward mine.

Skippy jumped up, landed on my chest, and started dog-licking me instead. I made a weird "Aack" noise. The oven buzzer went off.

"Uh, brownies." I'm so good with clever things to say. I felt nervous and warm, along with being achy. I sat up.

Evan exhaled and went to get the brownies out of the oven.

I pointed out a seat at our kitchen table, when the brownies were cool enough to eat. "Sit there." Then I sat on the opposite side. I don't completely know why. The steel scooper was slightly shaky in my hand, so I put it in the ice cream carton he brought. "So—here's how you do it. We're eating dessert first. And even before that, we take our ice cream in our bowls and mash it and stir it with our spoons so it's creamy and perfect to go with warm brownies."

We did, and it was warm and wonderful, even with the aches, to sit with Evan, eating the brownies he made and the ice cream he brought. Then, while I lay down again with my little damp forehead compress, Evan rinsed the bowls and pan and spoons and put them in the dishwasher and cleaned up the counter, so there was no mess to annoy Mom.

He started to pack up the eggs and milk.

"Uh, could you leave some milk?" I was embarrassed. "For my cereal in the morning?"

"You don't have milk?"

"Yeah, but like three weeks old. By now, it's chunky style."

Evan pulled ours out of the fridge. Then, because he's a guy, he opened the cartoon and sniffed it. "Eww." He wrinkled his face and poured it down the sink, watching the slow gloppy splatter with fascinated horror. "That's cottage cheese." He sniffed again. "From dead goats. Zombie dead goats. It's *moving*." He washed it down the sink and ran the disposal and rinsed out the carton and put it in the composting. He put the good milk he'd brought into our fridge.

"My hero. Saved me from a headache and boredom and zombie dead goat milk."

"You're my hero," he said. "Trying to save Beep."

"Only if it works. Not if it kills him instead." It's only in Beep's shooter videogames you get to be a hero by killing people. I was being such a downer. I wanted to be friendly and fun and funny, but somehow my words all got stuck on honest.

I stood up, and Evan walked over, until he was really close. He put his arms around me. I was looking right into those pretty brown eyes. He licked his lip, a quick nervous flick of the tongue. He leaned his face toward me with his lips slightly open. He looked scared. I could feel his breath on my skin. My heart was beating really fast. All I had to do was lean into it.

I tilted my head down instead. Put my forehead on his shoulder. "I need a hug," I said. "I'm scared." And I was, actually shaking. If we kissed, right before I donated bone marrow to Beep, what if the donation didn't go well and Beep got sick? Would I be afraid forever that it was because I got germs from Evan?

Evan hugged me. "Scared about Beep?"

"Yeah," I said. That was one of the things I was scared about. We hugged each other, but awkwardly, because somehow our arms weren't in the right place, like we needed more practice. The alarm went off on my phone, startling us both. Time to take more ibuprofen. And Mom would be home soon. Probably best if she didn't find me wrapped around Evan. "I, uh. Probably time to go," I said. But I didn't stop hugging him, and he didn't stop hugging me.

Finally, I let go, and then he did, and I took a step back. My headache was back. I walked him to the door, looking down.

When he left, I closed the screen door, and put my hand up on it. "Thanks."

Evan put his hand on the other side, so we were touching hands through the mesh. "My pleasure." He kept his hand there. After a long, long pause, I finally dropped mine.

"You have to keep being my friend." I swallowed. "If my cells don't work and Beep dies. Because I'll really need you. And I might not be my friend anymore."

"Okay." He looked somehow sad. "Always." He opened his mouth to say something else, but didn't, then gave me a little wave.

I watched him go, and, with the headache building again, instead of thinking *that was awesome*, I felt more depressed, like I'd gotten in my own way and screwed things up that could have been even more awesome. *Not quite good enough, Kat.* I hoped it wasn't a bad omen for the transplant.

20

Mom blew three and a half gaskets over Evan stopping by. Typical. But it was like she was speaking Sanskrit—her lips were moving, but only ancient nonsense came out. She was upset about "no supervision" with Evan here. Also, didn't I know I shouldn't get exposed to germs? And why had he come over? Another thing—brownies aren't nutritious.

I said I'd given Evan the health grilling before letting him in, and reminded her I wasn't Rachel—so there was no making out involved—and added that, since I had to eat dinner with Tyler's family once a week, I hung out a bunch at Tyler's unsupervised, and Tyler was also technically a boy, even when his parents weren't around.

"That's different," Mom said.

"How?" It hurt my head to raise my voice, but I did anyway. If stupidity was contagious, Mom would make me a moron right before I gave my dumb cells to Beep.

"Tyler's not Evan."

And I'm not Mom, which only made it harder to understand her insane babbling, especially since Evan studied with me at Tyler's.

"What?" I gave Mom my you're-not-making-sense look and sat up, which made my headache worse. "Never mind. It *was* weird having Evan here—someone in our house who cared that I had a headache and who tried to do something about it, who even brought milk so I have something to put on cereal. Completely different. From everyone around here."

"I left you girls grocery money," Mom said, ignoring the rest.

"Rachel did the shopping. Remember? The vegan?" It was like talking to Dad, all of a sudden. "She bought *almond* milk."

"You could use that."

I snorted. "If God meant us to drink milk from almonds, he would have given nuts cow udders." I looked at Mom. "It's bad enough he lets nuts have daughters."

"What's that supposed to mean?"

Mom's you're-out-of-line-young-lady voice doesn't work on me. "It means I have a killer headache and have to go lie down, to concentrate on growing blood cells for tomorrow's 'harvest.' Because that's all I am around here—a blood bag. So stop upsetting me, messing up my only usefulness."

I stormed off to my room and slammed the door, which, with my headache, bothered me more than it did Mom.

But I left my sports bottle behind and was supposed to be drinking lots of water. After my brain-rattling door slam performance, I wasn't slinking back downstairs to get it.

Five minutes later, Mom came upstairs to bring me my sports bottle and also to explain or apologize, but I didn't want to get into another fight, so I told her I'd just lie in the dark and maybe we could go through that some other time, when my head didn't feel like it was mashed under a collapsed bridge.

⟲

After dinner, when my headache was pounding even worse, and my elbows and knees ached, Rachel knocked on my door. I couldn't remember the last time that happened.

"Brought you ibuprofen," she said.

"Thanks." I was surprised. "How'd you know?"

"You were moaning. Wimp."

"I was not."

"No," she smiled. "I read about the side effects online. And saw your blog posts."

"Thanks." It was almost time for another dose of ibuprofen. I washed them down with water out of my sports bottle. "What do I owe you?" I joked, not knowing what else to say about Rachel being nice.

"Just—make Beep well, okay?"

So: No pressure. I gave her a scared nod.

The next morning, at the Blood Centers of the Pacific donation site in San Francisco on Bush Street, a block from Dad's office, I sat in a brown, one-armrest lounging couch for the three-hour "harvest," while the regular blood donors came and went, because my donation took six times as long. A Filipina nurse named Norlissa in a white medical jacket supervised, and the apheresis machine clicked and whirred, separating what it was pulling out of my blood for saving Beep from the stuff it sent back. The only creepy parts were (1) the blood they put back into me came back in cold, so I could feel this long chilly line s-l-o-w-l-y moving up my left arm then through my chest toward my heart. I put my right hand on where it was coming back from the left side, and felt the cold advancing. Eww. And, of course (2) there was no guarantee my stem cells, parked in Beep, wouldn't kill him.

They gave me this little tape-wrapped gauze about the size of the cardboard center of a toilet paper roll, which I was supposed to roll around every five seconds in the hand of the arm they were taking the blood out of. While I twirled and squeezed it, I sent little messages to my stem cells. *Make Beep well. Don't get rejected. Make healthy blood cells, in your new home. Don't kill my brother, guys. Be good for him. Kick leukemia's ass. Save my brother. Please.*

Beep was so zonked from the chemo, he didn't even remember getting my transplant. When the docs put the drip in, he was way too out of it to remind the little cells of what to do, and those cells didn't have any actual brains in their tiny selves. So I was worried they might already have forgotten my advice from a few hours before.

Beep played nearly dead for a couple of days, then slowly started getting better.

21

Kat's Make-Up Paper

Philosophy of Life Part 1:
Boys, and How to Impress Them:
The Nineteen Names for Barf Dating Secret

If you're a straight high school girl who can't seem to get along with other girls—like me, for example—your philosophy of life paper should probably include something about boys. Here is mine: Boys are different from girls. Deep, right? My first piece of evidence is their (generally) different attitude toward shooter videogames: Boys actually enjoy them. No wonder they're less mature than girls: Their brains are bludgeoned into a late-developing stupor by the boredom of repetitive videogames— See enemy guy. Shoot. Repeat.

Second, and even more profound: Our different attitude toward barf. Girls—correctly, I'm thinking—look at stomach content rebounds as disgusting and not to be discussed. Boys, though, think it's funny. There's the guy fascination with the gross plus their humor reaction to the uncomfortable. Like a movie where some dude gets kicked in the crotch: In a theater full of guys, the reaction is . . . laughter.

I can't explain it, but I know how to use it. To talk with boys, all you need to know is a little bit about shooter videogames. I used to grill Tyler Harris for tricks and tips at popular videogames, to pass on to Beep. So I actually speak Videogamese. As a result, I've had continuous conversations for several minutes with Tyler about a topic other than sports, something no other girl at our school (or, probably, on our planet) has managed.

Even more impressive to boys is if you can talk to them about alternative names for the big spit: Despite spending their entire childhood wandering the *World of Warcraft* or playing *Modern Warfare* online, even gamer guys have a vague sense that girls are different, that we don't go for the same level of grossness. So flip that stereotype: Meet their euphemism for barf and raise them two.

I discovered this by accident, because my brother Beep got such a kick out of alternate names like high-volume hiccups, coughing for content, and liquid laughter—even when that was his life's central unpleasant experience. Then I tested it on other guys in the PICU. They also cracked up. So I claim original research credit for this important discovery. I even used it to get a semi-actual boyfriend, chatting up a cute senior cancer kid named Hunter Lange online.

22

The weeks while Beep and my bone marrow were still deciding how much to fight with each other, I had trouble sleeping. Way across the country in his hospital room, Hunter was so wired on prednisone that sleep wasn't a regular option for him. Instead, we spent hours in the darkness, shooting messages back and forth. He said I helped distract him from his situation, and I needed something to take my mind off the growing ache of worry for Beep. One night in late November, we exchanged complaints about school.

H: *Was supposed to escape high school for good in June, but even if I get well fast they'll make me repeat at least a semester, cuz I missed so much.*

K: *(*Shudder*) Since I haven't done any of the assignments, they might make me repeat a whole grade. The student equivalent of being regurgitated. They'll feed me the same b.s. homework over again, to make me hurl. A whole year of making street pizza and eating lunch to match my shoes.*

H: *LOL. But don't get me started—I know lots more words for barfing than you.*

K: *Dream on, shiny head. I'm a cancer sib. I entertain my cancer kid brother with names for the big spit. I've forgotten more ways to say yak than you know.*

H: *Wanna bet?*

K: *Sure. My bone marrow against your heart. (With chemo, your liver and kidneys, probably not so good.) I should warn, though—it's not clear yet if my bone marrow is so great either.*

H: *No prob. Last girl I gave my heart to threw it back, bruised. And any bone marrow is better than mine. You're on: Hurling, horking, heaving. Hacking up a hairball.*

Hmmn. Upping the degree of difficulty by starting with the same letter? Easy.

K: *Barfing. Booting. Blowing gravy. Big spit. Bouncing breakfast. Burping biscuits. Barking chow.*

H: *Spitting up. Spaghetti speech. Stomach acid shoe shine.*

That was a new one to me.

K: *Tossing cookies. Talking to Ralph on the round white phone. Throwing up. Tossing a street pizza. Tonsil-tickle tossup. Technicolor yawn.*

After half a dozen more messages back and forth, Hunter conceded.

H: *Wow. You win.*

The poor guy never had a chance. He'd never heard of the power burp, let alone anti-gravity gargling. I dazzled him with my synonym skills.

H: *Where do you want the heart delivered?*

K: *I'll get back to you on that. Take good care of it in the meantime, so when I claim it, it's cancer free.*

H: *I'll do my best.*

That's when Hunter started calling himself my "possibly DBF," for possibly Dying BoyFriend. I had this weird pang, because I thought about Evan, but I played along anyway. Hunter was 3000 miles away, and a senior, and would either bounce back to the healthy world and leave me behind or be dead in a few months. Also leaving me behind. I figured it was like, when you're a girl getting a haircut, why not play-flirt with the totally gay late-20s guy hairdresser? You both know it won't go anywhere, but it's fun, maybe good practice for later in life, and basically harmless.

I wish.

☙

That week, Drowningirl disappeared on me. Or, technically, disappeared on her online friend Cipher, but I was the one who felt bad about it. There were two last heartbreaking poems and a final message.

> *My House 1*
> *I was born in a smoldering house*
> *And watched it slowly burn.*
> *My brother left for a hospital bed*
> *Now where can I turn?*

> *My House 2*
> *Crazy lives in the master suite;*
> *Cancer, one door down.*
> *Love was here once, long ago*
> *But can't get to my room.*
> *Too little left. Too many stairs.*
> *It's a simple floor plan, our house.*
> *But I'm lost. Again.*

D: *Too much gravity here. I'm too crushed to type anymore. Going to use all my energy pretending to cope. I'm turning over a new leaf, and will only email when I have something cheerful to type. If ever. Love and goodbye. Thank you. Be well.*

I sat there, stunned. I was worried about her, but also feeling abandoned. How could she do that? I was mostly there for her, but if things got worse for me, I figured she'd be there for me, a helpful expert on how to keep slogging through misery. And even if she was trying to protect me from her bumming me out more, didn't she know that it helped me to be needed somewhere? I'd never told her how much our connection meant.

C: *Don't go. I need to hear from you. I'm very alone where I am. Don't disappear on me. Please. I don't write poems like you, but I'm living one of yours. I feel like you're writing about me, too. Don't leave me alone with all this. It's too much. Please email me back. Love, and* not *good-bye. 1-800-273-TALK. Or write. Real soon.*

But I didn't hear from her.

23

Along with all the other things trying to kill Beep, after the transplant there was one more:

Me.

My borrowed bone marrow cells attacked Beep. Like I always go after everyone with sarcasm. Except no one has to gobble bowls full of colorful meds to keep my sarcasm from killing them.

Bone marrow, borrowed or otherwise, doesn't just chill, hanging out in the middle of your bones. It's one big twenty-four-hour-a-day factory, cranking out every kind of blood cell, including the infection-fighting ones, which are supposed to wander around attacking everything that's not you, as part of your immune system.

You can see how this might be a problem. Kat-style white blood cells, made by Kat's borrowed stem cell marrow in its new Beep home, are cruising down a Beep artery on their way to work one morning when Beep starts playing some first-person shooter videogame, like *Call of Duty* Roman Numeral Zillion Eight.

When the new Kat white cells realize he's enjoying that, they go "Holy crap, this *can't* be me, because I'm made out of Kat-stuff" and start attacking everything around as one giant foreign something-or-other that's not them.

It's called graft-versus-host disease, or GVHD, and it's like one of Beep's violent videogames: Everything attacks everything else. Except there's no restart, if you die.

GVHD can be mild, where you're a little sick from your whole body wanting to throw itself up. Or it can be bad. Gangrene, death, organ failure, or even death. Also, death.

To keep it down, they gave Beep buckets of pills to make his immune system tardy, on vacation, or almost completely absent, like human feelings of kindness, say, from the Tracies. Or me, say, from school, in early December.

Almost everybody was careful to describe Beep's GVHD as "mild," at least around me, but I was never sure how much they were lying. Beep was really sick, and I kept remembering how the *Johns Hopkins Patients' Guide to Leukemia* described even heart failure as "mild." The hospital people were probably trying to make me feel good about what I did, playing down how much my borrowed bone marrow was chomping on Beep.

Only Rachel wasn't so careful. Beep's transplant going bad had put everyone on edge, so Rachel and I got even more snarky with each other. A huge surprise, because even I hadn't thought that was possible.

She came back from the grocery store one afternoon, after deliberately not getting the eggs, milk, and meat on the list. I'd even written bacon bits and salami down, so she could leave two things out and claim moral superiority while getting the rest.

"Are you *trying* to starve me?" I asked. "Some of us prefer to eat chickens than to survive on what they eat."

"I got seitan instead of ham." Her expression was seriously annoyed. "And Tofurky bacon."

Vegetables are fine. If Mrs. Miller counts, I even have one as a teacher. But as far as I'm concerned, they have their own thing going and should stick to it, not pretend to be bacon. "As much as Brian nibbles on you, I thought you'd develop some sympathy for us carnivores."

"Shut up. Now."

"Put actual bacon in my mouth, and I'll stop talking long enough to chew."

"Why don't you stop talking, period? All you do is spew hateful things," she said. "It was bad enough when you were participating in killing animals. Now you've moved on to people."

"What?"

"I'm as sick of you as Beep is, and you're killing him."

I stared at her, mouth open, speechless. Stricken. My breath caught in my chest. I stormed upstairs to my room and slammed the door so hard, books fell over on my bookshelf.

Rachel knocked at my door a few minutes later.

"Go away." Sometimes, when you get a deep cut, it takes a bit for the pain to catch up with the injury. I'd been lying on my bed, thinking about how horrible it was that, across the Bay, my blood cells were attacking Beep. They gave me a whole pamphlet of risk factors, but they left out the most important: What if it didn't work and my cells killed Beep instead? How could I deal with that?

Rachel opened the door and came in anyway.

"Such great listening skills." I stood up. I didn't want her settling in for a lengthy let's-make-Kat-feel-even-worse session.

"I went too far," Rachel said quietly.

"What? With Brian? Didn't realize you had a limit."

"I came by to apologize." Her face reddened and she stopped.

As opposed to actually apologizing, I guessed. "I know I'm killing Beep. Okay? I can't get the homework done, but I'm not *stupid*." I looked down, at Rachel's red toenails in her cute, stupid sandals. "I'm not perfect, like you. I'm screwing everything up, including Beep's blood supply. I get it."

Rachel looked at me like we'd never met. "I—"

"How about you leave." Leaning in to shove her out of my room, I got a whiff of her perfume. It was like wrestling with an orange-scented lavender field. "Before you say something that makes me beat you until *you* need blood." I grunted and pushed her toward the hall. "In case. You hadn't noticed. Transfusions. Aren't going great. In our family." She tried to not get bulldozed out, but I had an advantage.

Soccer midfielders shove girls around all the time. "Oh, wait—between Brian-climbs you did notice. Even reminded me. That I'm killing Beep." I shoved the door closed between us and clicked the lock. "Thanks," I finished through the locked door.

☙

That night, Mom joined us for "family dinner" while Dad was at the hospital with Beep. We were having vegetable stir-fry with rice. Mom added some chicken to mine—which she'd picked up at the store—and scattered pale tofu sponge-cubes on Rachel's.

"Could you pass the soy sauce?" Rachel asked, because tofu—made of soybeans—still needs soybean sauce for flavor.

"Sure you want me to touch it?" I picked up the bottle. "With my blood-spattered hands?" I set it in front of her.

"Do you have a cut?" Mom's eyes widened in alarm.

"Relax. It's metaphorical blood." From a metaphorical cut all the way through my soul.

Mom looked at me with the same eyebrow-crinkling I give to people rattling off rapid French: No idea.

Except there's no fourteen-pint limit to the metaphorical blood supply. Maybe you just keep bleeding forever. I could have hassled Rachel more, but with my bone marrow chewing on Beep, there was already enough of me attacking siblings.

24

Drowningirl didn't answer my Cipher emails. When, as Cipher, I tried to post on her Facebook page, I got a message she'd terminated her account. Which left me terrified: Had her brother died? Had she finally jumped off a bridge?

I still hung out with Evan at lunch and we did homework together on Tuesdays at Tyler's, but it seemed like my personality was mostly sucked out by sadness, and it felt weirder and weirder to flirt with Evan electronically while I was pretending to be Cipher. That left Hunter as my only online buddy, and with him, it got intense. We exchanged a flurry of messages every night in early December, when I couldn't sleep. I'd sometimes page back through his past Facebook timeline about the developments with his AML. Man. He had no idea how to post in Mom Calmese. A teensy, say, raw.

I sent him the link to my blog on mastering the language of Mom Calmese and explained he ought to have a special Facebook page for updates in Mom Calmese on his medical condition. He said there was no way his condition could be explained calmly. I said I had mad skills and could translate anything. He called B.S.

K: *Try me.*

H: *My liver's the size of a football. Have jaundice and am turning yellow.*

K: *Although he hasn't gotten any sun, Hunter's looking tanned. More blood tests soon.*

H: *Latest round of chemo was the worst ever. Barfing everything.*

K: *Hunter's body is responding quickly and dramatically to the latest round of medicine. We're optimistic. This seems like the most powerful dose of chemotherapy he's had. We're hopeful about this new round of treatments.*

H: *ANC is 320.*

That was absolute neutrophil count, and the number meant he had practically no immune system left.

K: *We have to put on masks and gloves and poufy hats when we visit Hunter. We probably look like visitors from Mars. But he seems happy to see us.*

H: *What about when I die?*

That was a tough one.

K: *Hunter left us last night, after fighting as long, and as bravely, as anyone could. He was tired by the end, and he's finally in a better place, beyond pain. He was wonderful, and we were lucky to get to know him and for every minute he was with us. We'll miss him and remember him always.*

That one got blurry while I was typing it, because I'd really gotten to know Hunter, in the months of messaging, but hit send anyway. There was a delay before anything came back.

H: *I'm afraid. Think I'm going to die. Soon.*

That was even harder. It took a while before I could answer.

K: *Hunter is sharp mentally and making plans about the future. What's your phone number, Hunter? I'll call you now.*

H: *Don't want to be a bother.*

They didn't let patients use their cell phones in his hospital's ICU, but there had to be a landline in his room.

K: *Give me your damn phone number, tough guy. I've got info, from my brother Beep. It might help.*

H: *You can't. They don't put calls thru after 10. East coast here, girl—it's after 1 A.M.*

K: *Ha. If I can't work them at the nurse's station to get through, I deserve to be fired as a cancer sib. Send me your number, and I'll talk to you in five minutes. I promise.*

Hunter gave me the nurse's station phone number and his room extension. I took a deep breath and called. There was no receptionist at that hour, and the first nurse gave me serious pushback, with a side of attitude. "Are you on Hunter's team?" I finally asked. For the long-term stays like chemo and bone marrow patients, at UCSF they have a specific team of nurses, so there's continuity and you get to know them. I figured the deal was the same at Johns Hopkins.

"No."

"Then can I *please* talk to someone on Hunter's team? He's having a hard time, and somebody should know."

After a long pause, a professionally crisp, but more cheerful voice came on. "Hello, this is Nancy. I'm on Hunter's team."

I asked if she had a couple of minutes to talk, because I knew ICU nurses are insanely busy. She said it was quiet. In the meantime, I shot Hunter an email: *On the phone with Nurse Nancy.* "Thanks for taking great care of Hunter. I'm Kat, Hunter's best friend, from out in California." Which was kind of a lie. But I did limit it to California.

Then I worked Nancy like a pro. I explained that my twelve-year-old brother had ALL and AML and I knew it was against their general policies, but I'd been exchanging messages with Hunter, and I had to talk to him. "He's at a low spot. He's afraid of dying. There was a thing my brother Beep went through that might help with that. I promised Hunter I'd use my cancer sib skills and get through."

It took another couple of minutes before Nurse Nancy agreed. In the meantime, Hunter had emailed me, *Nancy's my favorite nurse*, so I even mentioned that.

"Okay," she finally said. "But don't make this a habit. And if he doesn't pick up on the first two rings, I'm hanging up on you. And don't keep him up too long. He's already having enough trouble sleeping." Yay, Nancy.

Hunter picked up on the first ring.

"Hey. It's Kat."

"Hey." He sounded shy, which somehow reminded me of Evan. "It's Hunter. You got through."

"Of course," I said. "I work miracles. They just don't let me pick which ones."

He laughed, so I knew right then, one way or the other, he'd break my heart.

Despite Nurse Nancy's warning, Hunter and I talked for two hours, in the middle of his night and what was turning into the middle of mine, while I sat in the darkness lit by the blue of the computer screen. We talked about ourselves and each other, and then other important stuff. I told him about Beep's near death experience, and Beep's seeing what went on in the next room during the code, and the tunnel of light. I told him how Beep didn't seem afraid of death anymore. Like he'd seen the trailer, and decided the whole death movie would be fine.

Maybe it wasn't fair. Hunter was a senior basketball player. I played the my-twelve-year-old-brother-is-not-afraid-of-death card. Maybe Hunter had to give up fear, because of the guy macho code. But I like to think Beep's experience touched him. Anyway, in the meantime, Hunter got more morphine, from his favorite nurse, Nancy, who didn't even hassle him—or me—about being on the phone at 3 A.M. his time, which added her to my long list of official cancer nurse heroes.

"You're an angel," Hunter said.

I snorted. "And you're getting spacey on morphine. If I'm an angel, I'm the angel of sarcasm." That somehow made me think of Evan, and how much I liked to make him laugh.

"Better you than the angel of death. She can come another night. Sarcasm Angel—I like that."

After two hours of talking, he slowed down, until he was drifting off, between sentences. "Should I take it as an insult, you falling asleep on me?" I asked

"Compliment. I'm not anxious. Between you and the drugs, I can go."

"Sweet dreams, Hunter."

"G'night, Kat." Then I guess he lost track of who he was talking to, drifting off on poppy juice. "I love you." There was a click and a dial tone.

Okay. What?

25

My replacement bone marrow was supposed to make cells that would hunt down all the mutated cancer leukocytes in Beep and destroy them.

But it didn't work.

Maybe it was because Beep was so sick before the transplant, they'd reduced the intensity of the chemo to not kill him. Or my bone marrow sucked. Or both. But Beep's AML came back.

In the meantime, Beep caught a fungal infection in his lungs, aspergillosis, and the side effects of the drugs they gave him to fight that were awful. Even by cancer kid standards. He got some new videogames and a little more time, but he didn't get well.

Treatment boiled down to two options: The docs could try repeating the transplant or "let the AML run its course." (Weirdly, even in hospital ICU wards, where they're occasionally carrying bodies out in bags, they don't call it "death." It's "letting AML run its course," like we're spectators at a microscopic obstacle track the leukocytes jog around.)

I tried to talk Beep into another transplant. Rachel said we should use her cells this time (since mine were obviously defective) but the docs shot that down because I was a better match. Plus, Rachel was stuck-up, so her clotting factors were bound to be off. Also, she has the disposition of a hissing tarantula, so what were the chances of a match with a human sibling?

It didn't matter. Beep said he wasn't going through pre-transplant chemo again, and that his original deal was that he wouldn't have to. The docs chimed in that even a reduced regimen of chemo and radiation to get Beep transplant-ready would almost for sure kill him, especially with the lung fungus.

Mom leaned hard on Beep to say yes to another try, but she could see it wouldn't work unless he miraculously got better first. The docs had run out of other ideas. And even Mom was getting tired of medically torturing Beep to try to save him.

26

Kat's Make-Up Paper

Philosophy of Life Part 2:
The Role of Hope I: A Weed?

Hope is a weed.

You find weeds growing in small cracks at the concrete edges of busy streets. In the most unlikely places, with the tiniest scrap of possibility, they're still there, still alive, reaching for the light.

Until almost the end, there's always a tiny crack of possibility, where the weed of hope can grow: Spontaneous remission. New clinical trial. Newly signed up marrow donor who's a 10/10 HLA match. Miracle drug. Or just plain miracle. Or all of them, one right after the other, which is sometimes what it would take.

Because hope is one thing cancer and chemo and radiation and GVHD and drug-resistant staph infections, even piled on top of each other, cannot kill.

27

It was a typical Thursday morning when I was cutting school again to be with Beep while Mom worked, long after it was clear, at least to me, that my bone marrow was attacking Beep and the immunosuppressive drugs were messing him up. Along with the lung fungus, Beep was fighting mouth sores and thrush and joint pain and a swollen liver, and there was a hospital-wide contest between the viruses and bacteria and fungi to see who'd kill him first.

"I'm done." Beep turned to me, flopping his head over on the pillow. "I want to stop and go home." His voice was strong.

A surgical mask was tickling my cheeks and nose, and the plastic hair net was crinkling my forehead. I scratched my cheek with the back of my medically-gloved hand to keep from getting more germs on him. "To die," I said. That's what it would be.

"This isn't living," he said. "I'm going anyway." He and I had talked about this for a week, and he'd been certain the whole time.

Hard to argue with, but I blinked tears anyway. "Are you sure?"

"How about a second opinion? Do you think I've suffered enough?"

"Too much." I looked away. "I wanted it to work."

"Me too. Sorry." He said it like he'd let me down. "Can you help me tell Mom? She doesn't always listen. Like, today?"

Chestopher, my favorite nurse and Beep's too, was on that morning.

"Hey." I caught up with him out by the nurses' station. He could probably see I'd been crying.

"Are you okay?"

"As much as I'm going to be," I said.

Chestopher squatted, like he did when he talked to the little kids, so I was looking down at him instead of him looking down on me.

"Beep wants to stop. He wants to go home." I was sniffling, but I didn't wipe my nose—that would put deadly germs on my hands.

"I know." His face was concerned. "He told me. He's wanted that for a while."

"So what do we do? Who do we talk to?"

"There's a medical team meeting this afternoon. At three. Your mom and dad should talk to them."

That would work. Mom would be done touring houses by late morning and back at the hospital. Dad was a short Muni ride away, downtown.

I called Rachel on her cell phone during the passing time between first and second period.

"This better be important." She sounded annoyed, as usual.

"Yeah. Beep wants to stop treatment and come home. He wants to go over it with the docs and Mom and Dad this afternoon."

On her end, there was the babble of students in the halls, talking, and a locker slam over her long pause. "Is he sure?" Sounded like tears in her voice.

"Why don't you come talk to him and see?" As a senior, Rachel had already gotten into college and could get an excused absence for being at the hospital to talk to her brother about stopping treatment—at least in my view. My World History teacher Mrs. Miller might disagree, but I'm right.

Rachel said she'd drive over.

I sent an email and left a voicemail for Dad, saying there was a conference with the docs at three today to discuss stopping further treatment and sending Beep home, and Dad *had* to come. Then I called Mom, and left her the same message.

In the bone marrow transplant isolation rooms, the hospital only lets in one visitor at a time. Rachel stayed for half an hour. When she came out, she took one look at me and started crying so hard she couldn't say anything, so I gave her an awkward hug, and held it for a long time, while she shook and we cried.

Then Dad showed up, *hours* before the three o'clock meeting, and he went in to see Beep and didn't come out for an hour and a half. When he came out, his eyes were red and wet. His shoulders were slumped, and he looked like something had broken inside him.

I gave him a hug, so he wouldn't have to talk, and then Rachel was hugging both of us. Someone was shaking our group hug with little sobs. Me.

After half a minute, Dad cleared his throat. "We have to talk—" He cleared his throat again. "Talk to your mother. Beep shouldn't have to take her on. Alone."

"No," I said. "We'll all talk to Mom." I squeezed Dad harder.

"Together," Rachel said. "So Beep doesn't have to."

Dad cleared his throat again, but didn't say anything. He just nodded, making our group hug bob.

So we sat, on the couch in the too-bright waiting room outside the PICU and its bone marrow unit, waiting to ambush Mom. Dad sat between us. Rachel held one of his hands, and I held the other in my chapped one, rough from the months of washing and hand-sanitizing to keep from getting germs near Beep. Dad's phone vibrated dozens of times, in his suit-jacket pocket, from incoming emails, but he never touched it.

My phone and Rachel's dinged at the same time. I pulled mine out. Mom had texted Rachel and Dad and me.

In lobby. There in 2.

I showed Dad the text. We all stood. I moved toward the PICU entry, like I was going to physically block Mom from going in there from the elevator. I took a deep breath. It'd be a huge struggle to get her to accept reality.

The elevator's arrow lit up in red. The doors slid open, and there was Mom, clutching her purse, with her face already crumpled and her eyes wet.

She stepped forward, into the lobby, and then just looked from Rachel to Dad to me, as if begging us to tell her it was something else.

"Oh." It wasn't a word, just a long sound of hurt. She burst into tears and put up her hands. "I know. I know."

Then Dad hugged her and they both sobbed. As I stood there watching my parents trying—and failing, utterly—to comfort each other, I knew: Beep was coming home.

To die.

28

Beep had been out of it most of the evening before, so I didn't get a chance to talk to him about my scheme. I told Rachel, who thought it was great. Evan thought it was great too, when I called him to get a second opinion. Mom was so flipped out about bringing Beep home, probably to die, there was no talking to her about anything.

We left UCSF Benioff Children's, for the last time, a little after seven in the morning. Seven o'clock was change of shift, so a lot of Beep's regulars were there, coming on or off shift. Beep was popular. Half a dozen nurses, including Chestopher and Adrienne and Terry and Chris, walked us out to say good-bye, following our family in a little scrubs-wearing knot, as we wheeled Beep down the hall.

Beep looked small in the wheelchair. He'd lost so much weight. He had my 49er ski hat on to keep warm, and a jacket a size too big. Rachel pushed him, and when we got to the front door, down on Parnassus, she glanced at me, and I nodded. She set the brake.

"C'mon, Beep," I said. "Get on up. We'll hold you, and you can walk out of here." Rachel had stopped his wheelchair a couple of feet short of the outside sliding doors, close enough so they opened. Beep looked over, not understanding. Mom looked anxious.

"It's giving cancer the finger, Beep. To walk out."

Beep smiled.

"Honey, you don't have to do this." Mom put a hand to her mouth. "I'm not sure it's safe."

"We're totally doing this," Beep said.

So Rachel and I each took one of his arms, carefully lifting, and pulled him to his feet. He set his right foot down just inside the

144

threshold, barely putting weight on it. Then he touched his left foot down across the threshold. Applause broke out behind us.

Beep closed his eyes, taking it in, then opened them. "Okay. Now fly me." He held his arms out to the side, like a little kid pretending to be an airplane.

Rachel and I exchanged a quick look and then linked arms under his chest and legs as he leaned forward onto them so we could hold him. We carried him a few steps while he held his arms out and flew. Applause broke out again. The Beepster left that hospital in style.

Someone pushed his wheelchair out to the sidewalk, and we put Beep back in. He closed his eyes briefly, breathing hard, but with a big grin. He waved to the nurses who followed us out, some in tears, and we wheeled him across to the parking lot and to our car.

Not everybody gets well. But there are other kinds of victory over cancer.

෧෨

So Beep walked out on the hospital and its bad food, and we brought him home to hospice care. "Hospice" isn't French, but it might as well be, because it's just a fancy word to disguise the meaning: "keep someone comfortable, instead of curing them, while you say good-bye." The ladies from Pathways Home Health and Hospice had it organized: Beep had his own hospital bed set up in our living room, with a nebulizer and a wheezy machine for concentrating oxygen. He also had separate oxygen tanks to wheel around if he wanted to wander all the way to the back yard.

Along with his antibiotics and his drugs for the fungus-lung, they gave us an eyedropper with a bottle of liquid Valium we could squirt in Beep's mouth if he was nearly in a coma but got restless that made him look anxious. Somehow, though, just being home made it so Beep didn't hurt as much. It even seemed like he'd gone into miracle spontaneous remission, or my borrowed bone marrow was finally kicking in, a little late.

When Dad carried Beep through the front door, Skippy wagged his whole little body. After we set Beep in his hospital bed, with his clear plastic face mask hooked up to his oxygen compressor making wet wheezy noise, Skippy jumped up on the bed and tried to lick every exposed part of Beep's face, while Beep giggled.

For the first time in ages, Mom didn't haul Skippy away, worried about germs.

29

Most other families—even if their mom has an anxiety disorder—probably don't take a body bag with them on a camping trip, expecting one of their kids to croak. But we brought one for our expedition to Big Basin. Beep had always been interested in space, and for his Make-A-Wish, he said he wanted to see a meteor shower. It was a little outside the Make-A-Wish Foundation business model to send a giant space rock our way (although if they can do that before I have to repeat a whole grade, that would be good). What they did instead was help organize a camping trip with Beep, away from the city lights, so he could watch a meteor shower in the middle of the night, when the moon was down and the shooting stars would be easy to see. Beep managed to hang in there for it for two whole weeks, to get to the night of the Geminid meteor shower, which was way past the doctors' expectations.

Along with the body bag (light) and tents and standard camping stuff, we had oxygen canisters (seriously heavy), saline drip bags, antifungal medicine, a portable cot with handles to carry Beep in on, and enough antibiotics to sterilize the coastal range. Make-A-Wish also supplied a nurse and burly porter volunteers in lumberjack shirts, including two cute college guys, which was pretty awesome, but weirdly impersonal. The nurse and a couple of the guys stayed in an RV in the parking lot, a quarter mile from our campsite, and for a while I wished I'd invited Evan, except that would have been a distraction and probably would have freaked out Mom.

We were excited about the trip, until we got to the trailhead, under a sky of solid gray. Watching a meteor shower is dicey. First, you have to have a night with meteors. They're fleeting, and rare, but a few times a year a family of them—like the Geminids—arrives on schedule. Second, you have to get away from the lights, so you can see the meteors. Third, you need a clear night, since clouds block seeing all the way to space. That was a problem, because it was completely overcast on the hike in.

Some of us Monroes were a tad cranky with God to begin with, over Beep's ALL, AML, two relapses, and failed transplant. So, with the heavy clouds on the hike in for his one last chance to see a meteor shower, we were all "well, *this* figures."

Not everyone gets a miracle cure. But come on—couldn't we get a clear night for all those prayers, as a consolation prize?

But Dad was optimistic, looking at some weather app on his phone, babbling about "rising barometric pressure," and that there might be clear skies by midnight.

Beep was dozing off and waking up, being carried in on his little cot/stretcher. "What?"

I almost said "God farts," I was so upset. But I was still hoping for a miracle, and even I didn't want to be that blasphemous. With my luck, I'd lurch against Beep's stretcher when I got hit with the lightning bolt, and take out everyone. "Dad thinks it'll clear up. The air pressure will drive out the clouds."

"Oh. Okay. Cool."

After we hiked in and set up camp, our Wish-a-porters left. We had dehydrated "backpacker meals," which, I guess, are used to punish backpackers who don't do their homework. We added water and cooked them on a camp stove, because apparently someone thought the Monroe family hadn't suffered enough. Mom brought some actual real spaghetti for Beep and a jar of sauce, because he had definitely already suffered enough, and it might be his last meal. Beep didn't even taste it. He just had a little melted ice cream, which had turned liquid like a milkshake. Because there was no meat in the sauce, Rachel split Beep's leftovers with me.

The Geminids were supposed to show up and be easiest to see after the moon set, around 2 A.M., so we were supposed to sleep for a few hours first. Beep nodded off before eight, and Rachel and I roasted marshmallows, while Mom complained we would set a National Forest on fire, which made us overcook them more, until they burned like little tiki-torches.

Mom and Dad slept in the big tent with Beep. It was still overcast at 11 P.M., and we couldn't see a single star. The closest thing was drifting sparks from poking the campfire. I figured if Beep was out of it enough, maybe we'd just fake a meteor shower with drifting embers. Thanks, God.

Rachel and I shared a little tent, which was actually okay. In case of emergency, a bear would go for her first—she looks more delicious, and she's already been tenderized, over time, by boyfriend slobber. Even mosquitoes go for Rachel over me, which for once was fine.

Dad woke us up around 2 A.M. The clouds had cleared completely. It was face-hurting cold outside. Rachel and I kept our sleeping bags wrapped around us as we crawled out of the tent, stood up, and awkwardly shuffled over to Dad and Mom and Beep by the dead campfire, making rustling noises as we shambled like giant standing caterpillars. I thought of starting a caterpillar fight with Rachel, like we'd had when we were little and camped out in the back yard, but I didn't want to annoy her. On Beep's meteor night, it seemed out of place.

We were lots of miles from any towns or major roads, and the moon was down. There were zillions of stars in the cold, clear sky. Dad had Beep out there in his sleeping bag, looking up, with only his face poking out, the little cannula oxygen tube at his nose. Dad pointed out Orion, the easiest constellation to find in the sky because of the three-in-a-row belt. To its left was Gemini, the two stars of Castor and Pollux.

And out of there, every few minutes, a yellow flaming space rock would come out and streak silently across the sky, burning up in the atmosphere. It was awesome.

"Ooh," Beep said at the first one Dad pointed out. Then "Aaah" at the second. He kept that up, for dozens and dozens.

God's own flare gun, signaling "It's beautiful up here. Join us." Or, if you insist, just space rocks burning to dust and ash, with their own message: "Be at peace. Even dying can be beautiful. People will remember your bright spark."

Either way, it worked for Beep. His face peeking out of the sleeping bag had the broadest smile. We must have seen forty meteors in two hours. At a break between incinerating space rocks, Dad pointed out the Milky Way. It was a band of lighter sky from one horizon to the other, because of so many stars in it, the spiral arm of the galaxy we're in.

"I'm going there," Beep mumbled. "When I catch the bus."

Dad shined the flashlight over at Beep. Beep squirmed a hand out of his sleeping bag, by his face, and waved it. "Good-bye meteors. Good-bye stars. Good-bye night." He waved again.

I pulled my sleeping bag over my head then, so as I cried it wouldn't spoil the moment for everyone else.

30

Beep didn't die that night, so we didn't need the body bag, but in the morning I did suggest sticking Rachel in it when she whined about how long it took to get coffee going.

Our cute team of buff porters returned, and we packed off for home. While our husky Wishlings carried Beep's stretcher, I walked next to it, holding his hand.

"That was great," he said about fifteen times, drifting in and out.

I guess we got our miracle: Beep lived long enough to get to the Geminid light show, and the winds carried off the clouds at the right time, leaving us a night sky perfectly dark and clear. It was the best Geminid shower for decades, according to an astronomy blog.

Not the miracle we'd have picked, for a fill-in-the-blank test, but you make do.

∞

Two mornings later, the Beepster died at home, surrounded by all of us.

It was a Saturday, and Dad was home. Mom had been up the night before with Beep, on death watch, and at one point when she barely dozed off, Beep started making gargling, rattling noises until she put his oxygen mask back on. Mom was exhausted. She went off to bed with Dad, while Rachel and I sat up with Beep, after promising to get her and Dad if Beep seemed like he was about to go. Beep hadn't been conscious in a day.

Rachel and I talked quietly, mostly about Beep, and watched him. At some point, he started shifting, rolling to one side, then the other, and arching his back, like he couldn't get comfortable, even unconscious. I looked at Rachel. She said, "Should I get Mom and Dad?"

I didn't know how I knew, but I knew he was going, like she did. "Yeah. Now."

Rachel rousted them, and they trailed in after her, still groggy.

Standing at the head of the hospital bed in our living room, Rachel started singing songs from Green Day, Beep's favorite band. (Beepster was an old-school little guy.) She started quietly, then her voice got stronger, perfect, clear, but with a little quaver, the part about how summer is gone and innocents don't last.

I was holding one of Beep's hands. Dad was holding the other. Mom was stroking his smooth small head, where his soft, tufted hair had come back in.

"I love you. I'm so proud of you, son." Dad's voice broke, and he started crying, and he couldn't say any more.

Mom was murmuring, over and over. "My little boy. My little boy. I love you. Please don't go."

I was doing counter-programming, telling him it was okay, and he should. "We'll be okay, Beep. We love you. Go toward the light. You don't have to hurt anymore. We love you so much."

Rachel kept singing, with that beautiful voice, the part about pain falling from the stars. Then Beep stopped breathing, but we kept holding him and talking to him, while Rachel sang. Rachel went on to another Green Day song, "Last Night on Earth," about how Beep could rest assured that she was sending all her love to him. It was the most beautiful good-bye gift. She prepared it all for Beep. Rachel doesn't even like Green Day—their music was too interesting.

Rachel's voice quavered on the final line, holding that note so long. Then we hung out quietly, together, around the hospital bed in the living room. We hugged each other and cried and talked about Beep, and about how he never needed the Valium dropper. I told Rachel her singing was the most beautiful thing I'd ever heard. Dad turned off

Beep's oxygen compressor, and when its gurgling wheeze stopped, the house got way too quiet.

After a while, Dad called the funeral home and the hospice ladies and the medical equipment company, and pretty soon a bunch of strangers were in our house.

The hospice ladies came and hugged us all, those long nurturing hugs that last half a minute. They put Beep's time of death on some official certificate, and one of them signed a form, while the other one took the Valium dropper bottle.

"Kind of a shame to have that go," Rachel said. "It'd be nice if we could squirt a little liquid Valium under Mom's tongue, as needed."

"Yeah." I put my arm around Rachel and leaned in to whisper. "But that little bottle wouldn't last twenty minutes."

We wrapped Beep up in a white sheet and the guys from the funeral home let Dad and Rachel and me carry him out to the back of their car, a beetle-black long dark station wagon like a vampire prom limousine, with curtains in the back. While we watched, they took my brother away.

Then Mom collapsed, sobbing, on the sidewalk. We surrounded her, first trying to pick her up, but that turned into a kneeling group hug while we all shook. Then there was an awful, awful howl, like a siren, but full of agony and loss and something broken and gone, and it went on for seconds before I realized it was coming from me.

31

My Last Post for Beep

Richard Bud Nelson Monroe, AKA the Beep, died at home this morning in his sleep, surrounded by love and beautiful music. There are no words.

It's not fair that there is sunshine, in a world he can't see anymore.

Good-bye, Beep, our shooting star: Bright, amazing, and here not long enough. He burned fiercely and fought bravely. Cancer never beat him. He finally went to a place it couldn't follow. He doesn't hurt any more. Now we do. We miss you Beep, and the best part of us—our hearts—go with you.

32

Rachel sang again at Beep's funeral, and I joined in on vocals during the chorus and played electric guitar, especially butchering the opening to "Wake Me Up When September Ends." Mom's friend Mrs. Castlewitz played electric violin, so between her and Rachel's great voice, we had plenty of production value to cover my mistakes.

When we got back to our seats, Calley Rose and Amber gave me little hand hugs, reaching from the row behind me to squeeze my shoulders.

"You sang perfect. Beautifully," I whispered to Rachel. "Sorry I played so bad."

"You were fine." She put her arm around me. Under that comforting touch, something broke in me. I leaned into her, and buried my face in her shoulder, grabbing her with one arm, like I was never letting go. She wrapped the other arm around me, and I put both of mine around her.

During the eulogy part, someone's cell phone went off and I whispered to Rachel, "It's resurrection calling."

Afterward, we stood outside, shaking hands with everyone as they left, and eleven zillion or so people shook our hands and hugged us. They all said "What a beautiful service" and told Rachel how wonderfully she sang and fibbed to me that I also played and sang the chorus well. And every single one of them said "I'm *so* sorry."

I wanted to say back, "Apology accepted. But I'm pretty sure it wasn't your fault." I didn't, though. Turns out, even I can keep a lid on it in extreme circumstances.

On the way out, Evan didn't say anything. He just gave me the longest hug. Which was way better than "I'm so sorry" eleven zillion and one.

We had an after party at our house that Mom called a reception. I didn't feel like hearing "I'm so sorry" twelve zillion more times, so I mostly hid out in a corner with Evan and ate poppy seed cake with ice cream.

Evan leaned close. "Don't let your parents try to make you forget Beep"—approximately the weirdest thing he'd ever said.

Before I could ask him what he meant, Mrs. Umbriss tottered over on stiletto heels under piled-up dark hair. "I guess God needs little angels." She wiped away a tear.

"Excuse me?" I said. "If God is all-powerful, he can solve his staffing shortages without child labor. Recruited through freaking *cancer*." I wanted to pelt her with cupcakes and then shove her face into a plateful of macaroni salad—give her another something to cry about. Instead, I grabbed Evan's sleeve and pulled him away and toward Mom. "You're coming with me, but you have to promise to not talk."

"Okay." He leaned back slightly, though, as I dragged him along.

I told Mom we were walking to Thousand Oaks Park, where Beep used to play when he was little, to say good-bye to him.

Mom compressed her lips into a *how will I explain you're not here* tight white line, but I had her. Was she going to say, "No, Kat—you're not allowed to mourn your brother your way"? No. Besides, it would be even harder to explain if I started bashing her guests for saying stupid things or shoving their faces into little plates full of food until they couldn't even mumble.

On my way out, Rachel shot me an annoyed look, maybe because if she thought of it first, she could have used the saying-good-bye-to-Beep-at-the-playground excuse to sneak off with her actual boyfriend Brian. But now the excuse was taken, because I said it first. As usual.

So Evan and I walked the few blocks to the park and sat in the swings, like little kids. It was overcast and had rained, so the playground sand was wet, under gray clouds.

Finally I just sat in the swing and cried, closing my eyes while the tears trickled out, pretending I was invisible. When I opened them, Evan was finishing a message he'd dug into the wet sand of the playground with his heel. I walked over. In big letters, it read, *There will be sunshine again, someday.* Then he drew a heart shape with his heel. It was cheating on the no-talking rule, but I didn't mind.

I gave him a quick hug to say thanks, and stepped away. "We should go back," I said.

He put out his hand, offering to hold mine on the walk.

I just looked at it.

33

Six totally stupid reasons I didn't hold hands with Evan:

1. I was so freshly wounded from Beep dying, I couldn't bear the hurt of also maybe messing up my friendship with Evan. We were back to best friends, and I didn't have anybody else. I needed him to be there, not just be some boy who might break up with me.
2. I didn't want to use my brother dying as the excuse to get a boyfriend. That didn't seem right. Plus, I didn't want Evan to be only a pity boyfriend.
3. If I walked back in holding hands with Evan, Mom would have freaked, that I'd snuck off from Beep's wake to hang out with a boyfriend, without even changing my name to Rachel.
4. My hands were rough from the hand-washing and hand-sanitizer-rubbing that comes with hanging around a cancer kid with a missing immune system. For Evan, it would have been like holding hands with a chapped sandpaper brick.
5. Hunter, 3000 miles away, was calling himself my (possibly dying) boyfriend. Even though I wasn't Hunter's actual girl-friend, holding hands with Evan would have made me feel weirdly disloyal to a possibly dying guy.
6. I have no idea. Those first five reasons I made up afterward. At the time, I wanted to take Evan's hand, but somehow couldn't. I was afraid. What I did instead: crossed my arms in front of myself and gave him a shake of my head.

He looked forlorn, and let his hand drop, and I knew I'd blown it. Except when he's playing guitar, Evan is shy, and I'd rejected him. He wouldn't be offering to hold hands again.

34

We had Beepster cremated and put him in a dark lacquer urn, a little bigger than a water bottle. It was closed and looked like a polished flower vase with a clamped lid. Like some sealed magic bottle for a genie—except, of course, that when you rubbed it (a) no genie came out and (b) no magic wish came true. I tried.

Next year, when the Geminid meteors would be back in Earth's atmosphere, we were going to scatter Beep's ashes near the campsite where we saw the shooting stars. In the meantime, Beep-in-a-bottle hung out on the mantle above the fireplace in the living room.

The Monday after the funeral and reception, we had to go back to school and to work, to the rest of life, still bleeding from this huge new hole in our world.

So I went from doing something important—taking care of Beep, being there so Mom could get a break and cling to what little sanity she had, even talking Beep through it when he went on to find the light—to doing algebra problems in a daze, in the back of class where the other girls were tying themselves into square knots over who was or wasn't invited to Tracie's birthday party. (There was a rumor that Sara might be on the outs. And on the ins—*moi?* Nope. Somehow I wasn't on the invite list. Shocker.)

Except I wasn't ready to let go and move on. And I was trying to figure out how I would make up for not saving my brother—and for maybe helping to kill him—with my borrowed bone marrow.

So I kept writing my cancer blog, and posting on the blood cancer Facebook page and AML cancer forum, and Skyping and emailing with Hunter.

I did let go of one thing. My hair.

I couldn't think of what else to do with myself after Beep died, so a few weeks later in January, I had my hair chopped off.

This was not as completely stupid as it sounds, because I donated it to Locks of Love, which makes hairpiece wigs for cancer kids. Radiation and chemo kill fast-growing cells like hair, so cancer kids' hair falls out. It's especially tough on girls. When they go out in public, ignorant strangers hassle their moms ("I can't believe you let her cut her hair like that") or call them boys—despite the pink dress.

I was nervous, though. My prior donation, stem cells, hadn't worked out so great. Plus, my hair wasn't super-long, so I'd have to cut it almost completely off to give Locks of Love enough to work with.

Also, I wasn't sure I'd look even semi-okay. The woman at Heads on Solano sold me on the new look by showing me a picture of this cute woman with short spiky red-tipped hair, but the picture was of a gorgeous model, which I didn't have going for me.

I went with it anyway, short, spiky dyed-red highlights in the middle and all. After my bone marrow killed Beep, or at least didn't save him, I wanted to be a different person.

35

I sat there crying while the hairdresser maimed my hair with scissors and clippers. I was saying good-bye not just to my hair, but also to Beep. And what I had left, when she finished, looked like red squirrel leftovers from a blender, on my head. Not, you know, in a good way.

My old, light brown hair was in a bag or in little bits on the floor. And in the mirror was an absolute horror. It was Marine-Corps-guy super-short in the back and the sides, with a longer spiky thatch left on top, sticking up, tipped with red highlights. Augh.

Rachel stared at me in sick horror when I got home, probably imagining what life must be like to be less good-looking and without piles of gorgeous hair. Or almost any hair.

The best Hunter could manage in our short Skype session that night was, "Uh, that's *really interesting*—and much better looking than my haircut." Which wasn't saying much, because Hunter was cue-ball bald. I had a sick pit of misery in my stomach, instead of hair on my head, after I logged off from that conversation.

"I'm proud of you," Mom said, the next morning at the breakfast table. A better reaction than Rachel's or Hunter's. "Some girl will be very happy with your hair."

"Sure—she got the best part." I hoped she'd have better luck than Beep did with my stem cells. Probably would. It's hard, even for me, to kill someone with just my looks.

"Honey, are you okay?"

"Mom, a red squirrel died, in a lightning storm, on top of my head. Not super okay."

"You're beautiful," Dad glanced up from the work stuff he was reading, to show he pretended he meant it.

"You need to spend more time at home." I shook my head. "The beautiful one's Rachel. The blonde." I looked like Donald Trump's love child with a short-haired Medusa. Maybe Dad didn't know any better. His idea of fashion was putting sunglasses on top of his head, in case his bald spot grew eyes.

"You can wear a hat," Rachel said. "You want to borrow one?"

Right. Like one of Rachel's hats would fit. My head's not *that* swollen. Plus, hers are designed for piles of beautiful hair underneath. Which I don't have. As the kids at school reminded me, later that day.

36

I'd posted a warning on my blog and on Facebook that I'd chopped off my hair to donate to Locks of Love and instead of feeling noble, I was suffering from extra ugliness and hair-butchery-shallow-person's remorse. I put on my 49er ski hat before going out to carpool, as if the dead squirrel on my head still needed to keep warm.

"Hey," Evan said when they picked me up. "Take off the hat. I want to see."

"Sure. When summer comes."

"I bet you look great with short hair."

"Rachel offered to loan me hats—plural—so she wouldn't be embarrassed by the extra ugly sister, even at a different school." That was the only time Rachel had ever offered to let me borrow clothes. "So—no."

We picked up Tyler.

"Kat's going to show us her haircut," Evan said. "She donated the rest of her hair to cancer kids."

"Cool," Tyler said.

"I'm not showing you my hair."

"Then I'm calling my Massive Lifetime Favor," Evan said. "And buying your hat."

"You are *not*."

"It's either that, or you have to come over for an all-night songwriting session at my house Friday."

His mom's strangled noise carried from the front. I frowned at Evan and crossed my arms.

"If your hair doesn't look great," Evan said. "I'll loan the hat back, and you won't owe me a favor anymore."

I sighed. "No laughing allowed, okay?"

He nodded, and held out his hand. I took off my hat, and handed it to him. I closed my eyes. I couldn't bear another look like Rachel's.

"You look great," Evan said. "Like Chloe from *After Darkness*, but with even shorter hair." That's a videogame with zombies. I hoped Chloe was one of the live people. Evan ran his hand through my hair, from the back to the front. "Wow. Feels great to touch."

I wanted to push my head into his hand, like Skippy did when he got petted. My stomach did a flip-flutter, but I wished he wasn't petting me like a zoo animal. "That's sweet, Evan. But give me back the hat."

"If I give back your hat, the only reason will be because you look so great, all the other guys will want to run their hands through your bristly hair, and you won't have time for hanging out with me."

Did he mean that? Probably just trying to cheer me up.

"Before you give her the hat," Tyler said, "could I touch Kat's hair?" An actual complete sentence. From Tyler. Before 8 A.M. He has a long arm, so he reached over Evan. "Wow," he said, running his fingers through what was left. "*Awesome* haircut."

"Thanks, guys, but petting zoo is closed." I pulled away from Tyler's touch. "And I can't face the Tracies like this."

"Actually, you should," Evan said. "If you wear the hat, they'll sense weakness, and close in for the kill."

I wavered. He might have a point. "You think I'm weak?"

"You're the strongest person I know. But the Tracies won't see that, if you wear the hat."

Evan thought I was strong? I couldn't even do homework. "Won't see what? Bad hair?"

"That you're different. Not afraid. And your spiky hair sticking up in the middle? It gives the Tracies, and everything they care about, the finger."

"Totally." Tyler laughed. "The hair finger."

37

By the time we got out of the car, I'd let Evan talk me into not wearing the hat. The crazy idea that doing good trumped looking good rejected everything the Tracies thought was important.

Evan stuffed my hat in his jacket pocket, so I wouldn't chicken out. "Can I *please* touch your hair one more time?" he asked, after Tyler shuffled toward the school doors.

That was the least I could do, since I owed him a Massive Lifetime Favor, and it'd probably make me feel better about the hair butchery. "Sure."

He reached up and ran his hand through my short hair, from the back of my neck to the top of my head. "Ummmm," he said.

This was in plain view of everyone arriving. I looked up.

Tracie was fifteen feet away, looking shocked and horrified, standing frozen next to Ashley. Then her expression changed to tight-lipped fury. Like I'd personally insulted her by having my head touched by her ex-boyfriend while I was this ugly.

She spun and stalked into the building, and I thought, *uh oh*. I doubted that, even with her look of horror, we were done.

I made it work in first-period World History, telling people how I cut my hair for Locks of Love.

Unfortunately, Tracie and Ashley were in my first-period class, busy playing whisper-and-glance and passing notes back and forth. Which gave them plenty of time to plot how to deal with my short-haired presence in second-period Algebra 2. That class has all five of the Tracies and three of the Tracie-Wannabes.

I went to my locker and exchanged useless unread textbooks, made a stop in the bathroom, and then headed for Algebra 2, and the trap they set for me.

38

I was almost late to class, but Ms. Clarke wasn't at her desk yet. All the kids, though, turned around in their chairs to watch me come in. As soon as I came out from behind cover, several burst into laughter, the mocking ugly kind. Jenna put on an exaggerated mouth open expression of shock and horrified delight, both palms at her cheeks. Sara covered her eyes with a hand, as if it was too awful to see. The laughter crested.

I bowed, like they were laughing at one of my jokes, not at me. "Locks of Love," I started to say as the laugh receded, but my throat was dry, so I couldn't make it come out loud enough.

"Lots of *ugly*." Tracie said, to renewed laughter.

"I donated—" I tried to say.

"My fashion sense." Ashley drowned me out.

"Bald Ho Monroe," Kayla Southerland yelled, to even more laughs.

I couldn't speak. They were making fun of me because I tried to give my hair to a needy cancer kid. I was afraid I'd cry if I opened my mouth. And those little verbal barbs I always threw disappeared, or I couldn't find the grip to hold them. It was like being Rachel, except not beautiful.

So I held both hands up, turned the palms toward me, extended a leg behind me in a gymnast's curtsey, and flipped off the whole giggling class with a double-barreled one-finger salute.

"Kat Monroe!" Ms. Clarke snapped from the door right behind me. "What are you doing? Sit down *now*."

The rest of the class thought that was even more hilarious—me getting in trouble—but Ms. Clarke silenced that by smashing her book down on a desk so hard it sounded like a gunshot. She had a stack of photocopies in her other hand, which she'd apparently made down at the office. She glared at me. "I don't appreciate someone entertaining everyone while I was gone. I could hear you all half the way down the hall. What's the meaning of this, Kat?"

She thought I'd orchestrated it. Me—the victim. I stared at her in wounded, tear-welling outrage.

She got it then, since it's hard to teach high school and be completely clueless about group cruelty. "I'm sorry," she said. "Kat, what's going on?"

I shook my head, in mute injury. I wasn't saying. I couldn't exactly whine about how everyone was mean. That's just high school background noise. When I got my voice to work, I said, "Some people think I'm having a bad hair day." More laughter, at that.

I spent the rest of the period with my head down on the desk, hidden in my arms. When Ms. Clarke had her back turned, writing an equation, I got pelted with a couple of folded notes. One I brushed out of my lap was folded in a triangle and said "great hair—not." The other said "Bald Ho Monroe—is all your hair now down below?" Nice. Looked like a guy's writing. A third one hit me on the elbow and then fell on the floor, late in the period, but I ignored it. When classmates fling notes at you, they sting less when they bounce off your arm than if you read them.

The snickers and comments followed me to third-period girls' P.E., when I was picked in the last half of kids for volleyball, even though I'm a good player, because three of the Tracies were in the class, telling their captains not to pick the girl "with mange." I ended up on a team with Ashley, whose lips curled into disgust when I got picked, as if bad hair was contagious. When our game got under way, some of the girls on the other team made a point of not trying to return my serves, because they might catch lice or cooties. Which would have been awesome, except after my sixth service ace, Ashley, near the net, turned around and said, "Way to go, Bald Ho Monroe."

She gave me a smirk, then turned back to face the net. Her ponytail swayed, dark against her white tee shirt. I gritted my teeth. The gym was full of the squeak of running shoes on floorboards and the *ba-doom* of a volleyball landing one court over, but it seemed to get quiet and time almost stopped, as I tossed the ball up for my serve. A serve, nearly supersonic, that ended up in the back of Ashley's head.

While they were retrieving her glasses from behind the other baseline and she was clutching herself with both hands and wailing theatrically, I walked off the court and over to Coach Paulsen. "Either give me a punishment time out," I said. "Or call an ambulance for the next girl who gives me crap."

She looked at me, and, without missing a beat, raised her voice as if angry. "Monroe. You're in time out. And dismissed. Go dress in street clothes." Before I crossed into the locker room, I heard her yelling. "Enough volleyball, girls. You're not even going for the ball, so you can run wind sprints the rest of the period."

I shoved my red gym shorts and white tee shirt into my locker and then just sat there, as the other girls ran, again and again, right to the edge of the dry heaves. It would make them—especially the Tracies—hate me more. So what. Beep fought cancer, and for him, some days, the edge of the dry heaves would have been an improvement.

39

I kept thinking about it while dressing. Tracie and Ashley had set up everyone in Algebra 2 so the greeting wave of scorn was too high to surf.

Impressive. I can't even figure out how to tackle homework, and they choreograph mass humiliation? I was so blown away at that skill level—or something—it must have shown in my face when I got to fourth-period English, Mr. Brillson's class.

"What's wrong?" Mr. Brillson asked.

"Kat's having a good hair day," Tracie said, from behind me, to general snickers.

Mr. Brillson used his patented teacher stare. The snickering stopped. I sat down, in the front. The bell rang.

"Are you all right?" Mr. Brillson asked.

I cleared my throat. "I donated my hair to Locks of Love, so a bald cancer child could have a wig. Now *some people*"—I nodded at Tracie—"think I look stupid." I dropped my eyes to the desk. Actually, pretty much all of us, me included, thought I looked stupid.

Mr. Brillson said, "That's a great essay introduction. Our free writing assignment today is to write for fifteen minutes about a sacrifice we've made, or would make, to help someone else." I don't think, for a second, that was in his real lesson plan. But I think he's awesome for it. "Kat, you might already have a topic. Okay, everyone. Fifteen minutes, and hand this one in. Go."

You'd think I'd write about the damned hair, with that soft lob pitch. Nope. I managed exactly four sentences and put my head down for the rest of the time, while Mr. B walked up and down the aisles, looking at our work in progress.

Once upon a time, I wrote, *I thought if I donated my stem cells to my brother, I could make him live.*

I donated, but he didn't get better, and he died anyway. Or maybe he died because my cells killed him.

So what do I do now?

At the end of the fifteen minutes, everyone else handed in their pages. I crumpled mine and threw it away.

ᏫᎤ

At lunch, where we always met outside, Evan took one look and gave me a hug. "Toby told me about Algebra."

"They're calling me Bald Ho Monroe."

Evan clenched his jaw at that, which was sweet.

I sat on the gray concrete steps, chipped from skateboard grinds. "The secret is breathing," I said. "If you put your head down on the desk, and concentrate on breathing, your shoulders don't shake when you cry, so people don't know."

"Oh, Kat. It's my fault . . ." He put his arm around me.

"Don't," I said, and started crying. What I meant to say was *Don't blame yourself,* but I couldn't get the words out. He pulled back his arm, which made me cry harder, because I wanted his arm there and was misunderstood. I finally managed, "Don't blame you. It's not your fault. You're a nice guy. A great guy. You don't understand how mean other people are."

"I thought if you didn't wear the hat, they wouldn't go after—"

"Yeah." That might have been right, if I could have carried it off. But there were too many of them, and somehow I couldn't pretend it didn't bother me. "It was Tracie and Ashley. They organized the whole humiliation. Planned it in first period." What if Evan ever got back together with Tracie? I put my head in my hands. "Don't ever let them get you to stop being my friend." Dr. Anne says you only need one friend. Just one person on your side. Then you can hold out against the rest of the world.

Even if Evan was just a pity friend, I would take that over not having him at all.

"I won't. Ever." He offered to get my former hat out of his locker, but I shook my head. I was taking the afternoon off. I hadn't studied for the Biology test, and had enough humiliation for one day, so I went home. I sent Mom a text explaining I wasn't feeling well—which was true, given the emotional carnage—and was bailing on school.

Of course, now that we're in the enlightened digital age, abuse can follow you home, wherever there's phone service or an Internet connection.

40

By that evening, I had emails and messages that I'd been tagged in pictures and posts. When I clicked on them, I discovered a fun online group activity: Various gross pictures (winners of ugly dog contests, animals with tumors, people with facial sores and genetic disorders) were tagged "Kat Monroe" and forwarded to me. Maybe it wasn't so smart, whacking one of the popular girls with a volleyball.

There are limits on what you can put on Facebook and Instagram, but other ways to forward disgusting images. Text or email it. Send a link to where it exists online. Or put it up on YouTube, like userloser69 did, a whole slide show titled "Things not as Ugly as Kat Monroe's Hair." Gosh, that comment section was fun. ("Q: What's the difference between Kat's house and a cathouse? A: At Kat's house, she'll pay *you* to do *her*." Below that, someone responded "Ho ho ho Monroe.")

The emails were especially nice, because by the time they got to me, thoughtfully forwarded by a concerned "friend" (thanks, Amber), I could see who'd forwarded them before and the "funny" comments those classmates had added, maybe not realizing it would eventually get to me. There was one nice reply to all buried in the middle, from Evan, saying "Stop being mean and awful," followed by one—surprisingly— from Elizabeth, saying "Yeah, stop. This is mean," but otherwise it was like looking at a horrible accident on the side of the freeway—sick, but I couldn't look away. Except that my reputation and I were in the twisted wreckage I was watching.

My stomach hurt. For the first time ever, I thought high school should give more homework. Some of my classmates have too much time on their hands. Also, there are lots of ugly pictures on the Internet.

Most of them probably didn't know my brother had died of cancer. Some hardly knew me at all, except as the girl with the weird hair they heard was a slut. The one you could make fun of, to get points with the Tracie-wannabes.

Evan called. I was surprised, since I was mostly getting email notifications that I'd been tagged in a post.

"So, uh, what are you doing?" He sounded worried.

"Reading emails," I said. "With pretty pictures. Pretty bizarre, anyway."

"Oh, no. Those got forwarded to you?"

"That's the point, Evan. It has to hurt." And make me wonder how much else I didn't see.

It was quiet on the line for a long time. "I'm so sorry . . ."

A shot of pure terror went through me. Had he at some point *contributed?*

". . . about the hat," he finished. Oh. Blaming himself for the hat thing. Which seemed like a million years ago.

"It's not your fault. It's not even the stupid haircut. I don't fit in. I never will."

"You don't have to. You shouldn't, not with awful people." His voice got quiet. "What can I do?"

My heart was still hammering from the adrenaline surge. "Be my friend. Please. Don't let them get to you. Or if they do, for God's sake, don't send me pictures."

After I hung up with Evan, I changed my privacy setting on Facebook so no one but actual Facebook friends could post on my wall. I stared forlornly at my email in box and emailed Hunter, with my stomach in a tight knot of hurt.

K: *Why are people so cruel and unfair?*

H: *Because life is.*

That quick answer should teach me to whine about mere teasing, to a boy who might actually be dying. I gave him some of the details anyway, and then he emailed back.

H: *That's awful. Even though they probably just thought they were "being funny."*

That left me feeling worse. I might have said something mean, once or twice, while being funny.

K: *I'm going offline for a while.*

H: *Don't.*

But I logged off. Which didn't do much good, because I couldn't sleep anyway. I was too damp, curled up in my own pool of misery.

41

The morning after my Internet-memification wasn't a carpool day. Evan came by anyway, to walk me to school, and he brought a little bunch of cut purple flowers from his back yard. Which meant . . . what? Probably just trying to make me feel less horrible, which it did, a little. The flowers people gave us after Beep died were long-wilted and tossed, as dried up as the Tracies' hearts.

"Thought you could use cheering up," he said, looking nervous, handing them to me.

"Thanks." I didn't know what else to say, so I reached for a joke. "You want to take a picture of them with me? You could email it to everyone labeled 'Kat Monroe sniffs the sex organs of another species.'"

Evan didn't laugh or even smile, so, as usual, I'd gone with the wrong impulse. He looked down. "What everybody did was awful. I disown the rest of my species."

I put the flowers on the table near the door and gave him a hug. "Thanks, Evan. You're the best." After a surprised pause, he hugged me back.

After I broke the clinch, he reached into his jacket pocket. "Brought your hat."

"Keep it. It's yours." I looked in the front room cabinet for a vase for my flowers. "I'm just going with the bad hair. Turns out my new hair isn't nearly as awful as some things. By comparison. Those pictures cheered me up."

"They did?"

"No, Evan. But that's my story, and I'm sticking to it. Beep went through chemo. I can take this." Or at least try.

In first period, Curtis greeted me, "Yo, Bald Ho."

"You wish." I said. "Even if I was, there's not enough money on earth to do you. Not that it's an issue. You'd just fall on your face."

His cheeks went pink.

In second period, Ashley tried to pass me a note. I raised my hand. "Ms. Clarke?" I said. "Ashley has a note she's throwing away in the trash now." Ashley did.

In third-period P.E., I worked a deal with Coach Paulsen—she let me run laps instead of playing volleyball, so we could keep the body count down.

And everywhere I went, all day, the looks followed. Two "Yo ho" greetings. Three "Saw your pictures yesterday." One "Wow, fugly hair, girl." With attitude.

It was nothing, compared to cancer. Nothing, compared to chemo. Nothing.

42

After school that day, I wandered into Beep's room.

Mom still hadn't cleared it out. His bed was made, with Ted E. Bear tucked in, and everything was in place. Beep didn't have time to mess it up when he was in the bone marrow isolation room or the hospice care rented hospital bed downstairs. It was still set up like he'd be back any day, from some long school field trip to New Zealand.

I ran my hand along the spines of the books on his bookshelf and over the collection of his *Star Wars*–themed Legos from the various sets he'd almost lived long enough to outgrow. I picked up his baseball glove. It was barely broken in.

I pulled open the upper middle drawer of his dresser. His tee shirts were folded neatly. I took the one on top, a maroon one with a picture of a taped-up duck on it, lettered DUCK TAPE. I sniffed it, hoping for a scent, somehow, of Beep. It smelled like folded laundry, a ghost whiff of detergent, designed by some chemist to remind humans of "fresh." Fresh loss. I put the shirt back and closed the drawer, then sat down on Beep's bed. I curled up on it and tried to smell him on his pillow. The pillow only smelled faintly of dust. I sniffed Ted E. Bear. He just smelled like cotton out of the dryer and the same faint detergent smell. Nothing like Beep at all.

"Hey," Rachel said from the door behind me, and I bonked my head on the headboard, startled. This was getting to be a habit.

"I was trying to smell Beep." I sat up, still holding the stuffed bear. "I can't."

"Mom washed Ted E. Bear last week," she said. "The smell was long gone anyway."

"What's *wrong* with her?" I tucked Ted E. Bear back in. "Why doesn't someone explain to parents that if your brother *dies*, they have to keep a shirt that he perspired in so for at least a month after, you can still smell him."

"His hat," Rachel said.

"What?"

"His hat. I have his baseball hat. In my room. You can still smell him."

"No way." Rachel must be teasing me.

"Way." She nodded. "I kept his little league baseball hat. In a ziplock. The old one he wore all the time. I stole it before Mom could wash it."

"Thank you." And I couldn't say anything more.

"You'd better blow your nose first," Rachel said. "Or you won't be able to smell anything."

I stopped by the bathroom and blew my nose twice, then followed Rachel into the sanctuary of her room. She brought her desk chair over to her closet, stood on it, reached behind a powder-blue sports bag and a stored rotating fan on the high shelf, and pulled out a gallon-sized sealed Ziploc plastic bag with Beep's little league hat sealed inside it. The hat was black with an orange "Giants" written across the front. Beep had been good at baseball—fast, and with a little strike zone, so he batted leadoff, except when he was out because of cancer.

She pulled out the cap and unfolded it, then passed it to me. "Sniff the hatband. There's just enough left. You can fill in the rest by imagination."

There was a first smell of plastic, and then Beepness. The faint scent of hair and perspiration and the yeasty warm smell of person. "Oh. Oh. Oh." I sniffed for a long time.

Rachel gently pulled the hat back. Then she sniffed the liner, a long complete inhale, like she would snort the fabric all the way into her lungs. She folded it, put it back in the Ziploc, pushed all the air out of the bag and pressed the seal closed. "When Beep was a baby, he had his own baby smell. Milk and baby powder and Johnson's Baby Shampoo."

"I don't remember back that far." We both sat on her bed, Rachel holding the plastic bag with the last smell of Beep, me with my hands in my lap. "I wish we could go back to how things used to be."

Rachel's eyes were as empty as Beep's room. "Yeah."

43

Hunter and I both had birthdays the same week in February. Hunter turned eighteen and I turned sixteen. On Hunter's Facebook page, lots of girls from his school posted "Love You!" with their happy birthday greetings, but they didn't put an "I" in front of love, which meant it was friend-love, not Big Romance Love. Several of them used three or more exclamation points, which just meant they need meds.

For his birthday, I sent Hunter a little bit of California: a red-and-gold baseball-style cap with the 49er logo. Early in the morning, when I logged on to Skype, he was wearing it over a big grin.

"Nice look," I told him. "After eighteen years on the East Coast, if you can come over to the light side and become a 49er fan, anything is possible. Even beating cancer."

"Ha. I'm only wearing it to impress my California girlfriend. If I ever root for the Niners, it'll mean tumors reached my brain. Go Ravens!"

"You're confused. You must be old. Have some cake and ice cream, while you can still chew."

He smiled. It looked like I caught him on a good morning. "I wish I could taste ice cream. Everything tastes weird now."

"Close your eyes. Really." I waited until he closed his eyes, there on the computer screen. When he did, I went on, "I'm sending you the taste of ice cream. Now. Keep your eyes closed. Just listen. And taste. It's sweet. Cold. Creamy. Vanilla, queen of the flavors. Keep your eyes closed! Because it's cold, even though it's the most wonderful thing there is, you can't rush. Break the rules. Mash it with a spoon until it's creamy. And always eat it first. Before every meal."

"Wow." He kept his eyes closed, looking blissed out. "I can taste it. Awesome."

"Of course. I'm very good at imaginary ice cream." And, apparently, at sending it to imaginary boyfriends.

"You know." He opened his eyes. "Our age difference isn't a big deal. If we get together in the real world. When I'm twenty-one, you'll be nineteen. Practically no gap at all. Unless I've been dead three years when I'm twenty-one. Then the difference gets fairly massive."

"There's the three thousand miles."

"No big. Maybe you could fly out this year, to solve the distance problem." He smiled. It looked somehow nervous. "If we meet while I'm still alive, fewer awkward silences and probably more fun."

I wasn't wild about where this was going. "Maybe. But it might not go well. You might want to kiss me, then die from it, because I didn't use enough hand sanitizer lip gloss."

"I'm all for dying happy. There are worse ways to go."

"Gosh. Thanks," I said. "Besides, in person, you might find me totally resistible. Most guys do."

"You sell yourself short."

"Nah. I'm the world's foremost expert on being me."

"Well, let's check. Why don't you come visit?"

"Live at least until summer and get your neutrophil count above 500 and I'll think about it."

We chatted and he flirted while I had this nervous empty feeling in my stomach, until I finally had to log off, to get ready for school. Cancer and the Internet are a weird combination for making friends. If Hunter didn't have cancer, and went to my high school instead of his, there would be exactly zero chance we'd ever be friends, let alone spend all our time emailing and messaging back and forth and talking by Skype and pretending to be boyfriend-girlfriend. He was a senior and hot—even hairless—and a basketball star.

I was, technically, me. So the difference was fairly massive anyway.

44

My birthday came and went without a big deal. When you're unpopular, having a party would be small, depressing, and lonely.

Evan baked me a little cake and brought it to school, then he and Tyler and Calley Rose ate it with me at lunch outside. Evan also made me a nice card, with a UA movie theater pass inside, good for two admissions. That made me fantasize about whether Evan wanted me to offer to go to a movie with him.

Amber and Elizabeth came by, looking slightly awkward. "Hey," Amber said. "Happy birthday." Then she looked down, like she felt guilty or something.

For some reason, I thought about Hunter, and how life was short. Maybe too short to stay mad at people forever. "Come have some cake," I said to both of them. There was enough left for a little piece for each.

"Are you sure?" Amber asked.

"Of course. You're totally invited." I didn't even hassle them for not inviting me to their birthday parties last year after Tracie turned them against me. It's possible I'm maturing or something.

Mom cooked my favorite dinner that night, salmon from the Japanese fish market on San Pablo. It wasn't vegetarian, but Rachel didn't even sneer at it, and Skippy got the skin from the salmon, which he thought was awesome. Also, Mom made sweet potatoes and vegan-tofu-whatchamacallit-ooh-barf-just-shoot-me-now for Rachel, so it all worked out.

I didn't get anything from Hunter except birthday greetings, but he had a few other things going on that week, between a final chemo dose and a spinal tap. Plus, I never gave him my actual physical real world address. When he asked, I told him I was too embarrassed, since I actually lived in a mental institution, which—with Mom downstairs— was close enough.

45

A week after Hunter's birthday, I was Skyping with him after the morphine kicked in on his end, and he said it again.

"I love you, Kat."

He tacked my name onto the end to make sure we both knew he was talking to me. A couple of prior times, under the late-night influence of morphine, he got confused about who he was talking to, even on Skype. (Once confusing me with his prior girlfriend, Leslie. And talking about the time "we" hooked up in a dressing room. Awkward.)

"No, you don't," I said. "You don't know me. We've never met. I'm just a voice. And words. A picture on your computer."

"I love your voice, then. And your words. And picture. That's all anyone is, really. I love you." He gave me a dreamy look, like he actually was in love—and on lots of morphine.

I didn't know what to say. "I have to go. I'll text you. In the morning." As in, tomorrow.

I disconnected in the middle of his "good-night" and stared at the computer, like it was a torture tool for scooping out my heart. Which was beating too fast, like I was panicking.

46

R U OK? I texted Hunter in the morning.

Possibly dying, he sent. *Otherwise really good.*

Are _we_ OK? I texted back.

We are great. Thanks for being my friend.

I'm glad I'm your friend, I shot back. *And you're mine. I'll email after school.*

Whew. Back to friends.

47

In soccer, the most basic—but really effective—move is the pullback. You're driving forward, then you pull the ball backward by putting your cleats on top of it and spin to reverse, to change direction again or pass.

That's what I did with Hunter. I wasn't sure I wanted to hear he loved me. My stomach clenched when he said it, and I couldn't lose another boy I loved to cancer so soon. And I liked him—a lot—but didn't Love-love him. I also wasn't sure what it meant when he did say he loved me, what with morphine, foggy chemo brain, and God-and-spinal-tap-only-knows how many leukemia blasts partying in his central nervous system.

So I went back to emails and text messages and Facebook private messages, not phone calls or Skype. If we texted, he'd have to be straight enough to type and hit send. And if we ran everything through a keyboard, maybe the computer's surge protector might protect my little heart. Yeah. Right.

It was still intense. We spent hours every night typing back and forth. It was like I was life and he wanted to hold on to me, and I didn't want to let him go either.

After a week in the no-Skype zone, Hunter sent, *Miss your voice.*

K: *Nope. It's right there in your mind. Like the taste of ice cream. You can totally hear these words in my voice.*

H: *Wow. You're right. Cool.*

Okay. Hunter definitely had morphine onboard. When you use words like "wow" and "cool" over imaginary voices, it qualifies you to sell tie-dyed shirts on Berkeley's Telegraph Avenue, except bald cancer guys can't grow old-hippie gray ponytails.

H: *We should go back to Skyping again soon, anyway. You know, while I'm still alive.*

At least *he* had legal painkillers for this talk. I typed back, before I could think better of it.

K: *So—how long is that going to be? When do you plan on dying?*

H: *Don't know. But talked to my grandma last night.*

That was a pretty random topic change.

K: *About dying?*

H: *Not only. But she is dead.*

K: *Then it must have been hard for her to keep up her end of the conversation.*

H: *Not really. She was here. We talked. Don't remember everything, but she said it would be OK.*

K: *That you're getting well?* There was an improbable electric surge of hope in my chest.

H: *No—that I'm dying. But it's OK. Death. She'd know, right?*

Sound of girl's heart breaking I typed, but didn't hit send. Instead, I held the backspace key down so long it should have erased not just those words but the whole last miserable year.

I started to type *how much morphine are you on?* but backspaced over that too. He'd give me the same answer he always did—lots, but not enough. And that wasn't the point. He was trying to tell me something. I was supposed to listen, not squirm away or joke or tell him he didn't know what he was talking about.

K: *Oh Hunter. Oh, my DBF.*

Then I put back in the sound effects, so he would know.

K: **Crash then squish, as my heart breaks and quivers wetly**

What else to say?

K: *Tell your grandma it better go well for you, or when I finally get to where she is, I will kick her wrinkled dead behind for eternity. Tell her I know karate and can kick a soccer ball the length of the field when I'm pissed. Which I would be.*

H: *LOL. That's why I love you, Sarcasm Angel. Love and xo, your DBF.*

Ah, xo—kiss and a hug. Or a hug and a kiss. I was never sure. Other girls get actual soft lip-kisses from their so-called boyfriends. I got two letters that don't even qualify as a Scrabble word. Please don't go yet, Hunter. I cried for fifteen minutes after I logged off.

48

If Hunter was getting visits from his dead grandmother, I figured he didn't have long left. So I gave up, and started Skyping with him again. When I logged on, in the computer window Hunter was wearing the 49er hat I sent him.

"Hey, girlfriend," he said. "Nice to see my Sarcasm Angel."

"You too, DBF. Great hat."

"My cute girlfriend sent it."

"Oh, crap. Now the cancer's affecting your *eyesight.*"

He laughed. I could almost always make him laugh. "I'm graduating from Chemo U. No more chemo after this series. One more radiation course, then they top me up with borrowed blood and send me home."

"What's your blast count?" *Please say zero.* I knew it wasn't close to zero.

"High. So I'll wait at home for a miracle, instead of hanging around here. You want to visit, and see if that helps?"

"I don't get the right miracles. Or the miracles right." I sat there in shock, while he filled me in on details. Not yet. No, no, no. They were going to let his immune system slightly recover from its whacking-by-chemo and then send him home. To wait for a miracle. Or, more likely, death.

෮෯

So Hunter and I went back to watching movies on Netflix "together"— at the same time. We picked mostly romantic comedies. Our lives were such a series of disasters, action movies were redundant. We shot messages back and forth. (*Weak. He should kiss her. Oh. Right. Maybe he should stop being a jerk first, then kiss her.*) A few nights after we'd started talking again, I was Skyping with him when our movie was over, just before 10 P.M. his time.

"So," he asked, from the window on my computer. "Are you going to change your relationship, too, on Facebook?" He smiled, like he had a surprise for me. So I split the screen on my computer and opened Facebook on the other half. There, Hunter had changed his Facebook status to "in a relationship." In response to the questions in the comments, he'd posted he had a "long-distance online girlfriend named Kat in California." His friend Michael commented that it sounded like having an invisible, nonexistent girlfriend from Canada. Ouch.

But that pretty much nailed it, even if we watched the same movies "together."

I didn't know what to say. After referring to himself as my DBF and saying he loved me a bunch, Hunter had announced I was his actual girlfriend. Okay—wow. No pressure, being a guy's possibly last girlfriend, ever.

My silence went on so long he jumped back in. "If you agree to be my girlfriend, I promise to stay alive for at least two weeks, so we can call our relationship long-term." He looked nervous and small, in the little Skype half-window on my screen.

"Sure. Of course. When you throw in a long, happy life, how can I resist? Swoon." I put my hand on my forehead. "I'll change my status."

He broke into a big grin then, like that was a huge relief.

But not for me. I didn't know what my status was. I got tingly sometimes, when I thought about being around Evan. But when I thought about going out to see Hunter, or even calling myself his girlfriend, I mostly got scared.

Fortunately, Facebook is like a multiple-guess test and there's a catchall none-of-the-above category. So I changed my status to that: "It's complicated." Which summed it up: Complicated.

49

Evan kept hanging out with me at lunch. "How are things going with your dying boyfriend?" His mouth twisted into a worried frown.

I completely did *not* want to talk about Hunter, as my boyfriend, to Evan. But even though most of what Hunter and I sent back and forth was by private messages, some of it was by public posts, so a fairly large tip of an iceberg was jutting into view. "I don't think he's really my boyfriend. But I have no idea."

"You don't know if he's your boyfriend?"

"If my life made sense," I said, "it wouldn't be mine."

"Well, uh, how's it going?"

"He's dying. So this is the exciting, swoopy part just before the plane hits the ground and everything gets painful and horrible."

"Oh. When? Will he probably . . . die?"

"Weeks. Or if he gets an infection, days."

Evan's eyes widened. "Whoa. Will you be okay?"

I teared up. About Hunter. About Beep. Maybe even about me. I probably wasn't going to be okay. "I'm counting on my sense of humor to save me. When everything else fails—chemo, radiation, prayers, borrowed bone marrow—that's what's left."

"Is that enough?"

"I pretend it will be. But it might get so dark, even I can't keep it light." I looked over at the fence by the tennis courts, like I was looking for something to climb, to escape from my life. I was behind on my paper, which was my last hope. "I'm flunking out, Evan. By this time next year, we'll be in different grades. If I'm still in school."

"Can I do anything?" He was so earnest, he looked in pain. It was sweet.

I thought about it. Having to repeat a whole grade was like being sick. "Sit with me, Evan. It won't fix everything, but it's nice."

☙

As we were sending emails back and forth late that night, Hunter asked about whether I had any other, non-dying boyfriends. In the real world. I said no, but that somehow triggered a long discussion about what had gone wrong between me and Evan the year before, and I ended up going through the whole story.

H: *He was probably trying to make you jealous and get you to notice he was boyfriend material, not just guy-friend.*

K: *Unlikely. And getting together with Tracie to make someone jealous is like cutting yourself in half to lose weight: Sure, it works, but—dang.*

H: *Maybe he was a jerk?*

K: *No. He's a great guy. Last year he was probably just all freshman-frozen-in-the-headlights when some cuter girl turned her bright smile on him. But it hurt. So he's confined to the friend-zone penalty box, where he can't hurt me again.*

H: *Then he's an idiot. Weird, though. You not letting a guy get close because it would hurt if he went away. (*Types her DBF—as in Dying Boy Friend—late at night, whose numbers are not getting better*)*

K: *I'm an idiot, actually. I'll have a hard time if you don't pull a miracle recovery. It's too soon after Beep.*

There was no reply for a long couple of minutes. I shouldn't have sent that. Hunter had it tough enough as it was.

K: *Sorry sorry sorry. It's not about me.*

H: *What? Your life isn't about you? Maybe you should learn how to take care of yourself.*

K: *Oh—says a guy in an ICU, full of tubes. Why don't you get better, so you can take care of yourself?*

H: *I will if you will.*

Which was a little random.

In my opinion, anyway.

50

The week in March after he stopped the last course of chemo, Hunter got better. Which sounds weird, since chemo was whacking his leukemia. But it made sense.

Beep once said that chemo is like a machine gun from one of his videogames, spraying streams of tiny bullets at all his cells. Those chemo-bullets do *more* damage to the fast-growing cells, like cancer. (And hair. And stomach lining.) But they're hitting everything, including good blood cells and bone marrow.

When they stopped chemo-drip-poisoning him, Hunter got better. Then all he had to deal with was cancer. He felt so good, he even asked me to a dance.

Hunter, it turned out, was going to his senior prom by phone, and would get the streaming video and audio on his computer, while he sat in his hospital room. That way, he could see his friends and classmates, and they could see him, and he could have the feeling of normal life. (Which is what? Sorry.) He also, though, had this goofier idea he should virtually bring me. "You can be on Google Hangouts or on Skype on the other computer," he explained. "And I'll pull up the video of the dance on a big window on one screen, and you can look at it at the same time I do, and people can see you in your video window along with me, and we can go together."

"I don't know anyone there," I said. "And I'm not sure how fun it'll be watching you dance by cell phone with ex-girlfriends and other girls."

"It'll be fine. I'll introduce you to everyone. My friends. By video."

"Yeah. Great. 'Hi, dressed-up dancing friends having fun. Here's a tiny video of my friend Kat, who's randomly sitting at a computer in

194

California, not having fun. What's she doing here? She doesn't know either.'"

"I want to take you," he said.

"And I want you to get all better, but that's not exactly on schedule either. You go, and tell me about it after."

In the end, he played the I'm-dying-of-cancer-so-you-have-to card, which was totally unfair. "Otherwise, I might not ever get to take you to a dance, Complicated Girl."

"Fine," I agreed after he wore me down. But I wasn't sure it'd be fine at all.

51

I didn't get a new dress for the big event, but I did put on the fanciest one I had, deep blue silk with a semi-plunging neckline. The hem was long, more go-to-funeral-and-be-solemn than go-dancing-and-get-flirty, but I wasn't planning to dance anyway. My hair was still a freakish disaster. Now that it had grown out a little, amazingly, it looked even worse—like my head had suffered some horrible lawnmower accident while I was sleeping in a park, but they'd missed a tuft at the top, which flopped over, now that it was too long to stick up. But I bought a blue-and-purple silk headscarf with gold highlights at Sari Palace on University Avenue, which covered the whole scene-of-the-hair crime. The colors made me look semi-interesting. I thought Hunter's friends might even cut me some slack, figuring I was another bald cancer patient Hunter had met. I helped myself to part of Rachel's vast collection of eye shadow, eyeliner, and blush, and I worked my way up to a dramatic look, trying to stop short of Kayla-Southerland-style scary excess.

At about the last possible moment, I signed on, and sat in front of the little camera in my computer.

"Wow," Hunter said. "You look great."

"Yeah," I agreed. "Completely covered up is my hair's best look. But you look terrific."

He did. His mom had rented him a blue tux, which he'd put on from the waist up. (The rest of him was under the covers of the hospital bed, so never mind.) He looked radiant—maybe a little loopy from a fresh morphine dose, but happy and excited.

Hunter's mom, standing by his bed, made a fuss, and insisted on taking a "prom picture" of the two of us, on split screen, in a computer window. Hunter couldn't stop smiling, and for a couple of minutes I thought the whole remote-prom thing would actually be okay-weird instead of awful-weird.

Then his mom set up the last bit of the technology bridge, to get Hunter to his prom by phone, with me tagging along, and excused herself. "I guess I should leave you two to your dance . . ." she said uncertainly, like she'd be happy to be invited to stay and hover.

"'Bye, Mom," Hunter said. "I'll text if there's a problem."

And then there was the boom of thumping bass and jostled wobbly video, and we were at his prom, carried around as a phone. The music blared in the background, too loud, and people had to yell over it into the phone to be heard. Hunter yelled back, and they could barely make him out. No one could hear me at all.

"Dude!" his friend Michael yelled, his face close in the phone. "Welcome to prom!"

"Michael, here's my non-Canadian girlfriend—" Hunter pointed, I guess, toward me on the computer screen propped up beside him on his bed.

"So great to see you!" Michael bellowed. But he was yelling to Hunter, not to me.

Different guys and girls kept carrying the phone out to the lobby, where the music wasn't quite so loud so they could have holler-conversations about who was there with what girl or boy and what different colleges they were going to next year, and how basketball season went. After the first couple of pointless tries to introduce me to people who could barely see my picture on the tiny phone screen, Hunter gave up introducing me at all.

I sat, with my hands on my lap, wearing a frozen smile. This was so fun. From that point on, the fact Hunter had "brought a date" went completely unnoticed. Different girls took turns dancing with the phone, doing full body scans of their skimpy prom dresses, spinning in awkward circles to the music, shaking the phone in nausea-making wobbles.

Then different girls took turns kissing the phone. From what I saw, while I was mostly trying not to look too much, so many girls kissed that phone it probably caused a schoolwide mono outbreak.

Then a couple of them went all "girls gone wild" on Hunter, putting the phone down the front of their prom dresses. What was the point? With the plunging necklines, there wasn't much mystery to begin with.

"Got to go," I said, after the third glimpse of bra and one actual nip-slip. I disconnected.

I'm sorry, I private-messaged Hunter on Facebook. *I'm glad you got to go to your prom. And I want you to get to hang out with your friends. But I had to go. It was hard for me (really hard) watching a bunch of other girls taking turns showing you their ta-tas. After kissing you by phone.*

I waited five minutes, but there was no reply, so I added. *I mean, after _they_ kissed you by phone.*

Five more minutes. No reply. I tried for funny. *On the plus side, you won't have to all weird them out at Make-A-Wish, trying to get into a strip club, 'cause now you've basically (1) been there; (2) seen that. Also, you don't have to ask the girls at school what's shaking, 'cause they've already shown you.*

I waited fifteen minutes, but there was no reply. I guess Hunter was still promming out by phone, and someone else's bra or nipple or tonsils up close was a lot more interesting than my mere words.

Good-night, Hunter, I finally sent by message, wondering what they were showing him by then.

Twenty minutes later, still no reply. It was 11 P.M. Hunter's time, but still early in California, 8 P.M., so I had a long wait before anything resembling bedtime. I posted on Facebook and my blog, *Having a miserable time,* then I signed out of Facebook as Kat, to keep from going all stalker girl and sending Hunter six more unanswered messages.

It was a painful reminder about where I really stood with Hunter, even though he typed "DBF" and claimed he was "in a relationship." He was eighteen and cute and a basketball star. I was sixteen and me, and 3000 miles away. He had lots of friends and knew lots of girls who would be happy to be more than just friends, at least if his hair grew back and his guy equipment started working again.

Maybe I was better than them at hanging out with someone who was sick. Maybe I sent funnier emails. But I wasn't okay with sending him pictures of my boobs. Which, for the record, looked small and undernourished compared to the down-the-dress look he was getting from those senior girls at prom.

I was just words. And I couldn't compete with live girls, once he got out of the isolation unit. If he got well, he'd turn back into a cute basketball star, and I'd turn into what's-her-name who used to send funny messages when he was sick. ("What *was* her name? Wait. I'll think of it. An animal, with a K. Kitty or something . . . ?")

I logged back into Facebook as Cipher. Put a status message up for her. *Even virtual girls have difficult times with boys.* Evan was online, so as Cipher, I shot him a private message.

C: *Hey, Skinnyboy—am having a bad night. (Really bad.) How 'bout you entertain me, while I untangle my poisonous tentacles?*

E: *Boyfriend trouble?*

C: *Not exactly, Skinnyboy. Noticed from your Facebook profile you're still single. Whew! So what could be wrong?*

E: *I think you're having boyfriend trouble.*

C: *More like, figuring I'll never have a real boyfriend. We elusive online creatures are like that. But then, the real world is full of broken glass and razor wire, so it's probably safer to drift through as an invisible, virtual girl. (And less scary for everyone else, since my poisonous tentacles don't show.)*

E: *You've never had a boyfriend?*

C: *Not exactly. Had a massive crush on a guy last year. Won't tell you details. He broke my heart, but probably didn't notice. Maybe he was my boyfriend. He just didn't know. Somehow, I forgot to tell him about the crush.*

E: *I'm sure he saw it. Too late. Then wished he could have undone the damage.*

I wish. Was he speaking from experience there? Scary, especially if Evan ever figured out Cipher was me.

C: *Never, Skinnyboy, underestimate the ability of a guy to miss seeing how he's stomped the female heart, right in front of him.*

That was a good description of Evan last year and tonight with Hunter. But I should add something reminding him I wasn't real, or predictable.

C: *Also, you don't know what you're talking about, with all that certainty. I'm a mystery.*

E: *Probably not as mysterious as you think.*

C: *I'm more mysterious than I think. I have no idea how I manage to screw up my life. But I am, clearly, more talented at that than even I can imagine, and I'm partly imaginary.*

As soon as I hit send on that, I knew I'd gotten the tone wrong. Gone all grim instead of flirty. So I speed-typed a follow-on.

C: *Sorry. Ignore that last. Honesty leaked through. Going back to Snark n' Flirt mode. We don't do reality here. Too limiting and depressing.*

E: *I wish I was your boyfriend. In the real world.*

What? Great. Now Evan was throwing himself at an online girl who didn't really exist. And, unfortunately, I had real-world experience with Evan being someone's girlfriend who wasn't me.

C: *Ah! On to fantasy. Well played, Skinnyboy. But no, you don't. I'm funny and flirty, but only online. You're one of the closest things I have to a boyfriend. (Pretty sad, since all we do is email and Facebook messaging.) I don't want to crash this beautiful, secret online thing into the tall wall of reality. In the real world, I'm a mess.*

E: *You're not that much of a mess.*

Okay. I'd already posted way too many facts resembling Kat.

C: *You have no idea, SkinnyB. My poisonous tentacles are so tangled right now, I'll have to comb them out with human bones for an hour, before I can use them again to spear more trolls online.*

E: *Can you be serious for a minute?*

C: *Yes. As serious as death and heartbreak. But not this minute. This minute I want to be all virtual, where none of the pain of the real world can reach me. I just want to flirt with Skinnyboy, without leading him on to any discussion that's not G-rated. 'Cause I'm a flirt, not a tease.*

E: *How about a friend? I think you count as a friend. You even sound like one of my friends.*

Danger. Damn it.

C: *Skinnyboy has it wrong, but breaks Cipher's heart anyway. She can only exist virtually. As he tries to shove her into the real world, even in the wrong place, she is nearly destroyed. She does the only thing she can do. She disappears.*

I logged off. Oh, crap. Was Evan figuring out I was Cipher?

52

I terminated Cipher's Facebook account out of panic, which I felt bad about, because before Drowningirl disappeared, Drowningirl used to occasionally post on that page. I still had Drowningirl's email address, though, and Facebook lets you reactivate a deleted account for thirty days.

The next day wasn't carpool, but Evan met me at my locker at the beginning of lunch, and I messed up the combination twice, trying to open it, while he distracted me with a butchered version of how he drove my friend Cipher off Facebook.

"Do you have her email?" he asked.

"You're asking me for another girl's email address?" I guess the movie pass in my birthday card was not a hint to take Evan to the movies. Also, I wanted to lay it on thick, separating Cipher from me in his mind. "Seriously?"

"Umm." He looked worried. "Maybe?"

I gave up trying my locker combination. "I have it on the computer at home." Also, in my brain, but I wasn't telling Evan that. "How about I send her *your* email address and tell her you want an email back, since you drove her off Facebook."

"Thanks. Uh, Kat? I—"

"Sorry." I cut him off. "I'm having a bad day. Like, beyond even my usual bad hair day. Maybe we could talk some other time."

He looked at me, searchingly. "I'd like that."

53

Apparently, after spacing out and ignoring me completely for an hour, Hunter eventually fell asleep and missed the end of his prom. He woke up and got evaluated during morning rounds before he figured out his "girlfriend" in California was unhappy about the dance. The day after the fiasco, Hunter sent me a pile of messages apologizing, and wanting to Skype. I was not, actually, in the mood. We could do it by text, I sent, and I was in hiding anyway, not being as photogenic as some girls he'd seen—a lot of—recently.

So we texted back and forth and partly smoothed things over, and in the evening I finally emailed:

K: *How about, in the future, the one of us who's not on narcotics gets to plan outings?*

H: *Fine. Your turn. What's our next date?*

K: *Next? Date? I'll get back to you. I'm not in a planning mood right now. But we could browse the Victoria's Secret bra collection online, to remind you of our last one.*

H: *Wasn't our last date. Will be more. I promise.*

K: *Ha. Don't send checks your fatigue level can't cash. And I'd have to agree. Also, let's not count that disaster as our first date, 'cause it sucked.*

H: *Of course not. Our first was exchanging sweet emails. About vomit.*

K: *Really? You romantic devil.*

H: *Yes. And dozens of movies we saw together.*

K: *Sitting 3000 miles apart.*

H: *See? 'The ultimate big screen experience.' Sorry about the dance. I screwed up. Will make it up to you somehow.*

K: *Excellent! Now you have to live for decades, 'cause that'll take time.*

H: *Great. Will work on it. (*Sends Kat a virtual kiss*)*
K: *(*Sends back the taste of ice cream*)*
H: *Yum. Why ice cream?*
K: *Sweet, but a little cold right now. Bye, DBF. Type to you later.*
Yeah, Hunter. Chew on that.

54

To: ciphergirl2@gmail.com
Re: Facebook and my friend Evan

Hey Cipher—
My friend Evan thinks he accidentally drove you off Facebook. He asked for your email so he could un-drive you away. I told him I'd send you his email instead. Could you email him? He tried to say sorry to me for something last year after he mashed my heart, but I didn't let him, because I was so bruised, so I owe him one on the let-him-have-a-chance-to-say-sorry front. Also, he's a great guy, and my best friend, so could you go easy on him?
Kat
P.S. You'd totally think he was cute, in person, if that makes a difference.

Then I listed Evan's email address.

That was pretty clever. I didn't say *I* thought Evan was cute, just that Cipher would think so (same thing, of course). And I mentioned enough other stuff so, when "Cipher" forwarded the message with her cover note, Evan would know I'd mostly forgiven him for the year before and I appreciated his being my friend, without getting mushy. In person. Or directly. Which somehow I have a problem with.

A few hours later, as Cipher, I forwarded that to Evan with a cover email.

Hey, Skinnyboy—
Your friend Kat says I should let you apologize. So get to it, and maybe I'll tell you the stipulations and limitations about communications.

If any. Communications, that is. (*Her poisonous tentacles quiver in anticipation.*)
Cipher

Dear Cipher—
I'm sorry if I drove you off Facebook. I promise not to pry anymore, if that's what you want. Can we be friends? Again?
Evan

Skinnyboy—
Sigh Was hoping for at least one grovel, to show you missed me. (If I drove you off Facebook? Yes. You did. Do you see me on Facebook? No.) You're a guy, so even if you don't know what you did wrong, you should make a sincere, deep, abject apology, in general. Face it: You must have screwed up somewhere, sometime. This could be your make-up apology opportunity. So: Maybe. I'll think about it. But even if the answer's yes, we're having Rules. Which I'm busy coming up with.
Cipher (who might come up with mysterious Rules, because yes she is. Mysterious.)

Dear Cipher—
I'm sorry. (*Grovel. Abject apology.*) And: You rule. Seriously, but mysteriously.
Evan

Skinnyboy—
That's better. So, here are the Rules: (1) I'm not a real person, so you don't try to make me one, or confuse me with one you know. You don't push or pry or guess. (2) We get to talk and joke, even flirt, but we're not crossing lines into racy stuff like "send me a picture of your boobs" or even "what are you wearing?" Not happening. (3) Turns out, even my tangled swirl of poisonous tentacles can't protect my tender self. So if you break any of these rules, I disappear in a cloud of invisible ink. Immediately, forever, no coming back. Delete my Facebook account and never use this email again, which will be a huge pain in the poisonous stinger, because it's how I keep in touch with other people I know online. Also, no talk about

being my boyfriend. I'm juggling enough already. Besides, with my poisonous tentacles, you should probably only date within your species, even online.
Tentacle hugs, Cipher

Cipher—
I agree. But with the boyfriend thing—you're allowed to change your mind later.
Your pal, Evan

Skinnyboy—
Of course. I may be invisible, but I'm a girl invisible friend. I'm always allowed to change my mind.
Cipher
(*Whose tentacles just changed color mysteriously, because she's changeable, she is.*)

The Cipher emails with Evan got me thinking. Maybe I could insist on self-protection rules with Hunter, too. I tried that an hour later, when Hunter and I were emailing back and forth, this time about other girls.

K: *Believe me. Once your guy parts start working again, the appeal of the cute girls in the short cheerleader skirts will be clearer.*

H: *You got it wrong. Also, cheerleaders are too coordinated to fall over themselves going after bald cancer guy.*

K: *Trust me. I know how romantic you are—cute senior boy fighting cancer.*

H: *Says the girl who captured her guy's heart with messages about barf. Figured you for a realist, not romantic.*

K: *Ha. Goes to show what you know. Scratch a realist, and you find a scratched, hurting romantic. Plus, I'm a girl. We're allowed to be complicated.*

H: *Another reason I love you.*

That was the opening.

K: *We have new rules, shiny-head: (1) You don't get to use the "L" word with me except "I loved what you wrote." Seriously. You're going to hurt me too much already. (2) No talk about us being together after you get well. It's a fantasy. I know you're just trying to keep up your morale, but it rips up my heart, a piece at a time. Got it?*

H: *My girlfriend Kat, who talks her way past the 10 P.M. no-call curfew, says silly rules are to be broken.*

K: *(*Crossing my arms over my small chest to protect myself, but then realizing that won't help, so trying once more, by typing*) These are rules for my protection, DBF. So you don't tear my heart out. I mean, even more. You have to follow them.*

H: *Or what? You'll disappear?*

I waited to respond, so he might worry that I'd disappeared already, even though I wouldn't, then typed again.

K: *Don't hurt me more than you have to. Please. On your way out. Or your way back. Either way, I'll hurt a bunch. I do hurt. Okay?*

H: *I'm sorry. Embarrassed. Ashamed. I wanted to not screw things up, but my brain barely works anymore, especially when I'm tired but pretending not to be. At least you know I'm not kissing other girls. With my ANC under 300, one little lip peck could kill me.*

That's the one upside of a possibly dying boyfriend. Who needs trust when there's rhinoviruses and drug-resistant pneumonia?

K: *Yeah. Especially after all those girls kissed the same phone. You've got one giant cross-contaminated female germ colony over at your school now. Plus—you forward one more picture a girl sends you of her nip slip, and maybe I'll kill you. Joking. I think. Still—don't be mean.*

H: *You worry too much about girls at my school. Why?*

K: *Oh, I don't know: A school full of girls who'd love to nurse you back to health, with large chests to use for that? Who sent you prom pictures of those chests? Gosh. No idea.*

H: *You have a self-image problem. And too much imagination, thinking about other girls' breasts in my face. First, I've always preferred the streamlined, athletic types, like you. Second, remember the dying part in possibly DBF? So probably not an issue. They can't even shove those chest pillows into my face in the casket, 'cause I'm getting cremated.*

K: *You type the nicest, sweetest things.*

H: *Back at you, Sarcasm Angel. (*kisses the computer screen, so Kat will know I say this with love and affection.*)*

K: *Argh. Someone is not reading my messages carefully. Or at all. Behave, or I'll tell Nurse Nancy to cut your morphine. Plus, don't kiss your computer screen. It's not hygienic.*

H: *I read everything you write. Then go back and reread it with the other things you wrote. "Love and affection" means I love (among other things) what you write. Love (what you write) and xoxo, your DBF. Also, actual Love love.*

Argh.

55

"So," Hunter said casually the next night, while we were Skyping. "I've got a DNR order now."

DNR means "do not resuscitate." If heart or breathing stops, no chest compressions, electric paddles, or breathing machines to bring him back. I didn't say anything. It felt like the world's biggest chest compression hit me. *No. Not yet.*

"Your DBF is DNR." He went on. He must have seen my reaction in the video window on his computer. "No, it's cool. Now if I hold my breath and an alarm goes off, there's no big fuss. So far, I don't miss the extra attention. You'll have to pay more attention to me to make up for it—like maybe come out in person?"

I couldn't say anything. The words stuck in my throat.

"Really, it's okay—just doing my part to save electricity."

"I'm not ready for you to go." My voice broke.

"I know."

But he didn't say he wasn't ready.

56

Kat's Make-Up Paper

Philosophy of Life Part 3:
The Role of Hope II: A Fire?

Hope isn't just a weed. It's also a pain. It burns, like the most caustic chemo through a drip that's already oozing and infected. Because hope comes with its evil twin: disappointment, the flip side of the spinning coin that sometimes comes up tails, once a kid has AML and a third course of chemo with no remission.

You fight anyway, like you play soccer when you're two goals down with a minute left. Not because you're probably going to win. But because there's at least some hope. Someone's going to come back three times from infections, from teetering right at the ragged edge of death. Into remission and into five years cancer-free and then a whole, long life.

Even when there's only a twenty percent chance of survival, someone will be that one in five kids who walks out of the hospital, leaning on a parent, hair starting to grow in again, stepping back, blinking, into the bright outside light of life.

Hope doesn't guarantee survival. I wish. Then they'd sell it, along with the silver helium-filled balloons, in the hospital gift store. But you use it, like you use the drugs and the radiation. Because that's the only way to play, when you're two goals down, without much time.

If you disagree, teachers, and complain I haven't provided two separate supporting evidence paragraphs, then it's *your* education that's incomplete. Spend a couple of months of your summer vacation at the ICU, which—on a bad night in a bad week—is a high-tech warehouse for the might-soon-be dead. You'll see how to play, two goals down, in life. Only then come back and hassle me about "needs citations for assertion."

57

I typed to Hunter late that night. After the part of my brain that stops the rest of my brain from blurting out the truth had gotten too tired to stop me.

K: *Can I send you one message? Then have us both forget about it and never talk about it again?*

H: *OK (*her DBF is a little curious and maybe afraid*) 'Sup?*

K: *I'm not sure I can handle your dying. Or be there for you. I like you way too much. I thought I was stronger, but I'm broken inside. Even thinking about it. Even when I'm not thinking about it. Maybe I'm just broken.*

H: *Is this the "it's not you, it's me" speech? Are you breaking up with me?*

K: *No. No. No. No!*

H: *OK. Cool. (Actually, yay!) Then—what?*

K: *I don't know. It's that I pretend to be together. I mean together as a person. Not just as a couple. Tough, been-there cancer sib. Maybe, compared to people who don't know anything about blood counts, I do know something. But I'm only me. Kat. Who can't get her homework done. I'm not sure I can do this.*

H: *Nobody can do more than they can. Just do what you can, Sarcasm Angel.*

K: *At least I'm using my awesome sarcasm powers for good, to entertain you.*

H: *See—that's enough. It's more than enough. It's one of the best things I've got left. You're up there way above ice cream. Or anything.*

K: *(*Kat's heart cracks. It will be broken later.*)*

H: *Then it's good you won my heart in an online bet—a spare!*

K: *Not sure it works that way.*

H: *Sure it does. Just imagine it that way. Like the taste of ice cream.*

I was almost empty. I talked Beep through it. I couldn't do that again. Too soon. But that's not what I typed.

K: *I'll try. But don't expect much. I'm. Just. Me. And kind of broken. P.S. This conversation never happened. (*Kat snaps her fingers. 3000 miles away, her DBF begins to forget... *)*

H: *What conversation? Depending on the day, I'm so spacey I can't remember anything.*

K: *Always remember someone here is thinking about you.*

H: *Some nights that by itself is enough.*

58

Evan changed the subject when I mentioned Hunter, and I almost never talked to Evan about him anyway.

Dr. Anne kept suggesting, in that therapist-asking-a-question way, that I was bug nuts crazy, for being involved with Hunter, so soon after Beep died. (She didn't actually use the words "bug nuts" or "crazy," but her eyebrows crawled into her hairline every time I mentioned him.) She had this weird notion that since I was in treatment for depression and anger issues, what with my brother dying and my flunking out, it might not be ideal to pile a long-distance dying sort-of boyfriend onto the heap. Apparently, they cover common sense in Ph.D. school.

Rachel got annoyed with how my next door clickety-click late-night typing to Hunter supposedly came through the wall to her bedroom and kept her awake. Also, she didn't quite get it, because what's the point of a boyfriend if you can't use him to collect neck hickeys?

Mom was the worst. After fluttering around for months like a giant moth, bumping over and over again into the topic of why I spent all my time messaging a sick boy instead of typing my massive make-up paper, she crashed into the walls for weeks in general Mom freak-out mode, which Rachel enjoyed. Little sis Kat was finally getting Mom meltdown-over-boy action, without even one little lip kiss. Story of my life. Mom finally tried a full-on intervention. She cornered me in my room, before another Skype-and-email night with Hunter.

She was, she made clear, *way* not okay with the DBF.

"Relax," I said. There wasn't much chance of pregnancy or Other Terrible Things, because of how Hunter was (1) infertile, because of chemo and radiation; (2) probably without fully-working guy parts,

215

because he was so sick; and (3) oh, 3000 miles away. "He'll probably be dead in a few weeks anyway."

"That's what I'm worried about. How will you be, when he dies?"

"Sad," I said. "I have practice."

"You know, honey—you can always talk to me about it. If you're feeling overwhelmed."

I looked up at the ceiling and wrinkled my forehead into a worried-about-your-nonexistent-sanity look. Mom's scale of 1 to 10 freak-out meter was permanently stuck at 15. She's not who you talk to about difficult stuff.

She looked forlorn. "Or at least talk it over with Dr. Anne."

"I do."

"Oh. I'm sorry, Kat. We haven't really been . . . With Beep sick . . ." She trailed off and tugged her hair. "I haven't been a good Mom to you. Not through this whole—"

"You've been fine. Good. It's been hard on everybody."

"Is this Hunter thing really about Beep?" she asked. "To keep Beep alive?"

It's nice, after Mom manages to make sense for a whole minute, that she veers back into nonsense land, to remind me she's Mom. "No. That's *not* what this is about. Beep's dead. That's why we keep his ashes in the urn. In case we get confused."

I Skyped with Hunter about it that night. "On the plus side, even my Mom thinks it's a bad idea to hang out online with you. So it couldn't be *completely* crazy. Everyone is worried, though, like I'll completely crack up when you die."

"Will you?"

"Maybe. Or I've bottomed out already. How about you get well, so we don't find out?"

Hunter was quiet. He bit his lip.

"Unless, I mean," I said, "that would interfere with your summer job, collecting the life insurance."

He laughed, but it was a nervous one, not a ha-ha funny one. "I'd like you to stick around. If you can. Until I can't."

"Sure. I can do anything, if it involves not doing homework."

As if.

59

"We're stopping," Hunter said at the end of that week. "No more dialysis or transfusions. I get to go home. If there's a problem, I won't come back."

That meant hospice. Beyond do not resuscitate. No more intervention. Dying. "Oh, God."

"My only hope left is a miracle," the smile was in his voice. "And you're taking God's name in vain?"

It probably was in vain, even if that counted as a prayer. "I've got no pull with God. It's been tested. If I did, I'd still have a brother."

"You do still have a brother. He's just dead." He paused. "You know, if I die, you still get to call me your DBF. 'Dead' and 'Dying' both start with D."

He was trying to cheer us up. But that was *my* job, and both of us were failing. He paused for a while, then kept his voice light. "You think you could fly out here in the next week? To say hi—bye. In person? Get to meet?" I was silent for so long, stretching to seconds, he jumped back in. "Look—sorry. Silly idea. I know it's—I didn't mean to . . ."

"No, it's a really sweet idea. A nice idea." Nice except for Mom's limitless freakout, over my flying alone out to the East Coast—to visit a guy I met online. Or, more likely, Mom coming with me, which would mean flying cross-country with her whacked-out self and anxiety disorder. Way fun. How would I pay for it? What did plane tickets even cost? And I'm not sure I could do it. Seeing Hunter might rip my heart out of my chest. "But I don't think so. I don't think . . . I can."

It was his turn for a long silence. "Okay." He tried to make his voice cheerful. It sounded like an effort. "Well, think about it. If something could magically work out."

"If I get one bit of magic, I'm making you well."

"You said it yourself: You work miracles, but they don't let you pick which ones."

"Well, if I get a vote. How long?"

"Maybe days. Couple weeks. A month. Depends on my liver. And whether I get pneumonia. But probably before the cancer messes up my brain. So I'll still be me."

"Well there's a relief." That had to be last-place finish for the silver lining award. "*That's* good."

He laughed. "I'm okay with it. Really. You know, finally."

I wanted to come up with something positive, but the best I could do was edgy. "If you *don't* get a miracle, Hunter, this death thing better work out for you, or I'll kick your dead grandmother's ass so hard she craps dentures for eternity."

Hunter laughed, bless his kind soul, but the sound couldn't carry over the crash and splat of my breaking heart.

60

While Mom was chopping endless vegetables for Rachel that night, to make some dish that looked like the farmer's market compost bin, I asked whether I could go see Hunter before he died. She made a sour small mouth expression, like she swallowed spoiled milk. Or vegan imitation milk.

"Not appropriate," she started, putting down the knife. Which was good, because she waved her arms once she got wound up. Mom covered loud topics ranging from no way to never, to not possible, to hell no, to not when hell freezes over, starting with why sixteen-year-old girls did not fly across country to visit boys they'd never met, to the cost, to how if I couldn't even do my homework she wasn't rewarding me with an expense-paid trip.

Rachel was smirking, enjoying that for once someone else was getting a hard time for wanting to go pretty far in the boy department.

"So," I cut in, when Mom paused for a breath. "I take that as no."

Mom was winding up for more. "Another thing—"

"Got it, Mom. It's no. I understand: No way. Ever."

She wanted to keep going, but I walked out.

I typed an email to Hunter that I'd asked about coming to see him, but my Mom said no.

What I didn't mention was an awful true thing: I was relieved. But at the same time felt, for letting Hunter down, like a screw-up and a bad person. As usual.

That night I wandered down to borrow Beep off the mantle, thinking that hanging out with his remains would leave me feeling slightly less awful and alone. But Rachel had the living room fully occupied, sitting in the chair closest to Beep-in-a-bottle on the mantle, reading *The Sun Also Rises* for her English class. The only reason Rachel hung out in the living room was to be near Beep, even though she pretended that wasn't. So I didn't have the heart to steal him. Instead, I sat down in the other chair.

She looked up, like she was going to skewer me with an icy Rachel glare, but when she saw my haircut struggling back toward normalcy, I guess she decided to have pity on me instead. She nose-exhaled a long sigh, and then said, "Hey."

"Hey."

"Are you okay?" she asked.

"Probably not. I'm flunking out and a total screw-up." Now I was even disappointing a dying guy 3000 miles away. Maybe I was bad for cancer patients. Rachel, by comparison, was getting straight-As and—in a new personal record—was still together with Brian, after six months. She looked almost infinitely sad, though, her mouth turned down and her eyes desolate.

"Are *you* okay?" I asked.

"No." She looked surprised the word had escaped.

"I'm sorry," I said. "You've got lots—" I waved a hand in a circle toward her, to take in her gorgeousness, her hard work, her basic non-screw-up self "—going for you. You'll be okay."

She looked at me as if I'd described a stranger.

"You will," I repeated. Then we both looked up at Beep, there on the mantle in his little urn, like he could add to the conversation.

She shook her head, as though my sisterly words of encouragement were too stupid to respond to. She looked scared. The silence after that weighed on me so much, after a minute I was surprised I could stand. "Well, g'night."

"G'night, Sis," she said, so quietly I could barely hear it.

You can call nights good as much as you want. They are what they are, though, when you realize there's still a Beep-sized hole in your sister, too.

61

Kat's Make-Up Paper

Philosophy of Life Part 4:
The Role of Hope III: Hope in the End

There's one last sad, beautiful thing about hope.

It's different than blind denial or magical thinking or goofy splashing in herbal tea with vitamin C as a miracle cure. Hope adapts: It changes shape, near the end, to fit reality.

Long past the death of hope for full recovery, or playing college basketball, or almost anything you would have picked six months before, some lives on: *I hope I can last long enough to see a shooting star. I hope I can leave this hospital and see my dog. I hope the cancer stays out of my brain long enough so when I die, I'm still me.*

I hope the pain isn't bad.

I hope on that final morning, when I move toward the light, there's something on the other side.

There's always some hope.

62

This next part is about, well, me being Evil. Not Kat-is-snarky evil, or even the Tracies-are-mean-to-less-popular-girls evil. Worse. So awful it excused everything the Tracies or Rachel ever did to me.

I bailed on Hunter, right before he died.

I. Totally. Bailed. Right at the freaking end.

Me, who was upset when I thought one or two docs stopped coming around so much when it got clear Beep wasn't going to make it. Me, who was blowing off my schoolwork to be online with Hunter. Me, who was all about the cancer blog and not bailing right there at the end.

But spring vacation was coming, and Mom and Dad decided we would backpack and camp near Yosemite. They'd gotten a permit, a year in advance, when there was some hope Beep would be well, and in all the craziness forgot to cancel it. They decided why not—let's go march around in big circles, snore at each other in small tents, and listen to Rachel swear at animals. We'd get to see the Milky Way every night and think about Beep.

Mom also had this whole Kat-has-an-Internet-and-Skype-addiction freakout going, over my online time with Hunter. She thought if I got away from the computer and cell phone coverage for a week, I could straighten up and become a total homework drone. Yeah. That would happen. Proof no reality pills were mixed in with Mom's anti-anxiety meds.

And it was okay with me. These were Hunter's last days. There'd be no miracle cure. Not for Beep, not for Hunter. I'd have to go through it all over again, losing someone who mattered. But my heart was completely wrung out. I could feel it, flopping weakly in my chest like a goldfish batted out of its bowl, gasping. With nothing left to give.

I had emailed Hunter that, because of the camping, I'd be out of phone range and off the Internet for over a week. Because I knew I was maybe going to bail on him, I also passed on that I wasn't exactly sure when we were coming back, because part of our trip was snow camping, which was insane and unpredictable—like Mom—so we might be delayed.

For the last Skype session with Hunter, the night before our 4 A.M. departure, I took Beep in his little urn and brought Skippy the dog, as moral support up to my room. I tried not to bring my heart at all, imagined it was in a protective box somewhere, because it was in no condition for this.

"Hey," Hunter said, when I logged on. He'd been looking worse and worse, and a couple of prior Skype sessions had even blocked the camera on his computer with duct tape because he supposedly looked too bad. Now he looked terrible. He was pale and there were yellow-brown circles under his eyes. Everything in his face was sunken. His arms in the tee shirt looked bony, and the skin on them hung. He was sitting up in a hospital bed set up in his house, and the 49er hat was on his head, slightly lopsided. "Wearing your hat." He paused, and his mom's hand came into the frame, holding out a little cup of water with a straw in it for him to suck on. He did, and there was a pause.

I had a bunch of jokes prepared, about snow camping, but instead I started crying.

"'S okay," he said. "Hat is just for show. Go Ravens."

I cried some more.

"'S okay to cry. Now, later. I know it's hard. But promise to smile and laugh someday. A bunch."

I nodded, but broke down completely. This would be even harder for him. I wanted to help instead of make things worse, but my sobs turned into a horrible wuh-wuh-wuh sound when I tried to say something. "I'm sorry," I finally wailed after blubbering. I was supposed to cheer him up. I couldn't even talk. I covered my face in my hands. "Sorry. Sorry." That turned into a long wail.

"I'm not going to say good-bye." His voice was strong. I looked up at the computer window. His face was there, staring right at my eyes. His eyes were wet too. "Just see you later."

The wuh-wuh-wuh sounds kept pouring out of me again, so I couldn't even say that. I think, after a while, his mom turned Skype off on his end, because after a long sob-a-thon, when I looked up again, he was gone.

So our family drove off to the hills, and we snow-camped and were off the Internet for a whole nine days. Which proves I wasn't addicted, because I didn't shake or drool or vomit or anything. Not even when Rachel talked about herself constantly. But I ended up thinking about Hunter anyway, while we were hiking around, staring at rocks and trees. There were trees that were hundreds of years old, and when I heard that, it made me mad. Really? *Really?* Freaking *trees* get to be three hundred, and some kids die before thirteen? Or nineteen? The only good thing about it was that every night we could see the Milky Way. Two times, I even saw a shooting star. I thought of Beep being somewhere forever, even if only in my memory, and thought of Hunter being with him.

When we came back home, I sat in front of my computer and stared at its green-grass-and-blue-sky wallpaper and icons, glowing in the dark of my room. I couldn't bring myself to log on. I didn't check Facebook. Or post on my blog. Or check messages. Or even plug in my battery-dead phone. I sometimes stared at the screen, sick to my stomach. For three more days.

It turned out, while I was gone, Hunter had sent me messages and posted some things on my Facebook page. When I was camping, he'd posted a few short and funny messages about his days. Then, right on the first day I was back, but pretending not to be, he sent a "where are you?"

Kat R U back?

Kat. Would love to talk. R U around?

Hey Kat. Almost out of time.

Hey Kat—going now. It's OK. It was great hanging out with you online. Thanks for everything. I'll say hi to Beep, and we'll both see you on the other side. Like you said, always eat dessert first. Bye for now. Love love (more than you can imagine), Hunter.

The day after that message, Hunter went into a coma. A day after that, he died. When I finally found enough strength to log on to Facebook, I saw his mom's post that Hunter passed away in his sleep the night before.

So I never said good-bye.

63

I didn't know what to do. So I typed a Facebook status, in emotional-trauma Mom Calmese:

> My good friend Hunter died yesterday. I just found out. He laughed at my jokes, so he was kind. He was also brave and fun and deserved better than chemo and AML and only eighteen years, but he was ready to go. I wasn't, and I never got to say good-bye. RIP, Hunter. Love always, Kat.

I stared at that for a long forever, pretending not to be finished, as if until I clicked post he wouldn't really be dead. Then I clicked post. I'd wait a few days to change my Facebook status back from "It's complicated," to "Single." I don't know if that was horrible, or even what the waiting period is supposed to be when your complicated relationship with a DBF ends because he finishes dying. If that was heartless, it fit, because my heart felt torn out. I sent a condolence card to Hunter's mom and dad and little sister. I told them I was really sorry and I'd miss Hunter and he was a great guy. Which didn't even scoop the top inch of the ocean of what I wanted, or needed, to say. But for once I was out of words.

Mom asked if I wanted to go out to the funeral. A little late. I stared at her a long time. Not much point. Hunter wouldn't be there. And I'd already done the feeling awkward and out-of-place thing. So, no.

Mom looked relieved. I felt hollow.

I hope the music was nice. Hunter would've liked that.

64

The next morning, when Evan's mom picked me up for carpool, Evan was wearing a black armband made out of crepe paper stapled over a tennis wristband. He gave me one and then gave one to Tyler when we picked him up. Tyler looked at it, confused, which was understandable but also pretty much how Tyler looks at everything before 9 A.M.

"What's this?"

"Kat's good friend Hunter died day before last. So she's wearing a black armband. For respect. Because we're her good friends, we're wearing them too."

"Oh," Tyler put it on, stretching it out to get it up on his bicep. "Okay." A few minutes later, half way to school, he added, "Sorry, Kat."

"Me too," I said. But sitting next to Evan, who'd unfriended the Tracies on Facebook because those girls were mean to me, who'd said nice things about my awful haircut, and who brought us black armbands because Hunter was important to me, I felt . . . held. I was sinking, and he was trying to hold me up. I teared up again, and it wasn't just about Hunter.

We piled out at Albany High, and yanked our backpacks out of the trunk. Tyler shuffled toward the entrance, but Evan stopped, waiting for me.

"Thanks." I started sniffling again. "For the armband. You're really thoughtful."

"I'm sorry. That everything hurts." He put down his backpack and gave me a hug. The bell rang, which ordinarily sent Evan scurrying to class—he's always on time. But he kept hugging. I cried.

Eventually, I stopped. By then the second bell rang, and we were officially tardy. Evan, though, pulled a packet of tissues out of his pocket—those cute ones called Sniffs that have a cartoon cat on them—and gave me a tissue. I blew my nose and wiped off my cheeks and dabbed at my eyes so I wouldn't look like I'd been run through a car wash. I crumpled two of them, soggy, before it hit me. "You brought armbands *and* tissues?"

"Thought you'd be having a rough day."

Evan, a guy, brought tissues. For me. I stopped and looked at him. "You're—" I picked up my backpack. "Great. Thanks." We wandered to class, through empty, echoing halls.

At lunch, Calley Rose joined us, and even brought a soccer ball. I'd stopped carrying mine around in a mesh bag months earlier, because I was academically ineligible to play soccer anymore—the no-homework flunking-out thing. "Thought you might want to kick something," Calley said.

"Thanks. But I think that works for angry, not sad." And, unfortunately, not for self-loathing. "But we could pass back and forth." We did.

Amber and Elizabeth came by and gave me long hugs, and sat with me. Which I didn't deserve. Out of respect, Elizabeth didn't even flirt with Evan, for the whole hour.

Near the end of lunch period, Evan turned to me. "You haven't told one joke today."

Calley Rose's eyes went wide with alarm at that.

"That part might be broken." Or I was too stunned for it to work. Stunned that Hunter had actually died. Stunned that I'd abandoned him. Stunned that everyone else was being so nice to me. Especially since I was now officially a horrible person.

65

That night in the dark of my room, lit only by the computer screen, I was online as Cipher, half-heartedly playing with Evan by shooting messages back and forth. He went into full-blown flirt mode, and I couldn't take it.

Too soon, too weird. Evan was flirting online with a girl he didn't know he'd met, and he was a great guy. At some point someone nice— which (whew!) excluded Tracie—would take him up on that, and he'd have a girlfriend. Who wasn't me. But who he'd start spending all of his time with. Instead of with me. And here I was, as Cipher, giving him flirting practice with other girls. How insane was that?

But Evan and I probably didn't belong together anyway. Evan was great. And me? I was an awful excuse for a human being, for bailing on Hunter. We didn't exactly match. So I typed that to him.

C: *I have to go away for a while. Or maybe forever. I'm not well.*

E: *What's wrong?*

C: *(*Cipher is having poisonous tentacle remorse. If she was a person, Cipher wouldn't be a good one. *) Maybe I really am poisonous. Or poisoned somehow. Not safe for humans.*

E: *You'll be better soon. You're hard on yourself. I like being around you.*

Humph. Evan didn't even know he'd ever been around Cipher.

C: *It's nice your ignorance is so deep. I'll swim away in that darkness, hiding my awfulness from my friend Skinnyboy. (*Cipher smiles, sadly.*) Cipher's sick of herself. It would break her heart if Skinnyboy got sick of her too, and she's worried it might be catching. She's swimming away for a while, or maybe forever. She might get her gills working again someday.*

*Don't wait up, though. Thanks for playing, but I'm not sure I can be
playful anymore. Bye, sweetheart.*

Then I logged out.

◯◯

The next morning, when we got out of carpool into the milling tide of
students belched out of mom cars, Evan tried to talk to me about it.
Or about something, anyway.

"Uh, your friend Cipher . . ." He tugged distractedly at his hair
instead of heading up the concrete steps toward the front doors.

This, officially, I could not take. Before I could think, I said, "Evan,
if you ask me for another girl's phone number now, I'm going to hit
you until one of us cries, and I'm such a mess, it'll be me."

"What? Why?"

I didn't know what he was asking—why he'd ask for Cipher's
number, or why I'd hit him, or why I was such a mess. I shook my
head. "Never mind. I'm just having a bad incarnation."

"What's wrong?"

"Everything. Me." Or everything, but especially me. Evan was one
of the only persons left who liked me, so it would be awful if my self-
loathing turned out to be contagious.

"I think you're great," Evan said, like a mind-reader.

"Thanks. You're awesome. But between the two of us, I'm the only
good judge of character. You didn't even used to know that Tracie was
evil."

The bell saved me from further conversation. I didn't actually hide
from Evan at lunch, but I was miserable company. On our walk home
at the end of the day, I didn't even try to make conversation. His
attempts fizzled out.

"You'll be okay," Evan announced, when we got to my house, which
was only slightly out of his way. But he looked down at the sidewalk,
like even he didn't believe it.

66

I never managed to say good-bye to Hunter or answer his "I love you" with how I felt. So that night, before I changed my Facebook status to "Single," I sent Hunter a last email. Not that he was still picking them up.

Dearest Hunter, my DBF, I typed. *I guess the "D" in DBF does stand for dead now, instead of dying. I know you're probably not checking messages from the beyond, but I'm sending one anyway, because there are things I need to write, even if you'll never read them.*

I'm sorry I failed you, at the end. I finally checked, three days after I got back (I'm so sorry I waited) to find you were gone.

I was afraid to check, to see that you'd died. I was also afraid you hadn't died yet, and I'd have to watch that happen or try to talk to you, when you weren't all there anymore and didn't even remember me.

You said just to do what I could. Maybe (probably) I'm so pathetic that hanging in there with you until twelve days before the end is the best I could. Anyway, I'm sorry. If I'd known you longer, it might have been easier. When Beep went, I knew it was time. But I was just getting to know you. You were ready, but I wasn't.

Along with a last good-bye, there was another set of important words I never managed to say: I love you.

I love you. I do. I never did figure out if it was I love you as a friend or capital R capital L Romantic Love. Probably as a friend. But I don't know. We never kissed or even held hands.

But I loved your sense of humor and your spirit. I loved that in your last few months you were still making new friends (me). I loved your spark. I loved that you called me your Sarcasm Angel and that you called yourself my DBF. I love you.

I'm sorry, in the tens of thousands of words I sent and said, I never managed to say that, except that it was slightly obvious from the fact I was spending every minute talking and texting and emailing with you.

Partly, I never said "I love you" because I thought if I didn't turn us into Huge Romance, then when you died it wouldn't rip my heart right out of my small chest. But now I feel empty, like I have a hole in me, and like I have no heart left. So that didn't exactly work out.

If you were still alive, I'd pretty this up and put in jokes, but I'm too sad and too raw, and I'm really writing this for me. What's the point of kidding myself?

I miss you. I love you. You broke my heart. Again. When I thought there wasn't anything left to break. Good-bye, Hunter, my sweet DBF. I love you and I'll remember you always.
Love love forever, your sarcasm angel, Kat

67

Bailing on Hunter somehow came up in that week's depression session with Dr. Anne. Tissues were involved.

You'd think, with something as insanely painful as (a) having your cool friend die and (b) failing him by disappearing at the end, the last thing you'd do is spit it up in front of a trained therapist. Once you start chewing on that in front of a shrink type, you know it'll come up again and again.

And you'd think, sitting next to that sharp spike of emotional pain on the couch, you wouldn't just hop on it. Oww. No, you'd expect to sit nearby, pretending it wasn't there, blowing flat little lie bubbles in a monotone. "Oh. Fine. No. Nothing new." (Long silence.)

But that's not how therapy works. At least not if you have a low threshold of boredom, like me. Plus, I was trying to figure it out—how could I do that? And how come, at the end, Hunter said it was okay and still said "Love"? By then, he knew I'd bailed. When it was getting darkest, I'd unplugged my little night light from anywhere he could see.

"Everyone has a limit," Dr. Anne said, from behind her big frame glasses and little notepad. "Where we can't stay close and give anymore. To someone dying too soon."

I sat across from her on this couch in her little Berkeley office that's so crammed with ferns it was like rain forest therapy. I didn't say anything.

"What training do you have," she asked, "to take care of yourself while being there for someone dying?" Since she sticks "Ph.D." after her name everywhere in the building, Dr. Anne might be a little biased on the importance of training.

"Just life." Which had been way too much practice lately.

"Why was it your job, anyway, to be there for Hunter? You're sixteen and still hurting from Beep."

"I was kind of his girlfriend."

"Were you?"

Probably not. I shrugged.

"Why would that make it your job anyway? Why was it even your job to post the cancer updates for Beep, or spend Wednesday nights and Thursday mornings at the hospital with him, when your mom was showing houses?"

"Because I could." It was hard to explain.

"Do you know what a parentified child is?"

"A thirty-five-year-old guy with two kids who still plays shooter videogames?" Sometimes Mom pays the woman just to listen to my bad jokes. Which Dr. Anne rewarded, as usual, with a pained smile, then ignored.

She tried again. "In some families where the parents have problems, one child steps up and takes on adult responsibilities that really shouldn't be hers. People should be taking care of her, but she ends up trying to take care of them instead."

This was relevant how? "I don't even do my homework."

"No," she agreed. "You do things like talking your brother through dying."

"I didn't choose that. It just happened."

"But you chose to become Hunter's friend and support. And when he died, maybe it was too much for you."

Well, duh. "You think that's me?" I asked. "*I'm* all parentified?"

"What do you think?"

"I think this year sucked completely. And most adults are basically insane. They're not, like, role models. They don't even eat dessert first."

68

The call came after school later that day, when I was at the kitchen pantry, trying to figure out a snack, which was hard, because all we had were boring healthy choices. (No eating dessert, period, let alone first.) Mom had her hands in dishwater when the phone rang, so I grabbed one of the phones on the fourth ring, the same time Mom grabbed the other.

"Hello," the woman's voice was gentle, in response to Mom's greeting. "This is Joanna Lange, Hunter Lange's mom."

I was too shocked to say anything, even though I was holding one of the phones. I clicked mine off, set it on the countertop, and then stepped back, like I was afraid a poisonous stinger would poke out of it.

"I'm *so* sorry," Mom said, after the introductions, and they were off to tearful cancer mom bonding, talking about Beep and Hunter and their boys dying, like they were old best friends. That went on a long time.

I stood there frozen.

They somehow made a shift to talking about me. I could only hear my Mom's side of the conversation. "Yes, she really is only sixteen."

Good. Maybe Hunter's mom would only prosecute me as a juvenile, for disappearing on her son.

"Yes, Kat *is* special. And amazing." Mom looked over at me with shining eyes. "Of course, that would be okay. If it's okay with Kat . . . Of course I'll let you talk to her."

Mom handed me the phone. "I'm *really* sorry, Mrs. Lange," I said, like all those people said to me after Beep's funeral. "Hunter was a great guy." I couldn't say anything more, because I choked up.

Hunter's mom was nice on the phone, which surprised me. I expected "Girl, I'm going to rip your lungs out, for abandoning my boy." But it was like she was trying to take care of me, even though it was Hunter who died. Who I'd left by himself at the end.

"Hunter gave me his Facebook and email passwords," she said. "So I could read what you wrote him. I stayed up most of last night reading it." That was hundreds of hours of private messages over months. Some, really private. Well, uh oh.

She went on and on about how much it meant to Hunter that I'd sent him all those messages, and what a great friend I'd been to him, while I squirmed more and more.

"Um, Mrs. Lange?" If she'd read all our messages, she must have seen my last, about how I bailed on Hunter and never told him I loved him. I didn't know why she was saying nice things. "I let Hunter down. I disappeared. At the end. I never told him I loved him. So I . . ." My voice broke, and I couldn't go on. The waterworks on my end really kicked in. Mom was looking at me with alarmed wide eyes. This was news to her, I guess. I turned my back on her, to continue without unnecessary Mom-is-freaking-out distractions.

"Oh, honey. Don't ever think that," Mrs. Lange said. "Hunter knew how you felt about him. Knew it would be hard for you when he died. Was worried about you. He loved you. He was so glad he got to know you."

I sniffled for most of the conversation after that. And she went on about how much it had meant to Hunter, hanging out with me, even 3000 miles away. And how much it meant to her, to read my wonderful messages, what a present it was to her, to see her son's words back. She'd printed a lot of them out, and was putting them in a scrap book, with other things to remember Hunter by.

Okay. Wow.

"Hunter had a class ring. It meant a lot to him. He wanted you to have it if that's okay."

"Um, yes," I said. "That would be . . . yes, please."

I stood in silence for minutes after the call, still holding the phone. Amazingly, Mom just let me be. Hunter's mom wasn't mad at me. And she said Hunter had understood, and that he wasn't mad. Instead, he was sending me a present. I had done the worst thing ever, and my sweet DBF had sent forgiveness.

69

The buildup to the Worst Day Ever (When No One Actually Died category) was the next day. That's when Evan asked if we could walk to school early together the following morning, because he wanted to tell me something.

Which weirded me out all evening. Did he want to be my boyfriend, now that Hunter had died and Cipher wasn't returning messages? Or—oh no—did he have a crush on some other girl, and he wanted to talk to me—his "just friends" female advisor—about how to tell her?

I couldn't go through that again. Or did he want to form a band with me in it? Or tell me he formed a band, but I wasn't in it? Or that he knew I was Cipher and had fallen in love with me because of our online exchanges, like Hunter, but for real?

I went through another dozen even more bizarre possibilities and worked up sympathy for Mom: You can make yourself crazy worrying about unlikely stuff.

Finally, I cheated and went back online as Cipher to send Evan a message.

C: *Hey, Skinnyboy—long time no type. What's up, and how are you?*

E: *Glad to hear from you. Otherwise kind of worried.*

C: *Why? If you tell me, I promise not to jab you with my poisonous tentacles.*

E: *Revealing a deep dark family secret tomorrow.*

C: *Do tell. (*Cipher's tentacles quiver in excitement, so she has to fold them, to keep from injuring herself.*)*

E: *Sorry. You'll have to wait for my memoirs. It's a secret.*

C: *You can tell me. My unusually tiny mouth is sealed. Give it over,*
Skinnyboy.

E: *Sorry, mystery girl, you should know—some things are better left*
mysterious.

Even though I hounded him, he wouldn't say what it was. Evan
always sent playful messages to Cipher, so I figured he was being
random about the "family secret." And frustrating.

70

The next morning I put on my ruffled blue top with the long sleeves, not just because it's cuter than my other shirts, but also because it was clean. Ironic, what with the difficulty later of getting out the bloodstains.

Evan showed up fifteen minutes early, even for a non-carpool day. Mom gave me a puzzled, worried look on my way out. Rachel was still in the bathroom beautifying.

"He's briefing me for a test," I fibbed cheerfully, before closing the door with a thud to punctuate my lie.

Evan fidgeted with his backpack straps while we walked.

"You were going to tell me something?" I said when we were most of the way to school.

"Yeah. I told you that so I wouldn't chicken out." He looked down at his shoes, like he had speaking notes on them.

He'll say he wants to be my boyfriend. That thought brought a swirl of emotions. First, a jolt of terror, that it would screw up our friendship, then a warm feeling that I really, really wanted him to say it. But over the top of everything, a hollow echoing *No*, which didn't make sense. Evan was a great guy, and I loved being around him, but I had this weird feeling it was wrong and scary, especially if it *didn't* wreck our friendship. *What?*

"It happened a long time ago, but I never told anyone."

Okay, that sounded exactly *not* like telling me he wanted to be my boyfriend. The surge of disappointment was so huge, it was painful.

We got to the block where school was, but Evan turned up the path past the tennis courts to the baseball and soccer field, instead of heading toward the buildings. I followed. When we got to the sports field, he stopped and grabbed the fence for support.

I took my backpack off and set it down, to signal I'd wait, even if it was a long story. Evan kept his backpack on, as if he didn't want to get too comfortable.

"So." Evan had his fingers knotted through the chain link fence. He absently kicked the ground, staring out toward Portland Avenue. He looked like Beep used to, when he needed to have a serious conversation, but could do it only half-distracted by a videogame. "When I was six, Mom had a baby."

What? Evan was an only child.

"I got this 'I'm the Big Brother' tee shirt to wear to kindergarten, and Mom went off to the hospital. She was supposed to bring me a baby brother back home, and he'd be named Tony, after Grandpa."

Sometimes you know you're about to hear the worst thing ever, from the buildup and body language.

"But they never brought the baby home. There was something wrong with his heart. He only lived five hours, and the whole time, they knew he was going to die. Mom and Dad didn't want to waste Grandpa's name on a dead kid, so they never even gave him a name. After he died, he was just 'Baby Boy Ford.'"

I put my hand over my mouth.

Evan was still looking away, like he could see something in the distance. "Mom was messed up when she came home. Depressed or something. She barely even got out of bed, maybe for weeks. Long enough, anyway, so I can still remember. They wouldn't let me wear my 'I'm the Big Brother' tee shirt. I threw a fit, because I *was* the big brother, so they took the shirt away. The rule after that was we were never supposed to talk about my dead baby brother. Ever. And we don't. I only found out the whole no-name story from my aunt."

How could they? How could they not give their dying baby a *name*? How could they ignore him and pretend he never existed at all, because it hurt when he died? How. Could. They. It would be like us pretending there never was a Beep. "That—" My voice was raw. "—is such total, utter, complete *bullshit.*"

Evan looked shocked, like I'd slapped him. Which stunned me. Was he going to defend his parents? For that?

"It's not!" He was flushed and there were tears in his eyes. "It's true. I just never told anyone."

I reached out to touch his arm, confused, not understanding his words. I knew I'd said something wrong, but was still floored by the nameless dead baby brother thing.

Evan pushed my arm out of the way. "Forget it." He brushed past me and stomped off toward class. I had to grab my backpack, before I could chase him.

"Evan!" He had a big head start and was moving in almost a run. "Wait."

"No," his voice was tight and furious. He didn't turn around. "Screw you."

I stood there, stunned. What just happened? I replayed our conversation. My stomach dropped. When I'd said "bullshit" to what his parents had done, Evan thought I was calling bullshit on him.

71

I couldn't find Evan at lunchtime. I'd sent him texts but just got an error message. Had Evan blocked my number? He wasn't where we always met outside, or at his locker. By the time I got to his fourth-period classroom, he was long gone. I looked all over, even got so desperate I went into the lunch room, on meat loaf day, to experience its dead-animal-baked-in-cat-box-and-ketchup smell. Which nearly made me join Rachel as a vegetarian, but didn't turn up Evan.

I wandered to my locker, and opened it to get my bag lunch, stuffed behind my books. Once I had it open, I stood there spacing out, thinking about how to apologize to Evan. I reached in to pull my books out of the way. The locker door banged off my hand. "Ouch!"

Kayla Southerland had slammed it on me. "Move it, Bald Ho."

I shook out my aching, tingly wrist. "Shut it, Southerland."

"Trying to." She shoved my locker door again.

This time I caught it with my hand.

"Why do you bother with the books?" she said, looking at the pile in my locker. "You never read them. Or do your part of group assignments."

Pretty much, but old news. "I'm having a bad day, Kayla. How 'bout we talk about that some other time?"

"Ooh—right." Kayla's dripping tone and incompetent locker slamming had caught the attention of some bored kids passing by, and a crowd was gathering. "Kat has a bad day, so the rest of the world has to stop."

I couldn't believe I was getting this, a week after Hunter died, and a few months after Beep. "What?"

"Never mind how it messes up things for the rest of us. You think you don't have to do anything, because your brother is sick."

"Not just sick. Dead. From cancer." Guess she didn't get the memo. "At twelve. He stopped treatment. Then died. So shut your badly-made-up face."

The crowd we were drawing grew and now included Curtis and a couple of the Tracies. Great. Maybe even Kayla realized she went too far with the dead brother thing, though. She licked her lips, but not enough to remove the excess lipstick. "Well, my dad kicked my ass—literally—because of my grades. Thanks to your screwing up our group assignment. Because you think you're too good for homework."

"Not too good for homework." What did she know about it? About anything? "Ignorant raccoon girl. Go scare someone else."

I didn't expect what happened next and had books in my hands, from pulling them out to get to my lunch. Kayla hit me, with a big half punch, half slap that slammed the back of my head into the locker behind me.

It clanged. I shook my head at the sharp pain, my mouth full of the coppery taste of blood from a cut lip.

I threw my books at her. Then punched her hard in the stomach. She snapped forward and I slapped her face, with a hard clap sound. Then I shoved her backward so hard she stumbled over someone's leg and went down.

Curtis started with "Girl fight! Girl fight!" and a few clods joined the chant.

Kayla scrambled up, furious, her cheek pink. "Right now, Monroe. Outside." She didn't look nearly scared enough. "Behind the gym."

"I'm too busy wiping your makeup off my books. That idea is as stupid as you are." I gave her an out. I'd hit her, and was done.

"It's your funeral, Monroe. No, wait—that was your brother's."

A dam broke inside of me and furious burst through. I shut my books in my locker and I followed her. "You'll need the makeup. To cover black eyes."

We stomped outside, herded by a growing pack of gawkers. At least they'd stopped chanting, to avoid attracting teacher interest.

Behind the gym, the wide concrete driveway with trash dumpsters stretched, complete with the warm ammonia garbage smell, like last Friday's fish sticks were growing slime-whiskers. That must have made Kayla feel at home, because that's where she led us. On the other side from the gym, a short concrete wall and chain link fence marked the edge of the practice fields above. Kids were gathering up there too, to get the box seat view.

I took five years of karate in the off-season, when I first started soccer, because the coaches thought that would help us with our kicking strength. Kayla was screwed.

"Wearing the blue shirt and almost no hair," Curtis Warren boomed, in a fake announcer voice, pretending to hold an invisible microphone. "Is Bald Ho Monroe." That got a rippling laugh from the crowd.

"Which you'd know," someone yelled to him. The laughs got louder.

"In the other corner, protected by her jab and heavy makeup," Curtis went on. "Is Massive Scary Mascara Southerland." There was laughter at Kayla too.

I took a deep breath and then blew it back out. I wasn't going to fight for these jerks' entertainment. "No. We're not doing this."

Kayla glared at me, furious, like she still wanted to fight.

"Punch her, Kayla," someone yelled.

"Yeah!" Someone else.

Kids were still arriving behind me and were piling up along the fence up above us, not wanting to miss the school's two least popular girls punching each other into bloody suspension.

"Forget it," I said to Kayla. "If your face needs rearranging, learn to apply makeup."

Flat-footed, she put her up clenched fists, not high enough to do any good. "Let's go, Bald Ho."

I clenched my jaw. "You're not worth it, Southerland. It's too late to beat you stupid." Did she think she'd get accepted by the Tracies if she beat me up? Like that would happen.

Her voice got louder and ugly. "Quit then. Go ahead. Quitter Ho. That's what you are. A quitter. Like your brother."

I might have broken my right hand the first time I punched her in the head, but didn't feel it until the third and fourth punch with that hand. By then, I'd driven her back, completely through the crowd, up against the fence and low concrete wall, barely aware the madwoman roar was coming from me. My right hand in useless agony, I smashed her cheek with my elbow, and she slipped and went down. I jumped on her and tangled my hurt hand in her hair to hold her so I could keep punching her face with my good left hand.

She was wailing and bloody then, trying to get a hand in front to block. She caught my left arm. So I head-butted her, bashing her back into the concrete with a hollow thud. Hands grabbed me, pulling me off her. Someone carried me straight back about five steps.

I wasn't done fighting, so I struggled, even though I heard Mr. Brillson, my favorite teacher, yelling in my ear, "That's ENOUGH, Kat! Knock it off NOW!" Before I could think, I smashed my elbow backward. There was a surprised grunt of pain, and the hands let go.

I stepped forward, fists up, even the hurting one, to pound Kayla Southerland into bloody paste. Everything was in slow motion. Kayla was lying, curled into a ball, holding her face, blood mixed with tears. She howled an awful "No . . ." One eye was white and wide in terror, the other already swollen partly shut.

One of the football players stepped part way between us, holding his hands down in a calming gesture, his face full of fear. I looked around, and every kid, from Miranda to Jordan to Kelly and Tracie, was staring with scared eyes like I would kill someone. Even the kids behind me looked shocked. I saw Evan there, looking at me in horror. Next to Evan, his face white and scrunched in pain, Mr. Brillson was doubled up and clutching himself, below the stomach.

Apparently, I'd just elbowed my favorite teacher in the balls.

72

They caught me hiding in the girls' bathroom, sniffling and staring at tear-blurred graffiti in the dingy toilet stall. I wasn't hiding from punishment as much as from everyone's terrified look after I'd beat down Kayla and elbowed Mr. B. Like I'd sprouted poisonous fangs, and was about to bite them all to death. But there was no hiding from the awful feeling—if I hadn't been stopped, what would have happened? I was shaking, an adrenaline reaction, or maybe I was now scared of myself.

"Monroe, get out here," Vice Principal Janey "the Fritz" Fitzgerald bellowed.

I didn't know what to do or say. "Would you believe I have diarrhea?"

"*Now.*"

I wiped my eyes, blew my nose, and shuffled to my doom. The Fritz, compact and muscular, despite her gray hair, grabbed me by the upper arm and practically dragged me to her office, in a trot.

Fascinated clumps of students watched me get hauled off. Ashley's expression was glee.

⟲

Kayla Southerland was already sitting in a chair in the Fritz's office, her head tilted back, pinching her nose to stop the bleeding, with bloody tissues stuffed in both nostrils and an ice bag pressed against paper towels on one eye. That eye was swollen shut, and her other eye was blackened, a dark circle underneath. Her mascara had run with the tears, so it was hard to tell other damage from excessive cosmetics.

I was holding my injured right hand, which was purpling up on the little finger side of the palm. The side of my face stung with scratches, which I couldn't even remember getting. When I wiped my cheek, there was blood on my hand.

The Fritz pushed me into the chair next to Kayla's, then huffed into her chair on the other side of her big desk. She leaned forward, breathing hard. Her frizzy gray hair made her look like a curly-haired schnauzer. A furious one. "What was this about?"

"She started it." Kayla jabbed a finger at me.

"It was my fault," I said, at the same time.

The Fritz opened her mouth, then closed it into a frowning line. She looked less angry.

Back when we still got along, Rachel taught me how to deal with angry grownups: Ultimate Frisbee Blame Toss. When there's a serious problem, grownups expect you to deny everything. But if you start with that excusing, denying, blaming-others thing, it makes them bang on you harder, to get you to accept responsibility. Instead, with Ultimate Frisbee Blame Toss, you grab total fault from the first words out of your mouth—then explain the facts to show the other person did something much worse, flinging the blame with a little flip.

"It was my fault," I said again, in the silence. "She punched me and smashed my head against my locker, and when I said I wouldn't fight her, she called me a 'quitter ho' like my dead brother, who died after he stopped his cancer treatment. Then I lost it completely."

Kayla started sputtering, but the Fritz shushed her.

"I was out of control. Completely. There was no excuse for getting that violent." I swallowed. "I could have killed her. And when Mr. Brillson grabbed me to stop me from hurting her more, I wasn't thinking, and I elbowed him. In the—" I looked up. "—testicles."

"Yes," Vice Principal Fitzgerald said, in a clipped tone. "I heard."

"I'm especially sorry about that," I finished miserably.

"Did you?" Fitzgerald was looking at Kayla. "Call her dead brother a quitter?"

"I . . ." Kayla trailed off. Maybe she was having difficulty figuring out the right lie, because there were fifty witnesses.

"First she said I use his cancer as an excuse for everything. Then, when I said I didn't want to fight her, she said I was a quitter, like my brother." I repeated what she'd said, mimicking her tone.

"And did you punch Kat?" It was quiet in the office for a long pause.

"She knocked me down." Kayla was furious. Kayla was doing most of the bleeding, but also getting the hard questions.

"*After* you punched me," I lobbed in. "And smashed my head into the locker. Before you told me to come outside so you could beat me up some more."

The Fritz raised both hands to shut us up. "Do either of you wish to make a police report?"

I looked at her blankly.

"Seeking to have the other charged with assault and battery?"

I shook my head.

"Nuh-no," Kayla managed.

The Fritz leaned forward. "You are both suspended." After a beat she continued. "For the rest of the day. I'll think about further appropriate punishment tomorrow. In the morning I want you *both*"—she looked from me to Kayla, with her gaze longer on Kayla—"to give to me and to each other a written apology for your part in this. And Kat—write Mr. Brillson an apology as well."

She waved us out, with a shooing motion and expression of disgust. "Hitting people is *never* acceptable. You are both released to go home. Have a parent sign your apology notes, so I know they've read them. And have them provide a daytime phone number."

We walked out into the sunlight, Kayla with her ice bag and the bloody paper tissue still sticking out of her nostril, like a red and white nose flag. A good look for her.

"I hobe you're habby," she said, through the plugged nose. "By Dad is going to *kill* me."

Right. My brother had, actually, died. Mr. Brillson had probably saved Kayla from brain damage, so it was already her lucky day. And my hand was killing me. "Keep using pressure." I put a finger on the side of my nose to show her. Beep used to get tons of nosebleeds from the leukemia, which was dangerous when his blood counts were bad.

Kayla stormed away, swearing.

73

My harsh punishment for attacking a classmate and octave-upping a teacher started with getting the afternoon off. Not exactly a rocket scientist score in the punishment-fits-crime contest.

You might think I'd feel great, after the Kayla Southerland beatdown. Nope. Horrified. Awful for hurting her, even worse that I'd been one Mr. Brillson–grab away from maybe causing permanent damage. And Mr. Brillson's thanks for trying to keep me from flunking out and then saving me from a mayhem rap was my bashing him in the balls.

When I got home, my hand hurt as badly as my conscience, throbbing fiercely. It was streaked black and purple, with swelling now all the way up through the little finger. Which freaked me out. Was that normal? The first sign of leukemia in Beep was easy bruising. I knew I probably didn't have leukemia, but I couldn't stop looking at my hand every two minutes. I mean, what if I did?

After they gave Beep my marrow-to-be cells, he got better for a while, but then got sick again. What if there was cancer in my cells too, and that's what made him worse?

Ibuprofen didn't touch the ache, and neither did the added Tylenol. Mom didn't answer my repeated calls. (Now that Beep was gone, she turned off her ringer when she met with clients.) I tried Dad at the office, but it rolled over into voicemail, so I hung up without leaving a message. I waited a few hours for Mom to wander home, then decided I'd better get my hand looked at. I'd go to UCSF Benioff Children's. There were closer hospitals, but that's the one I knew how to get to, from my practice with Beep, and it was on public transit, so I wouldn't have to ride my bike far, with the messed-up hand.

I left a note for Mom, holding the pen in two fingers like half a set of chopsticks, then shot her and Dad thumb-typed text messages: *Hurt my hand at school. Having it checked out. I'll text later.*

I got on my bike to go to BART, which would take me to San Francisco, except I couldn't grip the handlebars with my right hand. So I had to hold on with my thumb and first finger, like an old lady pinching a teacup handle. Going over the speed bump on Fairmount, my hand slipped and I bumped the black and purple part. My vision went dark, and I pulled over, as I almost passed out from pain. Ouch.

74

After the BART and Muni ride, by the time I got to UCSF, it was almost 7 P.M. Turned out, I didn't actually know how to check into a hospital as a patient. My massive hospital experience was with Beep already admitted, or sprinting to the front of the line at the emergency room over at Children's Oakland, pushing him in his wheelchair, while we tried to stop a clotless-cancer-kid nosebleed.

Seven P.M. was the change of shift for the PICU nurses, so I figured I'd wander up, ambush one I knew coming off shift, and get help to sort it out. Nurses help people for a living.

My right hand was a throbbing mess. The black and purple had spread down the palm almost to my wrist, and my little and ring fingers were hugely swollen.

The first person I saw coming off shift was Chestopher, my (and Beep's) favorite. Score.

"Hey." I waved urgently with my left hand, from the waiting room outside the nurses' station.

"Hi." Chestopher gave me a big smile, like it was totally normal to get visits from dead people's relatives at work. "Kat." I hadn't seen him in months, but he remembered my name. He still had gorgeous long eyelashes. "How are you?"

"Bad." I sniffled. Then, like a complete moron, I tried to wipe the tears with my smashed right hand, which hurt, so I cried harder. Then I started blubbering. "I beat up a girl, and it was scary, and I'm mad at everybody and I MISS BEEP." Practically howling.

He got me tissues, which of course they have in the PICU waiting room. "What happened?"

"I got in a fight with a girl at school and hurt my hand, and now it has this huge bruise." I showed it to him. "It's not—" I swallowed and my voice came out quavery, "—leukemia, right?"

He touched it gently, and I yelped. "Did this happen today?

I nodded.

"Ever have problems before with excessive bruising?"

I thought back. My hand throbbed. "No."

"Bloody noses? Tiredness? Joint pain? Swelling?"

I shook my head each time.

"Can you move your fingers? Make a fist?"

I tried. They barely bent on the little finger side, and it hurt too much. "No."

"I have some good news, and some bad news."

"Which is?" Throb.

"I'm pretty sure it's not leukemia."

"Okay." Throb. That was a relief, but I had this weird mixed feeling. If it was leukemia, life would somehow make sense.

"But you need to get this looked at by a doc. You might have broken your hand."

∾

Even though I wasn't an official patient yet, Chestopher went to get ice. "Keep it elevated." He put his own hand on the top of his head to demonstrate. So I put my hand up, in demented teapot pose, until he got back with the plastic bag of ice.

He handed it to me. "Where are your mom and dad?"

Uh oh. "Still in the East Bay." Assuming Dad was home from work.

"Do they know you're here?"

"Sort of." I looked behind him at some poster about diabetes, which had gotten interesting.

"Sort of?"

I was worried about how to get home and exactly how things would go after that. Maybe, since I might have a broken hand, they'd let me stay at the hospital overnight. I could use a night off from my life. "I couldn't get through, so I left them a message I was getting my hand checked out."

"Maybe we'd better try them again."

"Or we *could* figure out exactly what's wrong first, so they'll have totally accurate news and won't worry unnecessarily."

"They're probably already worried." Conversations with grownups always skitter off in the wrong direction.

They discourage loud cell phone conversations in the PICU, even out at the nurses' station. I went outside to call, where there was better reception anyway. Great. First, my favorite boy in the universe shared his deepest family secret, and thought I called him a liar. Then I beat up a terrorized girl, elbowed my favorite teacher in the nuts, and broke my hand. Might as well finish the great day as a runaway, calling the world's most freaked-out Mom. Chestopher came along for moral support.

Mom was predictably unhinged when I told her about what happened and where I was. When I finished, Chestopher took my phone and gently talked Mom down off the roofline, promising he'd wait with me until they got here.

We went back to the PICU waiting room, my home away from home, for the forty minutes it took Mom and Dad to drive in from Albany. My hand throbbed worse, even with the ice, and was just as swollen.

So he wouldn't think I was a complete dork, I told Chestopher the reason I was worried about leukemia. Beep seemed to get better after my transplant, but then got worse again. "I thought maybe he got cancer the second time from me."

"No, Kat," Chestopher said. "We test cells before we give them to patients. You didn't have leukemia. Beep's cancer came back from his body, not yours."

So I asked him about the other thing I'd worried about for months. "Beep got graft-versus-host. At the end."

Chestopher nodded.

"So." I cleared my throat. "It can be serious, you know?" I'd looked it up online. It can be fatal. "Did my bone marrow make Beep sicker?" Out of nowhere, I was crying again.

Chestopher put his arm around me, like I was a little kid. "No. Beep was lucky. You were a good match. Beep had a really, really mild case of graft-versus-host."

"Everybody called it 'mild,' but I don't know what that means." I told Chestopher about the *Johns Hopkins Patients' Guide to Leukemia*. How it called even heart failure "mild."

"Not like that. Beep's was about the mildest I've seen. Your transplant didn't make him sick, Kat. You just gave everybody more time to say good-bye."

I thought about that for a while and cried some more. But I felt better, as if a huge weight lifted off me. I'd have to find something else to feel bad about. "It was scary, when I beat up that girl. I could have killed her."

"Why'd you get in a fight?"

"She started it. Then, when I tried not to fight, she said I was a quitter—like my brother."

"She called *Beep* a quitter?"

I nodded.

"She's lucky you didn't kill her." Chestopher is some kind of nonviolent Buddhist, but he didn't sound bothered about my beating up the girl who called Beep a quitter.

"My hand *really* hurts," I said after a silence. "Maybe this is it for my boxing career."

He didn't laugh, but he did smile. "Retire as a prizefighter, undefeated?"

"Yeah. My prize is dealing with Mom when she gets here."

❦

When Mom and Dad arrived, it wasn't that bad. I guess when you've already lost one kid to leukemia and one of your other kids goes to the hospital with excessive bruising, it's a huge relief to find out she's just a thug—not, you know, dying. (Perspective. A good thing, but it doesn't come factory installed. When someone in your family gets cancer, it's the expensive upgrade.)

Chestopher took Mom aside while Dad was looking at my hand. Maybe telling her to go easy on me, because I was an even bigger moron than I seemed—thinking my bone marrow had killed Beep.

Of course, I was at the wrong part of the hospital, up at the pediatric intensive care unit, because instead I needed to go to an "emergency room," which was different. Weird, because you'd have thought cancer equals emergency, but bruised hand from punching a girl equals take-a-number-dumbass ward. Plus, although UCSF was fine for a little thing like fatal cancer, it turned out our insurance didn't cover a "routine" emergency room visit there, and instead we had to go to the ER at Children's Hospital in Oakland, back over near where we lived. So we piled into our car, me with my ice bag.

"Kat," Mom turned around to look at me in the back seat while Dad drove us back. "Your bone marrow didn't make Beep sick." Ah. Favorite nurse to the rescue.

"I know. Chestopher explained."

"Honey—" Mom started.

"Please. My hand hurts, and I feel like a total idiot. Can we talk about this some other time?" Say, when the sun burns out? Basically, about when I stop feeling like an idiot.

75

It turned out "emergency room" really was the take-a-number-dumbass ward, at least on a busy night when you don't sprint to the head of the line because you have a bleeding clotless cancer kid with you. Dad drove us to Children's Hospital in Oakland, where we sat in the ER waiting room for *five hours* while their docs took care of more urgent cases—car accidents, gunshots, and possibly even kids bored to the edge of death by having to repeat a grade because they didn't finish their make-up papers.

Here's an ultimate torture: At the end of the day you did the stupidest things in your whole life, sit for hours on a cheap plastic chair in a crowded waiting room full of coughing strangers and a blaring TV on the wall, with a clueless Dad and a Mom with an anxiety disorder who keeps babbling "Was the other girl permanently injured? Hank, can they sue us? Do you think you'll get *expelled*?"

Then, with the embarrassment setting way past please-make-me-die-*now*, dictate, out loud, apologies for your Dad to write out on a legal pad. Because, of course, your useless writing hand hurts too much and your apology notes are due tomorrow.

Surprisingly, Dad was reasonably cool about that. We went outside for twenty minutes, so I didn't have to stumble through the whole thing in front of thirty tubercular patient-wannabes.

When I finally got x-rayed, after midnight, the film showed a jagged broken bone below the little finger, and a smaller break in the bone below the ring finger. The Doc, a tired-looking young guy who needed a shave, said it was a "boxer's fracture," usually caused by punching something hard with a closed fist, turning the nice straight hand bones into splinters. Mine was apparently more messed up than most.

"I might have punched a few times, after it broke," I said.

"How'd you manage that?"

"I'm—" I shrugged. "I'm—enthusiastic."

They gave me Vicodin for the pain and put me in a splint and cast, which covered everything except my fingertips, and told me to keep the broken hand "elevated" above my heart, which was easy: After my blowup with Evan, my heart was sunken or missing completely.

76

When you want to overhear your parents (instead of standard mode, ignoring them when their lips are moving) pretend to fall asleep in the back seat of the car. Flop over, relax your face, and open your mouth into a big vacant O, like a dead goldfish. That's what I did on the drive home.

The dead goldfish face was key. It made me look like a kid, instead of a teenager who cared how she looked. It triggered parent suspicion-reducing awww-memories of when I was too little to back talk, and mouth-open drooling was normal.

"Kat?" Mom said, from the front.

I kept silently dead gold-fishing.

"Kat, honey? Are you asleep?"

The Vicodin made me loopy, but not loopy enough to answer back. The one skill I did get from skipping homework was how to fake the easy tests.

"She's out," Mom pronounced.

"No kidding," Dad said, driving. "With Vicodin on board."

"This is awful. She's *beating girls up*." Mom's tone said that was probably the worst thing, ever.

"At least she's acting out," Dad said. "Not pretending nothing is wrong."

"She's flunking out." Mom used her absolute doom voice.

"Kat's smart." Dad let out a long noisy breath, the background soundtrack for talking to Mom about problems. "She'll be okay. If she has to repeat a grade, it won't be the end of the world."

More like the end of the universe, if you ask me.

He went on. "It's Rachel I worry about."

"Me too," Mom said. "It's really scary that she calls herself 'drowning girl' online. Like she's dying."

"I thought you said she closed that Facebook account."

"She still uses it as her email."

Wait. *What?* I could barely keep dead-goldfishing, as my relaxed-O open mouth turned into a shocked-O. Rachel was Drowningirl? Drowningirl was Rachel? I opened my eyes into slits, to make sure this wasn't some nightmare hallucination caused by prescription painkillers. No such luck. We were stopped at a red light on Shattuck, alone on the otherwise empty dark street. Mom and Dad were, in fact, in the front seat talking about Rachel's online identity.

When we got home, I pretended to wake up, groggy. It was easy. I had the confused, disoriented, sleep-stupid stumbling bit nailed, without even trying.

77

Half an hour later, upstairs in my bedroom, I had more trouble imitating sleep. My hand ached, even through the Vicodin. I almost wished they'd given me Versed instead, like Beep used to take: Sure, it makes you hiccup, but the side effect is memory loss—at least it might make me forget what I'd heard.

Rachel was Drowningirl. Drowningirl was Rachel. My sister, who'd been the absolute, ultimate bitch to me, was also my secret friend, the only person whose life was twice as miserable as mine. The girl I had more compassion for than anyone.

It was hard to see the two pictures at the same time. Mean Rachel, so beautiful but snarling about everything, and desperate Drowningirl, with the miserable life and the sister who shredded her, and the parents who didn't love her at all, at least that she could tell.

When Beep was in the PICU, there was a little kid there, about eight, who'd had a stroke. The little guy got better and went to the step-down unit and to the floor, then back home to life, because he got well. For the first two days, though, before his brain adjusted, he saw everything double, and he thought it was hilarious. He'd shuffle along the hallway with his little rolling stand for the IV drip, and cheerfully explain there were two of you and ask, which girl he should he talk to—the one on the left or the right?

That's how I felt. Except it wasn't funny, and the two pictures didn't match at all. Snarling, mean, beautiful Rachel on the left, and her mirror image, wounded Drowningirl on the right, without words, except broken poems for her pain. I sat up and felt hot all over. I was always complaining that my sister was attacking me, and Drowningirl was always complaining about how her sister kept slicing her open, with the cutting remarks. She thought Mom and Dad loved me, but not her. She hadn't had a pregnancy scare. She had a suicide scare. She was in agony.

And I was responsible for a bunch of Drowningirl's—Rachel's—pain.

After another twenty minutes of tossing in bed, with a throbbing hand and conscience, I gave up on sleep. I got up and turned on the computer. Maybe I could at least try spraying a tearful apology on one bridge I'd burned, and send Evan a message. Especially since, if I got expelled in the morning, I wouldn't be talking to him in carpool anymore. I logged in.

I pecked out a Facebook update with my left hand

Broke my hand. In a cast. Can't really type. Tomorrow find out if I'm expelled.

It was about 3 A.M., too late for responses. I didn't see any Evan posts, which was weird. I typed his name at the top, which took me to his page. But not to his timeline. To a privacy notice, saying he shared information only with Facebook friends.

Evan had unfriended me. On Facebook and, I guess, in life.

I logged out and logged back in as Cipher, who, fortunately, was still a friend of Evan's. His status update was:

Told something personal to someone I thought was a good friend. She ripped into me. Then I saw her do something awful. Guess she wasn't who I thought she was. I've been there for her so many times, and thought she'd be there for me. Nope. Enough. Done. Blocked her texts and her emails. No more.

There were sympathetic comments below, asking for more information—what personal thing? Who? What awful thing the girl did? (Nearly beat Kayla into red wobbling gelatin, then whacked both balls into Mr. Brillson's corner pocket. Just a guess.) Evan didn't say.

I scrolled down. Evan, according to the cheerful Facebook notices, had become friends with Tracie and Ashley and Sara and Lauren and Jenna. Every one of the Tracies.

Ow. Ow. Ow. Ow. Ow.

Ow.

78

The next morning, at carpool, Evan was sitting in the front seat, next to his mom. His backpack was in the middle of the back seat, instead of in the trunk, to make sure there was no way he'd be forced to sit next to me. Evan has about twenty pounds of books in his backpack. My heart was squished underneath.

He met my "Hi Evan" with silence. He had the sullen face down.

When we picked up Tyler, I waved my cast when I said hi. Tyler actually noticed.

"Whoa. What happened?"

"Broke my hand in a fight with Kayla Southerland. Today I find out if I'm expelled."

"*You* were in that fight?"

"Tried not to be. Kayla picked the fight with me, and when I told her no, she said I was a quitter like my brother, because he stopped treatment." I said it loudly enough so Evan could hear. But he just stared straight ahead.

"Wait." Tyler leaned back in surprise. "*You're* the girl who elbowed Brillson in the balls?"

I nodded.

"Damn."

In the rearview mirror, even Evan's mom looked alarmed. For the record, gangsta cred is totally overrated.

When we got out, I tried to talk to Evan, even holding on to his backpack with my good hand, but he shook me off. Stony-faced, he stomped away.

I turned in my apology notes, full of self-criticism: When I was trying to tell Kayla we didn't need to fight, I should have avoided insulting her. Repeatedly. After the fight started, I should have stopped myself, before even beating some of the extensive crap out of her, instead of going all rabid wolverine on her and Mr. Brillson.

Kayla, it turned out, didn't have a broken nose, but she had a black eye and bruised ribs and face. On the plus side, with the black eye and the cheek bruises fading from purple to yellow-green, she could save on eye shadow and still have a colorful, dramatic look.

I was suspended for five days, put on probation, and given a behavior contract—in addition to my already existing make-up paper requirement—but not, at least so far, expelled from school.

I was expelled from Evan's life.

He wouldn't talk to me at all.

79

I stood outside Rachel's door that night, took a deep breath, and knocked.

"What—" The sound was muffled, over the thumping of angry girl-pop.

I pushed the door open.

"—do *you* want?" she finished, annoyed. She was at her desk, her lips pressed into a tight frown.

"To apologize." I sat on her bed with its red-flowered bedspread. "For being a complete bitch. All year."

She just stared.

"Okay—for more than a year. Hassling you. Sarcasm. Being annoying . . ." I trailed off. "Sorry. Everything sucks, but I shouldn't take it out on you."

She sat there, not moving, waiting for the "but" or follow-up attack. Finally, enough time went by so even she could think of a response. "That girl yesterday beat some sense into you?"

"Maybe." I shrugged. "Or it's the painkillers. If I don't hurt so bad, maybe I'll notice what I'm doing wrong. Anyway, I'm stopping. No more ripping on you."

Rachel raised one of those perfect eyebrows and shook her head. "Right."

"That's the plan, anyway." I looked up at her closet shelf, at where she kept Beep's hat, behind her stuff. "I've been so awful, I'm trying to be a new me."

"Maybe the new you could try going a week without calling me a slut." Her voice was ragged with anger, and it caught, as if she'd start crying.

I didn't know where to look, so I looked down at my lap, where my fingers were twisting together, one set sticking out of a cast.

"So what if I have a boyfriend?" she said. "There's so little love in this house. So what if I found it with Brian? I'm *eighteen*. But you nonstop slut-shame me. You have no idea what it's like."

Actually, I kind of did know. "I'm so, so sorry."

The next song came on, a horrible soaring slop-ballad from Jessica-Freaking-Simpson. But I didn't rip into her musical (non) taste. It was good practice for the new me. We sat in silence except for the grating pop. Finally, Rachel glanced at the door with a "you can go now" look.

I got up and retreated, trailing more apologies, and closed the door behind me. Which at least muted the tortured mewling of Jessica Simpson.

So, no "apology accepted" from Rachel or "thank you" or "I'm sorry too, for being bitchy and hassling you for allegedly killing our brother, and leaving you to deal with family craziness while I went off with Brian." But the point of an apology isn't to get one back. It's to say sorry. Especially if, like me, you've been a horrible, sorry excuse for a sister.

After that, I stopped fighting with Rachel. Almost completely. She'd say some bitchy thing, and instead of a verbal counterattack, I'd say "I don't want to fight." She wouldn't believe it, so she'd plow on with some follow-on snark, which I'd just let sit. Seriously.

She'd be all waiting-for-me-to-fight-with-her worked-up, then puzzled when I wouldn't, so she'd have to hunt Mom down to start a pointless argument. Which wasn't exactly hard, but at least it wasn't me hosting all the bitchfest reunion concerts.

80

The morning after my five-day suspension ended wasn't a carpool day, and Evan didn't show up to walk me to school like he'd been doing for weeks. I waited anyway, and was late.

I sat in classes imagining Evan surrounded by the Tracies at lunch, escorted out of my life forever. Or him avoiding me, until his heart hardened around the idea I'd called him a liar.

In fourth-period English, while Mr. Brillson was writing on the blackboard, my morose thoughts were interrupted when Tracie passed me a note. "I'm sorry about everything. Especially after your brother died," she whispered. The note had a phone number under a handwritten heading, "Angela hairdresser."

"She does my hair," Tracie whispered. "She could probably help you."

I looked from her to the note. From the note to her. Had absolutely no idea what that meant. Was this the closest thing to trying to make up for things, on top of an apology? Was she going to stop being mean to me now, because she'd finally won—Evan was out of my life, thanks to my own efforts? Or was it some further humiliation—when I called the number I'd find it was a dog groomer?

"Uh, thanks," I said finally, and put the paper in my pocket. I didn't even have Evan to talk to anymore, to try to sort it out. At that thought, something clicked into place. I *couldn't* let Evan leave my life. I had to talk to him before he got too far out of reach to ever pull back. So I got up, walked to the front of class, and asked Mr. Brillson for permission to leave early.

"Really?" Mr. Brillson raised his eyebrows. "As a special favor?" He looked over at his desk and my yellow folded-up apology note from my ball-bashing him the week before.

"I have to apologize to someone," I said.

Mr. Brillson glanced at my folded note again. "Quite the month for that."

"It's important." I was pleading.

He gave me a flat look. "You're not going to get in another fight?"

"No." At least, I hoped not.

He shook his head, as he was agreeing to something stupid, and knew it. "Go," he frowned and waved me out with a shooing gesture. Quite the month for that, too.

I hurried through the hallways and skidded to a stop outside Evan's classroom as the bell rang, to ambush him coming out.

If it wasn't too late.

๛

Evan frowned when he saw me. His eyes darted away, looking for an escape route.

"Evan," I started. Then ran out of the right words. If there were any.

He squeezed past me to bolt down the hall. I followed. He was walking so fast I had to jog, to stay at his elbow.

"I'm not talking to you."

"You *have* to."

"Why?" Evan looked at my cast. "You'll beat me up if I don't?"

"No. I'll beat myself up." We reached the cross corridor, and he was turning away, but somehow that stopped him. "I'm sorry," I said. "Please, *please* let me explain."

Somehow, I coaxed him outside, so we could talk not in the crowded hallway. We stood over by the concrete steps worn from skateboard grinds.

"I wasn't lying." His voice was strained. "About my brother."

"I know. I wasn't calling bullshit on you. I said that because what your parents did was complete B.S. Trying to make everybody forget your brother." I waved my cast around and teared up again. "I was mad, thinking how awful it would be if Mom and Dad tried to make me forget Beep. I just . . . said it in a stupid way so you didn't understand." I sniffed. "Which is typical." Then I rushed on. That might be taken the wrong way. "I mean, typical that I say things in the stupidest, worst way." I wiped my eyes with my unbroken hand.

"Oh. I thought you meant—" Evan uncrossed his arms. "I got that wrong." Time ticked. The pause was way too long, but then he went on. "And usually I like the way you say things. You're funny. You say what you think."

"I used to be funny. Then I got angry at the whole world. Now I'm just snide. Even when I don't want to be. *Especially* when I don't want to be." I put my face in my hands, the fresh cast rough on my wet cheek. "I'm sorry, Evan. You're the best guy I know. Have ever known. The best guy there is." Then I started doing one of those shoulder-shaking crying things, because once it starts, the whole miserable year comes out, and it's water-the-yard time. I sat down on the steps, crying hard, and after a while Evan sat next to me and put his arm around me, probably because guys can't take crying, and that might make it stop. Which, in a way, it did. "It's been such an awful year."

He gave me a tissue, and I blew my nose. I looked at him. Except for chemo kids who get a million nosebleeds or are always mopping up a power burp, what guy carries tissues?

I held it up, soggy. "You come equipped for sobbing girls?"

He smiled. "I'm full of surprises."

I looked up. This was at school, over lunch break, in plain view. "Be careful, or your friends the Tracies will tease you to death for hanging out with me again."

"I don't mind. I could be teased for worse."

I was trying to work that out, feeling his arm still around me. "Did you just compliment me or insult me?"

"Meant as a compliment, but it came out wrong." He started to move his arm.

"Then you should definitely stay," I said, and leaned back into his arm, to keep it there, because otherwise, if he moved it I'd topple backward. "I'm starting a club. For people who say things that don't come out right at first. As long as they come out all right at the end." His arm, around me, felt wonderful.

"It's hard, sometimes, to be your friend," Evan said. "You need to give me credit for time served, and take me off friend probation."

"If you promise never to stop talking to me."

"Deal," he said. "But only if you come over and write songs with me again."

"Sure," I said. He kept his arm around me. Before I could think about it, I blurted, "I thought for months my bone marrow killed Beep and nobody would tell me. But I talked to his nurse, and it didn't. I only failed at saving him. Not, you know, killed him. Like I thought."

"Oh, Kat," Evan put both arms around me and held me while I cried, and stroked my short little hair. "Oh, Kat."

81

That night, Dad was actually home, going through piles of papers in the living room and "preparing for trial," scribbling notes on a legal pad. Rachel was upstairs. Mom was off with some couple trying to buy a house in Berkeley, writing up their offer.

"So." I cleared my throat. "Rachel thinks you and Mom don't love her."

"What?" He peered at me.

"She thinks you love me, but not her. She and Mom are always fighting, and you never protect her from my sarcasm. She thinks you two don't approve. Of her. She gets hassled for hanging out with her boyfriend, but I don't even get in trouble for beating girls up."

"That's . . ." Dad paused, then just sat. He opened his mouth once, and closed it again, like a balding fish. "Ridiculous."

"It's how she *feels*, Dad. Don't argue with me." Dr. Anne says your feelings are feelings, and other people can't argue with them, you being the world's expert on how you actually feel. "One of her online friends finishes every message to Rachel with the suicide prevention hotline number."

Dad's eyebrows shot up far enough to crinkle his forehead. "Seriously?"

"Yeah, Dad. Even I don't joke about my sister maybe killing herself." That's poor taste way beyond barf jokes.

He set down the stack of papers on the little upholstered ottoman footstool. He sat there for a long time, like he was working something out. "Maybe I'd better talk to her."

"Good idea," I nodded. "But you didn't hear it from me."

So Dad, of all people, left his papers and legal pad behind, and tramped upstairs to have an actual conversation with Rachel. Which went on for twenty minutes. I couldn't make out the words, but Rachel yelled and cried and drawer-slammed. Then the low calm rumble of Dad's voice would go for a shorter time, and Rachel would be loud again.

An hour later, Mom came home, flushed with excitement that her clients had made an actual offer on a house, so she might even get a commission. Dad intercepted her near the front door. They went to the kitchen for a whispered parent conference, then both of them trooped upstairs.

Rachel cried and yelled some more, then there was the shorter murmur of parent voices between Rachel outbursts. It was a great sign that Rachel got all the long rants: For once, Mom might actually be listening. That went on for another half hour. When Mom and Dad came back downstairs, they looked shell-shocked, but Rachel didn't even slam the door after them.

That night, when I logged on as Cipher, there were two emails waiting from Drowningirl. I hadn't heard from her in months. The first was from the morning, before school.

You'll never guess what happened, she sent. *Last night BFH apologized! Seriously. For being a constant bitch. A little late, but still. Some other girl broke BFH's hand this week, for being so hateful. Maybe, along with mending her hand, BFH is mending her ways.*

Not exactly accurate about the reason for the hand break, but whatever. Also, since my name was only three letters long, there'd been no need all along to abbreviate it as BFH, for Brat From Hell.

Or maybe she's finally growing a conscience, Drowningirl went on. *That lets her care about people who aren't dying from cancer.*

Okay, ouch.

The amazing part, she burbled on, *is BFH says she'll stop being sarcastic. My sister without sarcasm. Right. That's like my mom without uptight insanity. She'll become invisible.*

Ha. Ha. Quite the wit, my sis. Maybe we're lucky she has trouble thinking this stuff up real time.

The next message was about her letting Mom and Dad have it. She'd told them about how it felt, living in their poisonous atmosphere of disapproval. They'd listened. And apologized. Again and again. And tried to explain they did love her and they'd screwed up badly if they hadn't shown her that, in a way she could see every day.

The best part was the end. *Email back*, she typed. *And, for once, no need to re-send me the prevention line phone number. Feeling so good, I don't need it.*

82

My next weekly depression session with Dr. Anne, I expected to talk the whole time about nearly pounding Kayla Southerland into mush and finding out Rachel was Drowningirl. But I covered that in the first ten minutes and spent the rest of the time trying to figure out what to do about Evan. Which was weird. Talking to a therapist about your crush was like paying an old person with Mom's money to pretend they're your friend for fifty minutes. (Which was pathetic. So it fit my life.)

But I couldn't understand it. I froze every time there was a chance to get closer to Evan—whether it was his saying I was cute, or his offer to hold my hand after Beep's funeral, or when he made me brownies and I got this weird idea he wanted to kiss me, or even now. The only time I could flirt with him was when I was pretending to be somebody else, named Cipher.

Dr. Anne went off on a therapist change-of-subject tangent. "You said there was no chance of things ever working out with Hunter, long term?"

"Right." Hunter was always going to be either (1) dead or (2) the healthy, cute, 3000-miles-away, senior basketball star exception to being a possible Kat boyfriend.

"So what did you get out of that relationship?"

I fingered my unusual necklace. I'd put Hunter's ring on a thin chain, and wore it like a pendant. "Some guilt?" Still, that was from bailing on him, not from the "relationship."

"But not an actual boyfriend. Because it would never work out, the relationship with Hunter was safe."

Not with the heartache when he died. I shook my head. No way. "Safe how?"

"You wouldn't have to open yourself to a long-term intimate relationship."

I frowned. Apparently, my trained therapist was suggesting I might need 3000 miles of distance, plus the gulf of approaching death, to feel "safe" enough to let a guy get close. That would work out well, long term. I gave her an annoyed look. Ph.D. my As.S.

She tried again. "Do you think you have permission to be happy?"

More like an obligation, with my promise to Beep to have fun—which I was breaking, every day. I shrugged. "I'm not big on asking permission."

"Then entitled? Are you entitled to be happy? Do you deserve it?"

That was easy. I shook my head. "I'm a screw-up. I don't do my homework. I bailed on Hunter. I've been a snarky bitch to Rachel. I beat up a girl." Even my bone marrow was useless. "No."

"You were there for Beep. And for your mom. You helped Hunter, when you were hurting and you never expected it to work out with him. Now you're even trying to get along with Rachel."

I shrugged. In therapist school, they probably teach their little Ph.D.s-to-be that whole glass-half-full-happy-happy babble, even for their total screw-up patients. It's unprofessional to say "Yup, gargle with drain cleaner."

"Have you heard of survivor's guilt?" she asked.

"Is that the zombie videogame sequel to *Left 4 Dead 2*?"

I couldn't even get a smile out of her. "When someone dies," she said, "the survivors sometimes feel there's no reason they—the survivors—should be alive. That they have no right to a happy life." She leaned forward. "You tried your best to save Beep, but it didn't work. And you wanted Hunter to make it, but he didn't."

I blotted a tear with my hand.

"Did Beep want you to be happy?"

"He made me promise—" My voice broke. "—to always have fun."

"Did Hunter?"

"He told me I should take better care of myself. And—" I thought back about what he'd said. "—to laugh."

"They died, and you survived." Her voice was gentle. "But they gave you permission to have fun. To have a happy life. They wanted you to. You *have* permission. They thought you deserve it, and they knew you really well."

Something huge and painful broke open inside my chest. I sat and sobbed, using up a bunch of what was left of Mom and Dad's money, while they paid a Ph.D. to sit and watch me cry.

83

For the record, it wasn't the talk-and-sob with Dr. Anne that made up my mind about Evan. It was my promise to Beep. How could I keep my promise to have fun, if I desperately avoided something that might be? Was I coming down with the grownup brain-damage virus early? If I never got closer to Evan because I was afraid of hurting our friendship, that wasn't eating dessert first—it was skipping dessert completely.

The next morning in carpool, I climbed into the back seat next to Evan. My left—unbroken—hand was touching his leg. As we pulled away from the curb, headed for Tyler's house, I took a deep, shaky breath and reached over and took Evan's hand in mine. I gave it a squeeze, then our fingers naturally interlinked, and I was holding his hand.

Evan gave me a wide-eyed *really?* look. I nodded. I gave his hand another squeeze. He squeezed back. I ran my thumb over the back of his hand, the smooth skin between his thumb and first finger.

And Evan gave me the most blissed-out smile, and then leaned into me, so our shoulders rubbed too. *Mmmmmmmm.*

Tyler didn't notice the handholding when he got in, but he doesn't notice much before 9 A.M. unless it's waving in his face or on fire.

When we pulled up to school, Evan announced, "This might be the best day ever."

His mom looked puzzled in the rearview mirror. Tyler glanced over. Evan smiled again.

"I have to let myself out," I wiggled our hands. I wasn't good yet, opening doors with my hand in the cast.

"More of this soon?" He squeezed my good hand.

"Definitely," I squeezed back, and then we both let go. I reached across my body and let myself out.

After we hefted our backpacks and his mom drove away, I pulled the UA theater passes Evan gave me for my birthday out of my pocket. "I have something for you." I showed them to him. "A great guy gave me these. If I give them to you, will you invite me to a movie?"

He took the tickets. He swallowed. "Come here."

But he tugged at my sleeve instead of taking my hand. And he wasn't talking about a movie. I followed him over past the tennis courts to where we'd had our talk about his baby brother, while I got more and more worried. The movie thing was a yes-or-no question. Was he dragging me out here to shoot me down, because of everything I'd put him through? The first bell rang. We were going to be late. Was I also going to be a complete wreck?

He stopped, and turned to me. We were at the exact spot he told me about his dead brother. He looked right into my eyes then slowly, slowly leaned forward toward me. Our lips were inches apart. I leaned in, instead of away.

His lips touched mine. We kissed. Soft, slow, long. I closed my eyes. His lips were even softer than I'd imagined. He put his arms around me, his hand sliding up the back of my neck into my short hair. It was fireworks. Or a meteor shower. It was like being a kid and jumping out of a swing and flying and never landing at all. I put my arms around him, maybe so I wouldn't fall, while I melted. Then I opened my eyes, because Evan's brown eyes are too pretty not to look at, during a girl's first real REAL kiss. The second bell rang. I completely did not care. Evan broke the kiss, and then kissed me again. And again.

"You're shaking," he said.

I was. Trembling. "Then kiss me," I said in a throaty voice that didn't sound like me at all. "Until it stops."

That took a long, long time.

"Would you go to a movie with me this weekend?" he finally asked.

"Yes. You pick."

"I . . ." He trailed off, then cleared his throat. "I want to change my Facebook status. To 'In a relationship.'"

"If you promise, no matter what happens, you'll always be my friend."

"I promise."

"Then me too," I said, and I gave my best friend, and now actual boyfriend, a hug. And then a long kiss. Then several more.

84

I'd already pounded blood out of Kayla, the day I tried to give her a cute upturned nose. Might as well improve the process, I figured, by having the Blood Centers of the Pacific collect whatever dripped out. So a few weeks later, Evan and I organized a school blood drive.

Mr. Brillson agreed to be our faculty sponsor, and Blood Centers of the Pacific agreed to send a bloodmobile. They gave us posters and piles of forms for signing people up ahead of time. Amber and Elizabeth and Calley Rose agreed to help, and we were off.

We set up a table near the entrance of the lunchroom, and for the whole week, it was Bring My Dead Brother to School Day. I had a poster-sized picture of Beep, in his bald cancer-kid cuteness, on an easel next to our sign-up table.

In California, they let you donate blood without a parent's permission if you're 17. At school blood drives, they also let you donate if you're at least 16 and have a form signed by a parent. Unfortunately, that permission slip has all those unlikely risk factors spelled out, and getting it signed by a parent ahead of time was a stretch on the planning front, since half the students are boys.

So we mostly concentrated on teachers, and juniors and seniors who were at least 17. To help with that, Rachel came over from Berkeley High on her lunch hour to be our gorgeous drop-in spokesmodel, to stand by my sign, attracting smitten seniors. Which, with her wearing a short sundress the first day, totally worked.

"You're only allowed to talk to the lovely Rachel if you first sign up to donate," I explained to the guys who drifted over. "Be sure to put your cell phone number on the form, though, to get a personal thank-you text from her."

"I'm using your phone for that, Kat," Rachel said in a short break in the crowd. "There's no way I'm giving my phone number to, like, two hundred guys by texting them."

"Use my phone," Evan said. "No way should those senior guys get Kat's number, either." He was holding my good hand at the time. I liked it.

Rachel drew a crowd of the most confident senior and junior boys, and that, in turn, drew a crowd of the senior and junior girls, like antibodies swarming to protect the male half of the student body from a powerful intruder.

Mrs. Miller, my World History teacher, tried to sneak by our table, but I called her out. "Donate! Standing in line at work to get stabbed is like having the even more exciting job of gladiator."

She waved me off, but did smile.

When Coach Paulsen went by, I said, "Donate blood! The only exception to always-give-a-hundred-and-ten-percent."

Evan brought his acoustic twelve-string, and when things got slow, he played and we sang Jonathan Coulton's song about corporate zombies, "Re: Your Brains," but with changed lyrics:

We're not unreasonable, I mean, we'll leave most of it still inside
All we want to do is take your blood . . .

Rachel joined in, harmonizing on the chorus. That girl can sing.

"For the record," I said to Evan at the end of the song. "Rachel's musical influences totally do not overlap with yours."

He squeezed my good hand. "Don't worry. As soon as you're out of that cast, you're in our band, and there won't be room for another front singer."

Tyler was hooked in with the male jock crowd, and got them into mass testosterone competitive frenzy, where they dared each other to donate as a macho thing, and that took off. Almost the whole girls' varsity soccer team signed up too, which I didn't expect, because Tracie was on the team. Elizabeth and Amber and Calley Rose wandered around with clipboards, buttonholing the juniors and seniors who didn't come to our table.

"If I get twenty more sign-ups in the next ten minutes," I announced with ten minutes left in the period, "our blood donation spokesmodel Rachel here will unbutton another button on her dress."

"Unbutton your own top!"

"C'mon. This is a good cause. We're saving lives here. They're donating blood. The least you could do is offer a glimpse of perfect skin."

"I'm bringing Brian with me tomorrow," Rachel said. "To keep you in line, so you don't start offering to take pictures of me in the shower for donor guys."

"Great idea. Have Brian wear that tight tee shirt of his and bring his soulful look. I'll tell all the girls he's a sparkly vampire from Berkeley High they're keeping alive."

Rachel shook her head at that, but she was texting Brian at the time, to make sure he'd show up the next day. I turned to Evan. "She's in total denial over the supernaturally good-looking guy that sucks on her neck."

"Should I wear a tight shirt too?" Evan asked.

"That'd be overkill. With you and Rachel and Brian here, we'll already have enough eye-candy to put a diabetic in a coma."

Near the end of the period, even the Tracies came over. As soon as I saw that approaching pack of human hyenas, I turned to Evan. "Get them to sign donor forms before they start talking you into crushing my heart."

"I won't crush your heart."

"Good. Don't. Especially not before Friday, when I have to give blood."

Evan got all five of them to fill out and sign donor forms and gave them parent permission slips. They laughed and flirted with him. I gritted my teeth into something I hoped resembled a smile. Good cause and all. At the end, while they were still hovering, he reached over and took my hand again. Then I gave the Tracies a real smile.

85

The last day of the blood drive—the actual donation one—Evan's mom helped us pull the poster of Beep and the blood donation poster out of the trunk for the last time. Evan grabbed them, because I had the box of sign-up forms. As he staggered up the steps with them and his guitar, I yelled, "Catch up with you at lunch." Then I turned to his mom.

"Mrs. Ford?"

"Yes?" she said, in that distracted grownup way, as if worried about getting her car out of the loading zone.

"They just did a ceremony, at the George Mark Children's House, for the kids who died in the last month. They put the memory stones in the fountain with their names on them."

She looked at me blankly. I went on, and explained how at the GMCH, after a child dies who ever stayed there—like Beep had stayed, for transitional care the first couple of times he was sick—you engrave their name onto a smooth memory stone, about the size of your fist, and it goes in the fountain, as another way to remember them.

Evan's mom's eyebrows were wrinkled in confusion, and she tapped the clasp of her purse, as if I was doing some fundraising thing, and if she pushed folded money at me, I'd go away.

You wish. "Some of the kids at the George Mark House, with birth defects, lived only for a couple of days, but they were still special, worth remembering." Like Evan's brother. I looked off to the side, so I wouldn't be distracted by her shocked reaction. This was hard. "I was thinking you could do that."

"Do what?"

"Figure out some ceremony or something. To remember your baby boy who died. Evan's little brother."

She took a step back, and her eyes were wide, as if I'd bashed her with my cast and was threatening to do it again.

"It's better to be remembered than forgotten, even if you're only here for a little while, like my brother Beep. Anyway—think about it." I bounced off to class while the bell was ringing, signaling I was late. I looked back before I went in the doors. Evan's mom was still standing by her car in the loading zone, her mouth open.

♋

That night, after we had set the East Bay record for a high school blood drive, Evan called. We'd already gotten to talking for over an hour every night.

"Kat, are you sitting down?"

I was.

"My mom talked to me tonight about my dead baby brother. We're going to visit him in the cemetery. He's at the one nearby, on Colusa."

"Wow," I said.

"She said you talked to her about it."

I went silent. Was that a bad thing?

"Thanks." There was a long pause. "Kat." His voice quavered with stress. "I love you."

"I love you too." I had for a long time, really.

After we hung up, I hugged my pillow, pretending it was Evan. I am totally going to borrow one of his tee shirts, to remind me of his smell, the little bits of time he's not around.

86

For the longest time after Beep died, I didn't have dreams about him. But a couple of weeks before the end of the school year, just before I woke up (the only time I ever remember dreams from) I dreamed I was at a picnic with Beep, except his hair had grown back, and he was healthy, and he even looked older, my age. Plates of cupcakes and little bowls of quivering red Jell-O cubes were spread out on a blue-checkered tablecloth on the grass. Beep had a huge smile. In the dream I was worried that I'd have to break it to him that he was dead and that would spoil everything.

As I was trying to figure out how to tell him, he reached over and squeezed my arm. "I know," he said. "It's okay. I *cleared the level!*" As if he'd won in a videogame.

There was something so electric about how happy he was, I woke up half an hour before the alarm. A great feeling filled the whole room, like the sunlight just coming in or the smell of baking brownies. It was so nice, I tried to go right back to sleep to finish the picnic, but of course it doesn't work that way.

87

Things are better now. I still see Dr. Anne and sit through the weekly depression sessions, but I'm used to it, so it's mostly okay.

Rachel and I gradually went from a one-way truce into getting along. Her helping with the blood drive, and me hanging out there with her and Brian and Evan almost like a double date, somehow put us on the same side again. She's happier, looking forward to going away to college, as if it's escaping from a cage. Which for her, it probably is. She's even started to believe in her Kat-sarcasm immunity pass.

She and Cipher are still online buddies. I never told her I'm Cipher. Somehow, even I know that would ruin things. Everyone needs a friend who's not her annoying little sister.

Over the summer, I won't have to deal with the Tracies. But even before the end of the school year, they tapered off their hating. After the Kayla Southerland smash down, maybe they got nervous that I'd beat them into a group coma. Or after I bailed on my DBF, maybe I became evil enough to be accepted by them, which would be even more depressing, so I don't think about it. I'm over the Tracies—you know, finally, as Hunter might have said. They'll never be my friends. I'll never be their friend. That's okay.

For the rest of life, I'll always be the girl who donated her hair to Locks of Love after her brother died. They'll be the girls who made fun of me for that.

I'll always be the girl who, after she screwed up so badly, tried hard to make it as right as she could, even if it wasn't easy. The Tracies, not so much.

I still wear Hunter's ring around my neck, at the end of a thin chain. It's like carrying part of him, so he'll never be completely gone. It's near my heart, to remind me that because Hunter and his mom forgave me, maybe I can forgive myself.

I don't post on the blood cancer Facebook page anymore or the cancer forums or my cancer blog. Even I have had enough words about cancer for a while. Life is so great when I'm around Evan, I'm trying the healthy non-online world for a change.

Every free minute of every day when I'm not working on my make-up paper, Evan comes over, or I go to his house, and we watch a movie or play music or hang out, or take Skippy for a walk holding hands. Now that my cast is off, I'm playing guitar again, and when we find a drummer and somebody ignorant enough to play bass, we're forming a band. In the meantime, it's fun to goof around. We wrote four more songs together. Evan says our latest, "Eat Dessert First," is his best, ever.

I don't really know if Evan and I are best friends who are also a couple, or boyfriend-girlfriend who are also best friends, getting better. I do know it's slow and great and it makes me happy. Evan makes me laugh. I make him laugh, and when I'm around him that's what I want to do. We are so obviously massively together, though, Mom has imposed all kinds of door-must-always-be-open-and-a-grownup-must-be-home-when-Evan-is-over rules, which are mostly unnecessary. Mostly. (*Kat sighs happily.*)

His friends are turning into my friends too, so I got a bunch of friends to go with the awesome boyfriend. They don't even seem to mind my weird hair.

It turns out Evan was ninety percent sure I was Cipher, all along. After both Cipher and I went offline for the long week when I went snow camping, he was ninety-five percent sure. Apparently, I sound like me, even when I'm pretending to be someone else. That stress I had about Evan flirting with Cipher while he was friends with me was mistaken: He's had a crush on me. For about forever. Ahhh.

And although I screwed up the entire school year, I've got this possibility of not having to repeat all my classes, in the form of my finished make-up paper, poised right here in my computer, next to Fate Almost Worse Than Death.

When I think about being done and getting to hang out with Evan even more, I get a strange feeling I haven't had for about three years. It's weird, but nice. I think it's happiness.

88

Kat's Make-Up Paper

**Philosophy of Life Part 5:
Getting Close to the End of the Journey**

If you pay attention and care, the world will eventually break you
somewhere. It's like that. Death and pain are baked right in, like flour
hiding somewhere in the brownie mix, waiting to ambush the gluten-free.

Life is a journey. Somewhere between that first map edge of birth and the
other edge of death, you have to wade through deep pools of pain. Sorry:
People die on you. Or some other way cut themselves out of your life.

That oozing hole of someone missing, the jagged broken connection,
will hurt worse than the ache of a crushed bone. (I have, actually, done
the research.) When you feel that, it means you still care. You're not
numb, and whatever the grownup brain damage is, it hasn't gotten you
completely yet.

You can deal with that pain, or the fear of it, different ways. Zone out,
like my brother Beep did sometimes with videogames. Try to bury it and
have it come out in a thousand different worries, like my mom. Or bury
yourself in something else, like work for my dad, or boyfriend-hugging
for my sister Rachel. Or you could try keeping people from getting close
in the first place. That's what I did, with my sarcasm, my not letting my
dying friend Hunter Lange get closer, and my keeping my friend Evan Ford
away.

You can even band together in a tight knot, like Tracie Walsh and her in-crowd, and try to stay above the rest of us and hold on to your closest friends through threats of social death.

Or deal with that pain by sending it other people's way, trying to shove it through your sarcastic words into their ears. But that doesn't get rid of it, just spreads it around so it hurts more people.

Worst of all, you can pretend the person gone never existed at all, which is just wrong.

But, in a way, understandable. Because nothing works. Nothing. Freaking. Works. Not to make that pain go away. But if you keep trying the impossible, working harder and harder to deny the reality of an essential pain, you'll end up a crazy grownup, who can't accept that there is such a thing as fatal childhood cancer. You'll get insane enough to argue that vitamin D cures cancer, or to say leukemia was dropped off at my house by God because my family could *handle* it.

Or you can even get so crazy that you don't hold hands with a great guy named Evan Ford after your brother's funeral and instead end up breaking that hand by punching Kayla Southerland with it.

But if you can forgive the world and life for their craziness and for being so wrong, you can survive the place where the world breaks you. My hand has healed enough that I'm typing this. And the hole in me and my life from my brother Beep leaving might be more healed someday too.

Here's the official Old Dead Guy Quote that no academic paper is complete without:

"The world breaks everyone and afterward many are strong at the broken places." —Ernest Hemingway, *A Farewell to Arms*

That's the famous part, but it goes on:

295

"But those that will not break it kills. It kills the very good and the very gentle and the very brave impartially. If you are none of these you can be sure it will kill you too but there will be no special hurry."

My brother Beep was good and gentle and brave, and he never broke, so the world killed him.

The world is in no special hurry to kill me, so I'll have plenty of time to learn to be better, and braver, and gentler. A nice start down that road would be a passing grade on this paper, so I don't have to repeat most of the catastrophe of sophomore year.

But on the last read-through before handing this make-up paper in, when it's too late to change, I realize it's an utter fail at giving you teachers a true philosophy of life. I make it sound as if I understand something, which is completely wrong. This whole miserable year, I mostly staggered around confused and in pain, as if I'd head-butted a goalpost. This stuff I wrote almost makes sense, which shows how completely I missed: Starting with brother Beep's cancer, nothing in life has made any sense.

Except forgiveness. If you can forgive your mother for being an anxious wreck, and your father for checking out, and your sister for being even crankier than you are, and your brother and another good friend for dying, then maybe, just maybe, you can also forgive yourself. And find a way to survive, and maybe even thrive, with your broken places.

Anyway, remember to eat dessert first. And to forgive.

Your hopeful future former student,

Kat Monroe

89
Kat's Afterword:
(After Lots of Words—a Few More)

Yeah—I passed. Whew. Studying with Evan helped my French and Algebra 2 grades, despite the distraction of his earnest brown eyes. And my make-up paper was a hit. Apparently, even a brain-damaged grownup of a World History teacher figured out it was even harder than the assignments it replaced. And, really: Would *you* want Little Miss Attitude Problem back in your class another year? No.

So I get to be a junior, in my actual junior year. Which counts as a major triumph these days.

Anyway, thanks for sitting with me through the worst year ever. As Drowningirl always says—although I'm just starting to understand what she means—be well.

Acknowledgments

A huge thank you to my agent, MacKenzie Fraser-Bub, who believed in this book for a long time, and to my editor, Jacquelyn Mitchard, for buying it and for helping me make it much better; to Suzanne Goraj, copyeditor extraordinaire; and to everyone else at Merit Press for sharing this story with the world. To my daughter, Alexandra, who read the then-only scene of this book nine years ago on the family computer and said, "This is really good, Dad. You should finish it." To Merriam Saunders, a terrific writer and approximately the world's best critique partner, and to my great writers' group members, especially Gloria Lenhart, Aline Soules, Laura Remington, and Nanette Heffernan. To my many fine writing teachers, including Margaret Muth, Mel Shields, Jeff Newman, Nick Mamatas, Annemarie O'Brien, Janis Cooke Newman, An Na, Susan Fletcher, Mark Karlins, Kekla Magoon, Shelley Tanaka, and especially David Macinnis Gill. To my classmates at VCFA, who I'm in awe of; to Deborah Davis who provided a professional edit to an early version; and to Daniel Meier who gave me great comments at the same stage. To the folks at George Mark Children's House for the extraordinary work they do and the difference they make. To Dr. Marcy Adelman, who is much better at what she does than the Dr. Anne in this book. To my friends and to my wife, Nancy Ricci, for everything.

You can find me on Twitter at: @deangloster and on the web at *www.deangloster.com*, where (among other things) the character Kat Monroe maintains a (mostly YA) book blog. Be well.